A Casualty of Power

A Casualty of Power

by

Mukuka Chipanta

WEAVER PRESS

Published by Weaver Press, Box A1922, Avondale, Harare.
Zimbabwe. 2016
<www.weaverpresszimbabwe.com>

© Mukuka Chipanta, 2016
<www.mukukachipanta.com>

Typeset by Weaver Press
Cover Design: Farai Wallace, Harare.
Printed by: Directory Publishers, Bulawayo

Distributed in Zambia by Gadsden Publishers, Lusaka.

This book is a work of fiction. References to real people, events, establishments, organisations, or locales are intended only to provide a sense of authenticity, and are used fictitiously. All other characters, and all incidents and dialogue, are drawn from the author's imagination and are not to be construed as real.

ISBN: 978-1-77922-297-8 (p/back)
ISBN: 978-1-77922-298-5 (e-pub)
ISBN: 978-998224-103-8 (Gadsden Publishers)

Mukuka Chipanta is an Aerospace Engineer and Program Manager currently residing in the Washington DC metro area with his lovely wife Sandra. Born in Zambia, he spent his formative years in the mineral rich Copperbelt Province near the border with the Democratic Republic of Congo. Mukuka has several degrees in Engineering and Business from the United Kingdom and the USA. One of his proudest professional achievements is having played an integral role in designing the Boeing 787 Dreamliner airplane. He has travelled widely across North America, Europe, Africa and Asia and considers himself a global citizen with a heart firmly rooted in Zambia. His passion for telling stories originates from many nights as a boy spent listening to the colourful tales told by members of his expansive family. He is currently working on a number of new writing projects which he hopes you will be able to read in the not-too-distant future. *A Casualty of Power* is his first published novel.

'Ici kupempula ecikulya.'
The thing that visits you is the thing that eats you.

A Bemba proverb.

常将有日思无日，莫将无时想有时
'Cháng jiāng yǒu rì sī wú rì, mò jiāng wú shí
xiǎng yǒu shí.'

When rich, think of poverty, but don't think of riches when you
are poor.

A Chinese proverb.

To my beloved big sister Eunice.
You were a ray of sunshine in our lives,
we miss you.

Chapter 1

A Son of the Earth

Chishimba Mine, Copperbelt Province, Zambia

October 2011

The crowd of African mine workers advanced in a clamouring wave past the guard post. The three wiry, baton-wielding security guards manning the gate were suddenly engulfed by the angry mob. Swinging their batons in a desperate attempt to defend themselves, the guards were flung forcefully against the wire fence.

Observing the mêlée from a distance, Jinan and the four other Chinese supervisors fled back into their tiny office and locked the wooden door behind them. They could hear the shouting of the angry mob outside. Over three hundred African mine workers were yelling and chanting; their voices had reached fever pitch.

Once inside, Jinan and his compatriots moved to shut the glass louvres and draw the thin curtains over the two windows on either side of the door. The asymmetrical criss-crossing of metal bars welded over the windows had always seemed sturdy and impenetrable, but at this moment, they seemed anything but secure.

Jinan reached into the bottom drawer of his desk to remove a grey metallic pistol with an ornate ivory handle. He had kept a weapon for protection ever since the lethal Maamba Colliery incident near the Zambia-Zimbabwe border. During that recent uprising, a band of African coal miners, angry over delayed wages and poor working conditions, had pounced on their supervisors – also Chinese, like Jinan and his crew – killing one and maiming the others. He had thought it unlikely that such an incident would rear its ugly head at Chishimba Mine – but here they were, cooped up in a tiny office with a bloodthirsty mob outside. Jinan had never fired the pistol before; but he knew how to use it from his days in the Chinese military. That now seemed a lifetime ago. The heirloom pistol was a gift from his deceased great-grandfather, who had served in Mao Zedong's revolutionary Red Army. He hoped it still worked. He was shaking uncontrollably as he emptied the box of bullets and loaded the pistol, pausing for a moment as he listened to the crescendo of footsteps and angry voices.

'Africa for Africans! Zambia for Zambians!' the mob shouted in unison. 'Africa for Africans! Zambia for Zambians!'

'What are we gonna do? They're gonna kill us! They've gone mad, mad I tell you!' Ping shouted with teary eyes. He was visibly distraught; his face was bloodless. 'The Africans have gone mad. They don't care about anything anymore; they're gonna kill us for sure!' He shook his head rapidly from side to side as if to will the situation away. 'Call the police again, call the police!' he demanded in desperation.

One of the men pulled out his cell phone, and with shaking fingers he dialed 9-9-9. They waited for a few seconds tense with anticipation. 'Ugh, no connection again. We're doomed!' His voice was heavy with resignation. The cavalry was not coming to save them. If they were to make it out with their lives, the solution lay within the confines of their claustrophobic four walls.

'What do we do, Jinan?' Ping's voice was shrill. His lips were trembling; beads of sweat had formed on his forehead. 'They're gonna kill us, they're gonna kill every one of us!'

Like the others, Jinan's heart was pounding furiously as if trying to escape from the depths of his chest. He glanced at each one of his compatriots; they all wore the same look of fear and desperation like a set of death row convicts helplessly pleading for a final stay of execution. One of the men crouched down, knees to chin, his eyes tightly shut, chanting inaudibly to some invisible deity. Two of the others lay flat on the floor in fear of projectiles they expected to come hurtling through the windows.

'Jinan, you must do something, you must!' Ping shouted hysterically. 'Please do something, you have to do something – they'll kill us for sure, they'll kill us!'

'Africa for Africans! Zambia for Zambians! Africa for Africans! Zambia for Zambians! Go back to China! Leave our country now!' the mob chanted. 'Go back to China! Leave our country now!'

The chorus outside grew louder. The mob moved closer; they were now only about ten yards from the tiny office building. The walls seemed to be caving in on them with every passing second. The chanting had become so loud that it drowned out Ping's panic-stricken ranting. Jinan's palms were sweating, the muscles in his back taut. His mouth was dry, as if he'd just completed a day of punishing labour in a Chinese rice field. He tightened his grip on the pistol, feeling the heavy weight in his hand.

Just then, one of the widows shattered into several pieces and the piercing sound of breaking glass broke through their fear. Shards of glass sprayed across the surface of Jinan's desk and onto the floor. The five men winced, fearing for their lives. The end seemed near.

'Jinan, you must use the gun,' Ping pleaded. 'You have to shoot or else they'll kill us. It's either them or us. It's our only chance! Jinan, you have to use your pistol, shoot now!'

'Africa for Africans! Zambia for Zambians!'

Two more stones came flying through the windows, flinging more glass across the room. Even the concrete floor was shaking from the thunder of footsteps outside.

Most of the mine workers were dressed in dirty navy blue overalls, boots, and hard hats. Many of them wielded sticks, and they seemed to be feeding off the euphoria of the moment.

'Go back to China! Leave our country now!' They continued to yell at the tops of their voices.

There was no way out. It was clear to Jinan that they were trapped, there was no help coming, they were grossly outnumbered, and the mob outside was beyond the point of reason. Their last hope of living another day was in his trembling right hand.

Slowly, like a man being led to the gallows, Jinan used his unsteady legs to push himself up as close as he could to one of the windows. He positioned himself underneath the sill and leaned his back against the wall. He paused for a few seconds to look up at the room. His compatriots were all lying face down on the floor in resignation to the terrible fate that was surely awaiting them. Another object was pelted, this time against the wooden door. A loud thud resonated through the room, adding to the feeling that death was imminent. Jinan removed the safety latch and cocked his pistol. He took a final deep breath, mustering whatever courage was left in his body. Then he turned and pointed his pistol outside. Taking aim in the general direction of the oncoming mob, he shut his eyes and fired two shots.

The pistol's loud cracks jolted the other men in the room who screamed in panic; Jinan lost his footing from the pistol's violent recoil, and stumbled to the floor. As he lay there, he imagined the mob scampering in confusion like a fist full of marbles across a smooth floor. The image was vivid, men at the front turning to run back in the opposite direction, confusing those who were still advancing. Mayhem as hundreds of bodies fell over one another like crabs in a barrel. He could hear guttural wailing and pictured the crowd parting and men climbing over the short wire fence fleeing to safety in the direction of the nearby township, while others made a beeline towards the processing plant, melting into the jungle of metal pipes and trusses. The mine workers were no longer acting in unison; it was each man for himself.

As the noise diminished, Jinan slowly conjured up the courage to peer through the broken window. He blinked several times as he became accustomed to the brightness outside. He could see the final vestiges of a fleeing crowd; men running heel to head for dear life. He cautiously scanned the area just outside their office to make sure the coast was clear. His breathing began to slow down and he could feel his tense limbs relaxing. Ping and the others began to lift their heads as they sensed the danger was over. A wet map had formed at the crotch of one of the men; but an air of relief filled the room leaving no room for embarrassment. Jinan blinked and refocused his eyes on the yard to reaffirm that their nightmare was over. It was in that moment that he realised what he had done. There before him was a limp body lying in a pool of blood.

What had he done? How had things deteriorated so badly to this point?

♋

Eight months earlier...

Kitwe, Copperbelt Province, Zambia

February 2011

Hamoonga stepped out and smelt the air. 'Yes,' he thought to himself. 'Yes, home again!' His nostrils absorbed the smells coming from the charcoal fire: steaming *nshima* – the thick maize porridge that was his daily staple – and fried kapenta fish sizzling with fresh onions and tomatoes all engulfed in one textured and flavorful aroma. This is what he had missed for so long. The feeling took him back to the good old days when life demanded little; a time when he had not yet grasped the finality of life itself, how each moment lived was lost, never to be regained.

He stoked the coals underneath the cast iron pot of *nshima* and thought back to the days growing up as a boy in Kwacha East, a high-density township in the sleepy copper-mining town of Kitwe. In Kwacha East, everyone knew each other, there was a certain symbiosis to how people lived their lives; I depend on you, as you depend on me. Elders were quick to discipline their neighbor's children as they would their own. Many a time Hamoonga had felt the lashing of a switch not picked by a family member but by a neighbour or a passer-by. Hamoonga recalled how his mother, Mama Bupe, would cook with her two daughters, Moonga and Beatrice, by her side. She put them through their paces like a stern army general: washing and cutting fresh pumpkin leaves, cleaning the kapenta, stoking the fire, stirring the *nshima* to a boil. Her handmaids knew better than to deviate from her sure direction, for that would result in a stern rebuke or worse still, a pelt from any object that happened to be within arm's length. On days like this, Hamoonga would play football with the boys of the neighbourhood. A testament to their ingenuity they always had a makeshift ball comprised of rolled up plastic bags and scrap rubber bands that they had retrieved from the numerous rubbish heaps marring the outskirts of the township. They would christen the morning soil, wet with dew, and play until dusk when they could no longer see their ball – let alone each other. They shared a pure, unadulterated passion for the beautiful game, a passion that life bestows only on children. Indeed, life in those days was stripped down to its bare essentials: playing football, climbing trees, making wire cars, and playing *icidunu*.

It was six years since Hamoonga had last been home. Much had happened. He was a changed person; he was no longer a naive, God-fearing, and ambitious son of the earth but a hardened, cynical man. He had left Kitwe in the green innocence of youth, believing in the promise of a great future for well-intentioned people who worked hard and cared about others. Now he knew the true nature of things: happiness was the preserve of the precious few who were rich and powerful. He also knew how perilous it was to interfere with the bounty of the rarefied elite. Hamoonga had been relegated from being a bright university student in the capital city to a mere labourer in a Chinese-owned copper mine under the supervision of a hard task master named Jinan Hu.

His journey to this point had begun a decade earlier.

⌘

Kitwe, Copperbelt Province, Zambia

Early 1990s to 2005

In his adolescent years, Hamoonga Moya had been a God-fearing child. Not that he had any choice in the matter; his mother had habitually employed a switch to straighten out the wrinkles in his character and drill the fear of God into him. In Mama Bupe's eyes, the primary duty of a parent was to raise an obedient child, and a parent who failed in this divinely instituted duty was surely destined for eternal damnation by hell or high water she was determined not to suffer that fate!

Hamoonga was Mama Bupe's first child and only son. Barely a year after the boy was born, she bore fraternal twin daughters, Moonga and Beatrice. Shortly afterwards, her husband, Hakainde, died from a lung infection, no doubt exacerbated by his many years working in the copper smelter at Nkana Mine. A torrid place to work, it was here that the copper ore was melted down into a molten sludge as it made its way through the harsh chemical extraction process to produce the pure metal. Many men suffered curious respiratory ailments in their years working there, but safety procedures never seemed to improve.

With three children in tow and zero prospects of remarrying, Mama Bupe struggled to make ends meet. She moved from the middle-class neighbourhood of Nkana West to the cramped dwelling of Kwacha East Township, not a squalid shantytown, but a poor township nonetheless. It had pit latrines, tiny houses with disintegrating walls, and erratic electricity. Mama Bupe's mother came from the countryside to live with them and help care for the children. With that welcome support, Mama Bupe was able to secure work as a domestic servant in the wealthy suburb of Riverside where she would commute an hour each way six days a week. On her meagre salary as a domestic servant, she struggled to make a living and provide for her children. She always imagined herself as a climber delicately balanced on a precipice; if she nudged too far one way, she would fall into an abyss.

Times were tough but Mama Bupe's dogged spirit held the family together as she raised her children. Hamoonga, Moonga, and Beatrice attended Kamitondo Basic School, a public school with paltry facilities, lacking desks, chairs, blackboards, and running water. Teachers were scarce and those who showed up were overwhelmed by class sizes in excess of eighty children. By God's providence, Mama Bupe's children made it through to high school. Beatrice and Moonga attended Good Hope High School, while Hamoonga attended Kitwe Boys High. Good Hope High was a co-education school notorious for truancy and high teenage-pregnancy rates.

Kitwe Boys High was relatively better, that is aside from the chronic shortage of teachers and rundown infrastructure, and it managed to send a handful of students to the main state university every year. Although merely an average student, Hamoonga scored high marks in English language classes but struggled with the sciences and mathematics. In contrast, Moonga and Beatrice laboured through school and by the time they were in eleventh grade, Moonga had fallen pregnant. Beatrice followed her sister's example six months later. The twin sisters both had their *'Ichombela nganda'* ceremonies and moved in with their respective husbands in short order.

Hamoonga continued with high school and was able to take his national examinations in the twelfth grade and graduate; but his examination results were not good enough to secure a place at either of the two five-year universities in the country. After eight months of applying to several lower-level, government-run three-year colleges, he was finally accepted to study journalism at Evelyn Hone College in Lusaka. And so, with one small bag containing a pair of trousers and two shirts, he boarded the Euro-Africa inter-city commuter bus and set off on the six-hour journey to Lusaka – Christopher Columbus en route to discover a new world.

Chapter 2

Lusaka

Hamoonga's arrival in Lusaka, Zambia

March 2005

It was Hamoonga's first visit to the capital, and the sights and sounds were as exhilarating as they were overwhelming. Lusaka was the city of his dreams. He had heard tales of people from the mining towns and the rural areas moving to the capital to make their mark and strike it rich. The thought of rubbing shoulders with fellow students, lecturers, business people, government ministers, European expatriates, and other power-brokers excited him. He imagined what lay ahead: it felt as if a heavy door had been cast wide open allowing in sunshine, hope, and infinite possibilities. He was determined to make it in this new world!

Hamoonga stepped out of the Euro-Africa bus and walked tentatively past the other passengers waiting to collect their bags from the undercarriage. He made his way to the edge of the perimeter fence in the direction of the blue-and-white taxi cabs parked to the side. A tiny man wearing a chequered beret was leaning against one of the cabs. The instant he saw Hamoonga approaching, he leapt into life.

'*Alo*, biggie man, *muleya?*' he asked expectantly, extending one arm in welcome and pointing at his cab with the other.

'How much is it to Evelyn Hone College?'

'Six *pin*, boss,' the cab driver eyed Hamoonga.

'Hmmm, no, six thousand kwacha, *pa* Hone? It's too much!' Hamoonga had no idea what it should cost to take a cab from the station to the college, but he knew not to accept the first price. 'Ahhhh boss, *ni* standard six *pin*,' the cab driver argued half-heartedly. Hamoonga shook his head.

'No, that's too much, I'll take a minibus.' Feigning incredulity, he started to walk away – a pretext which immediately prompted a counter offer from the cab driver.

'Okay, okay, okay, boss, just do *ka* five *pin chipwile mo fye*.'

'Three-five,' Hamoonga countered without hesitation.

'Okay, four *pin* five, you're killing me boss, I have to pay fuel and maintenance plus *Forex*, boss!' the cab driver complained.

Hamoonga acquiesced. 'Okay, let's go, four *pin* five.'

Pleased, the cab driver hurried to open the door for his customer. Once the young man was safely installed, he jumped into the driver's seat and slipped the car into neutral. With the taxi rolling on the slight incline, he began to turn the key and pump the accelerator. After several attempts, the engine reluctantly accepted the call to action and they were off.

The car was a 1990s model, 1.2 litre Toyota Corolla that had seen more life than its designers had intended. The steering wheel was a naked plastic and metal frame, the original upholstery having long fallen off. There was a huge crack across the windscreen that looked like a relief map of the Congo River with its many tributaries. The fuel tank gage was below 'E' and the odometer looked as if it had died of exhaustion many years ago. The cab was old and poorly maintained. The interior was covered in what looked like a furry purple carpet. There were three grape-sized holes in the floor of the left-back passenger side through which Hamoonga could see the road beneath him.

'New student?' the cab driver peered at the cracked rearview mirror.

'Yes, I will be studying journalism,' Hamoonga responded proudly.

'Ah, *ni* best biggie man, school is a good thing, boss' the cab driver declared. 'Me, I lost my parents *ku kashishi* when I was thirteen. After that I had to stop school to look after my three brothers. It was hard, boss, but now, *ya li balansa*. I make my own money and I have a wife *na ka kadoli* on the way!' He grinned ear to ear.

Hamoonga noticed that he and the driver were about the same age. It dawned on him how easily the tables could have been turned. But for the hand of fate, their lives might have been reversed.

'Have you been to the big L-S-K before?'

'No, this is my first time. I'm from Kitwe.'

'Ah-ah-ah, a *kopala* boy! You'll enjoy it here, biggie. Everything's here. You name it, you'll find it! Lots of places to enjoy yourself and the women, hmmmm *ni so tambe! Imbeka chi saka* and the way they're dressing these days eeeeehhhh *ni so tambe!*' He gave a broad, sinister smile as if recalling an all-too-vivid memory.

Hamoonga cracked a smile at the cabbie's theatrics. He enjoyed a good time as much as the next guy but he was determined not to get distracted. This was a once-in-a-lifetime opportunity for him to make something of himself, and he was not going to let any frivolous pursuit, or any woman, derail him.

'But biggie boss, I see that you're a serious man, you're here for studies, so watch out for these women. *Nga walya ku shako*, biggie man! And it's expensive here, biggie! Watch your pocket with those women, but enjoy boss, enjoy!' he declared triumphantly.

They soon arrived at Evelyn Hone College. The cab driver pulled into the driveway and stopped the car. Leaving the engine running, he turned to face Hamoonga. 'We're here, biggie man.'

Hamoonga produced a few crumpled notes that he counted carefully. Satisfied that he had the exact amount, he gave the cab driver the money. Putting the notes into his pocket, he offered some unsolicited parting advice. 'Biggie boss, remember a man must always have fun, that's how God made us. Have your beer, have your women from time to time, but *ku shako*, true story, biggie man!' And with that, Hamoonga exited the cab and the driver turned and drove off in a cloud of smoke and dust.

Chapter 3

The Hone

Life at 'The Hone' was anything but easy. Running water was a problem; one had to wake up early to catch a cold shower in the dilapidated communal showers before the water inexplicably dried up. The rooms were just large enough to fit two single beds with barely four feet between them. Each student had at least one roommate, but it was not unheard of for four people to share the tiny space, all packed tightly like corned beef in a can. Hamoonga, like most students, was on a full government scholarship. This meant that, in theory at least, tuition, room, and board were fully paid for and all one needed to do was to concentrate on studying. Rarely did things go as planned.

Government bursary payments were routinely late and when the students were finally paid, the money typically fell short of what they needed to pay for books, meals, and general upkeep. Like boats set adrift on a turbulent sea, students were left to survive on their own. They would pool their meagre resources together to buy cheap staples from street peddlers or from the local bazaars. They banded together in groups of four or five that were colloquially named '*kambies*'. They would purchase small bags of maize flour and cook their *nshima* on tiny makeshift stoves. A *kambies* would typically buy a bag of cheap kapenta, which they would fry in vegetable oil with onions and tomatoes, all doused in salt. On lean days they would pick the leaves of wild vegetables which grew in the open areas between the campus buildings.

When paid, the male students would venture into the surrounding township in search of *shabins*. Every time the government paid the student bursaries, there was a rush to spend the money in a few nights of drunken excess. It was something of a race to see who would finish their allowance first. But no sooner had the students exorcised themselves of the money demon, than they yearned for its elusive presence.

Hamoonga's roommate and *kambies* partner was Ken Simutowe, a first-year Media Studies student. Ken was a native of Avondale, one of the middle-class suburbs in the capital. His parents were both medical doctors at the University Teaching Hospital, commonly known as 'UTH' on Nationalist Road in the eastern quarter of the city. Ken was a gregarious, happy-go-lucky kind of guy. He loved Man-U and like many students, he enjoyed a beer with the boys around the television in the local *shabins,* each yelling feverishly at the fuzzy image on the screen, as if their remonstrations could alter events on the far-flung European football pitch.

Ken also loved everything American. TV shows like *The Fresh Prince of Bel Air* and *The Cosby Show* were his favourites. He worshipped American actors and actresses like Denzel Washington, Regina King, Taye Diggs, and Omar Epps. American R&B music was the credo by which he lived his life; he knew all the latest songs, all the artists and even the music producers down to who was dating whom, who had slept with whose girlfriend, and other such trivia. Ken felt he was destined for the United States, and that someday he would live out his dreams in the so-called home of the brave. '*Exsay,* have you *copped* the latest R. Kelly joint? Man, it's the bomb-Bee!' he would say, in his best fake African American accent. 'R. Kelly be killin' it, y'all don't hear me though!'

Despite their incongruous backgrounds, Ken and Hamoonga soon bonded. The latter would lie on his bed, attention drifting in and out like an ocean tide, while Ken talked for hours about American music trivia. Hamoonga indulged Ken as a grandchild indulges the meandering stories of his elderly grandparents; he found that his friend's enthusiasm alone was ample entertainment.

Like all red-blooded men in their early twenties, Ken and Hamoonga had many conversations about the opposite sex. Mostly it was Ken making fantastical declarations about what he would do to this girl or that; or how a certain woman's posterior bettered another, and so on. Hamoonga interjected with comments and prompts, but again, he was content to let his more flamboyant friend do most of the talking.

'Man, I think I'll holler at Temwani, I swear she's feelin' me, *exsay*!' Ken proclaimed one day in class. Ken was the kind of guy who somehow believed that every woman on campus harboured a secret crush on him. The size of his ego was matched only by his own Herculean exploits in his bountiful anecdotes. He once told of a time when he made love to three married women in a single night. He claimed that all three were so overwhelmed with his prowess that they swore to leave their husbands for him that very night. Hamoonga never believed any of his tall stories but he did wonder if Ken imagined he did.

'You know, *exsay*, chicks *smack* a guy that takes charge, steps up, and tunes the right vibes, know what I mean?' Ken said adjusting his New York Giants cap further down his forehead mimicking the American rappers in the videos he watched all too often. Ken had never in his life watched an American football game, nor did he know anything about the New York Giants, but that made no difference to him; he adored American urban regalia.

'Temwani's, serious, hardworking. She seems like a girl that needs an intelligent churchgoing guy, don't you think?' Hamoonga, volunteered.

'Na, na, na, homie, that's where you're wrong, *exsay*. You see, it's those churchgoing chicks that'll surprise you my man. They act all nice, all hallelujah, praise God and shit, but behind that, they're your biggest freaks! Just like *dem* rappers say – a lady in the street but a freak in the bed!' Ken laughed and stretched out his fist and Hamoonga completed the fist-bump.

'So how are you going to play it?'

'It ain't no *thang* but a chicken *wang*, *exsay*; I'll wait until after the Digital Media class at six tomorrow, and then step up to her. I'll need a wing man though!'

'What's a wing man?'

'What's a *wing man*? *Dang* man, a wing man is the dude that hangs around to run interference and talk to the friend while the other dude works on the main chick. Man, don't you guys know how to get chicks up there in Kopala City?' Ken chuckled. 'You know them girls walk in packs; you gotta isolate them and then work your magic!'

'Are you sure that will work? She looks like she won't fall for monkey tricks.'

'Sure it will, *dawg*. Have I ever let you down?'

'You're seriously asking me that?' Hamoonga replied laughing.

'Come on man, be a sport, I need this, *brah*. Show a brother some love, man. I needs to get my groove on! Don't stand between a brother and his *skezzah*, come on now, *dang!*'

'Okay, okay, okay, I'll do it. But if it doesn't work, don't say I didn't warn you!' It would, if anything, be entertaining to see how the 'Lusaka boys' chatted up a lady.

'My man!' Ken replied. Pleased with himself, he gave Hamoonga a wink and a slow upward check of his head – the aficionado of all things cool.

♋

Professor Farai Ndlovu shuffled through his messy stack of lecture notes on the wooden lectern at the front of his class. It always seemed ironic to Hamoonga that the 'Digital Media' class was taught without any use of digital media whatsoever. Professor Ndlovu was the only Zimbabwean teacher at the college. He was a fastidious lecturer. He prepared meticulously for each class with copious notes. He always arrived early for his lectures and demanded much from his students. He challenged them to have robust discussions about contemporary issues, prodding them to opine intelligently and unreservedly. His class was more interesting than some of the other classes that Hamoonga took at the college – certainly more interesting than the Journalistic Ethics class that was taught by Professor Maxwell Malunga. He spoke in a soft, monochromatic voice with the enthusiasm of one going to have his prostate examined. His monologues would extend for minutes on end, one sentence indistinguishable from the next, all adjoined end-to-end like an old freight train slowly chugging away on a monotonous track. Needless to say, attendance for Professor Malunga's class was patchy at best.

Today the Digital Media class was more than usually full. It was always this way the closer it was to examinations. During the exam season, students would suddenly become religious, and begin to attend the classes they had skipped throughout the semester. There were about a hundred students packed into the cauldron of a hall and a constant buzz of conversation as they milled around, sat on benches, exchanged notes, and gossiped about the day's events on campus. Professor Ndlovu looked up and paused for a second as he adjusted his low-riding, black-rimmed spectacles. 'Ladies and gentlemen, let's begin!' he said in a raised, nasal voice thick with a Zimbabwean accent. The students exchanged a last few words and settled down into their seats. The sound of papers shuffling could be heard for a few more seconds as they opened their notepads in readiness for the lecture.

Ken and Hamoonga sat next to each other halfway up the stadium-seating arrangement of the hall. Scanning the room, Ken leaned over and whispered, 'There she is.'

Instinctively, Hamoonga surveyed the room, not knowing in which direction to look. There was a bevy of women sitting directly below them. His eyes interrogated each one of them as if sifting through a dish of ripened fruit.

'There she is, up the room to your right. Temwani. She's sitting with Maya.' Ken nodded toward the front of the classroom. 'Boy she looks fine! We're definitely gonna make our move after class today, for *sho'*. It's on, *brah!*' Ken sounded triumphant. Hamoonga turned and stole a glance to his right. The two girls, Maya and Temwani, were seated next to each other. Maya was scribbling something in her notebook.

'Today,' Professor Ndlovu began, 'we will discuss the role of the Internet in the delivery of news in developing countries. Is it currently playing a role? If so, how, and in what forms? If not, is there a future for it, and what is that future?' With that preamble the professor proceeded to engage the students in a conversation about recent news events in the country; he provoked them to envision what a future with ubiquitous Internet connectivity would look like from the standpoint of press freedom. He gave the example of how the Internet had opened up the world to learn more about issues around land reform in Zimbabwe, the illegal trade of blood diamonds in Sierra Leone, and the brain drain across the African continent. He asked what role the Internet could play in long-standing conflicts such as in the Democratic Republic of Congo, or how journalists could influence commerce and trade in a connected African continent.

The class lasted for two hours with a ten-minute break. When Professor Ndlovu concluded his lecture, he gave an assignment that was due in two weeks. There was a collective grumble from the class as the students left their seats and began to funnel through the single exit, like the flow after the release of a tightly held spigot. Ken was one of the first to get up. He signaled impatiently for Hamoonga to hurry up so they could make their way towards Temwani and Maya.

The two men shuffled through the crowd of students, bumping shoulders – Hamoonga apologising for the two of them. Outside at last, they could see the two girls walking through an archway, engaged in conversation. His target identified, Ken tilted his cap, tugged at his shirt collar, and adjusted his gait to a rhythmic bounce. Intrigued, Hamoonga followed closely behind, observing everything as one would a daytime soap opera with B-rated actors – appalled at the poor acting but perversely drawn in to see how the plot transpires.

'Hey ladies, how y'all doing?' Ken opened with a less-than-stellar line. 'Do you mind if we walk with you?'

Temwani and Maya stopped momentarily, turning to face the young man. From the quizzical expressions on both of their faces, it was clear they were underwhelmed by the 'Lusaka boy's' approach. Undeterred, Ken continued with the confidence of a Spanish matador.

'How did you guys find that lecture? Professor Ndlovu seriously needs to get a life. His lectures suck, man!' Ken turned to face Temwani in an attempt to gauge her reaction, the way a mischievous adolescent craves validation.

'Huh, what?' Temwani retorted, screwing up her face as if smelling something foul. On cue Maya rolled her eyes in an overt expression of disinterest.

'I mean that guy is like straight from the seventies or something. Man, he needs to move with the times, you know what I'm sayin'?' Ken's *faux* American accent did little to impress the ladies; actually it did the opposite. Ken was a man in quicksand, sinking fast!

'What do you think…' Temwani began with scorn audible in her tone of voice, but before she could finish, Hamoonga swooped in to the rescue, a helicopter pilot coming in to save his embattled comrade.

'Maya, right?' Hamoonga jumped in. 'You're in my Journalistic Ethics class. I was wondering if you would like to join our discussion group on Thursday evenings. A bunch of us meet in Manda Hall to bounce ideas off each other. It's pretty cool. I remember you had some great insights on the unique perspective of female journalists during our last class. I think we would benefit from your input and I'm sure you'd like it.'

At once, Maya broke into a coquettish smile. Hamoonga's flattery had cut through the tension. 'That's kind of you. I'm surprised you remember.'

'Of course I do. You delivered your point so eloquently. I know you'd be perfect for the group!' Hamoonga piled on the compliments like a stack of breakfast pancakes. Maya smiled again, a little coy. She looked down to her feet before looking up again at the purveyor of the compliments. How tall and erect he was; her head barely reached his shoulders. He had an easy handsome face, naturally well-cropped eyebrows, a well-proportioned nose, and a deep set of brown eyes. She had noticed him before. He frequently kept to himself, writing notes and contributing only occasionally in class discussions – the consummate student. Now, she was chuffed by the notion that he'd noticed her.

'Who else is in the group?' she asked.

'It's me, Ken here, two other guys Ben and Brave; you may not know them but they're pretty cool. We also have a lady, Bernice, all good people. So you can see it would be great to balance out the numbers and have more female representation. You and Temwani would be fantastic additions!'

Maya looked at Temwani – a look that declaimed, 'Please let's do this.' Standing in the background now, the proverbial superfluous third wheel, Ken stared admiringly at his friend.

'When did you say you meet?' Maya asked with an inviting smile.

⌘

Temwani and Maya arrived on time at 5:30 p.m. for the Thursday evening Journalistic Ethics discussion group. Brave and Bernice were already present as were Hamoonga and Ken. Ben was missing from the group. He had gone off campus earlier in the day to visit relatives and would most likely be a no-show. Seeing the two women arriving at the door, Hamoonga rose from his seat to welcome them. Giving both ladies a warm embrace, he turned to the rest of the group: 'Hey guys, this is Maya and this is Temwani. I'm sure you've seen them in class. Temwani, Maya – welcome to the group,' Hamoonga smiled broadly. There was a collective, 'Hey!' before they proceeded to make individual introductions.

Both girls looked beautiful. It was clear to Hamoonga that Maya had made an extra effort. Her braided hair was neatly coiled into a bun at the back of her head; her brown lipstick complemented her almond skin. Maya had a round face; she was not beautiful in the conventional sense, but her pleasant smile had an inviting charm. A pale blue chiffon dress swung just above her knees. She wore a modest pair of slippers revealing her toenails, which she had taken care to paint in a dark brown gloss.

Temwani was classically beautiful with high cheekbones on a perfectly chiselled face and slanting brown eyes. Her natural hair was cropped and well oiled. A huge pair of wooden oval earrings completed her ethnic look. The two young women sat next to each other in the neatly arranged circle of chairs. Hamoonga and Maya exchanged glances like two lovers sharing an inside joke. She averted her eyes first.

Brave, who was sitting between Ken and Temwani, spoke first.

'So, as you all know, the topic for our next class is about how we, as journalists, should contribute to the social discourse on the recent takeover of the country's mining industry by the Chinese. How, essentially, should we cover the issue in a manner that is balanced and informative, without compromising our civic responsibilities as African citizens?' Brave loved open-ended debate; he liked to set the ball rolling and play devil's advocate in heated discussions.

'Well,' Bernice said, adjusting her braids, 'I think, first of all, that your preamble is flawed. Your supposition is that the mining industry is being 'taken over' by the Chinese. I think that creates a false premise that somehow the Chinese are the aggressors and the Africans are powerless bystanders. I reject that notion. We, as Africans, are equal partners at the table, good or bad; we are co-conspirators in what is happening within our mining industry. It's not a case of the 'Evil Red Empire' subjugating the African people; no, we're part of it!' Bernice was a great debater, with good previous experience in the Roma Girls Secondary School team.

'I agree with Bernice,' Temwani began as everyone turned to listen to the newest member of their group. 'We, as Africans, need to take ownership of the decisions we make. Yes, good or bad, we accepted the Chinese into our country and they are merely doing what was agreed to by consenting parties. I think that as journalists, we should be fair and cover the Chinese perspective as well as the Zambian perspective.'

'You say that they, the Chinese, are merely doing what was agreed by consenting parties,' Brave began his stern rebuttal. 'But was the negotiating done on an equal platform? I contend that our copper mines were sold off well below fair-market value. It was and still is daylight robbery! As journalists, being led by a strong moral compass, it is incumbent upon us to report this atrocity and let it be known to any ear that will listen that African nations are being bamboozled. The Chinese are robbing us of our children's inheritance!' Ken and Hamoonga shared a quick glance, taken aback by Brave's emotive views.

'Is it the fault of the Chinese if African countries don't present themselves well at the negotiating table?' Temwani asked. 'Is it not essential that African countries put their best foot forward and get the best deal they can when selling their assets?'

After a brief moment of thoughtful silence Brave responded. 'But what you have here is an imbalance. The Chinese come with a war chest of money. They can afford to get the best lawyers that money can buy, they have time to wait until we're desperate enough to make a deal and, above all, they can appease our corrupt politicians through graft.'

'But again, is it the fault of the Chinese that we're led by charlatans?' Temwani retorted. She raised her hands, as if daring the group to respond.

'Yeah, whose fault is that?' Ken interjected awkwardly.

A dismissive look flashed across Temwani's face. Ignoring Ken, she continued, 'I say, business is business. Who would pass up a good money-making opportunity? I believe that if the tables were turned, we'd do the same.'

'What do you think, Maya?' Hamoonga asked trying to broaden the conversation. The entire group turned to face Maya. The sound of footsteps echoed in the corridor outside as they all waited for her to speak.

'Hmmm,' she mused for a moment. 'Well, I see both sides of the coin, but let's get back to the topic at hand. I don't believe that it's up to the journalists to judge which point of view is right or wrong. Ours is to report on the facts and let them tell the story.'

Hamoonga was genuinely impressed. He smiled broadly at Maya as she fidgeted nervously with the hem of her dress. 'I like that perspective, yes, but being stakeholders ourselves, it's very difficult for us to remain impartial. I mean, the copper mines are the lifeblood of our country. We know we need to guard them jealously for generations to come, but we can't let that blind us to the facts. I think these are pretty clear: we have corrupt, incompetent leaders representing us at times. It is also a fact that the Chinese are not necessarily considering our best interests. They're looking out for their own; you can't blame them for that! I mean . . .'

'Hold on!' Brave interrupted. 'I think we can and we should blame the Chinese. They need to play by ethical rules. I'm sorry. I just don't believe that it's right for one country to knowingly enslave another just to capitalise on an arbitrage opportunity! No, that's colonialism all over again!' Brave's right fist was clenched.

Ken leaned back in his chair and lifted his arms in the air. 'Hey man, but it's all about the paper!' he said matter-of-factly. Temwani rolled her eyes. Ken was failing to impress.

Brave shook his head at Ken's comment. 'So as journalists, how should we cover a story in which over ten thousand out of a workforce of thirty thousand mine workers are laid off in a period of two years by the so-called Chinese investors; the same people who promised our government they would retain jobs? How are we to report on the loss of hospitals, schools, and other social services previously offered by government-run copper mines? How do we report on the massive influx of Chinese workers taking up jobs previously held by local Africans – and even including the menial jobs? Tell me, how should we report on Chinese owners that mistreat African employees, underpaying them and overworking them? How can we cover stories of Chinese firms that plunder our natural resources and pollute our rivers and streams, disrupting our farms and making our children sick?'

Brave's ruthless characterisation of the Chinese mine-owners had brought the animated discussion to a thoughtful pause.

'I guess there might be a place for the activist journalist then,' Bernice broke the silence. There were a few concurring nods.

'One thing I keep thinking about is how the media only seems to focus on the men who've lost their jobs in the mines. What about the impact on women?' Maya asked, offering a change in direction for the conversation.

'How do you mean?' Hamoonga asked.

'Well, as journalists, I think we should cover the effect that these job losses are having on women. You see, the typical family in the copper-mining towns consists of a husband who works long shifts, his wife, and three or four school-going children. It is the woman in this family who plays multiple roles: cooking, cleaning, taking care of the children, and in most cases bringing in a second, supplementary income to sustain the household.' Maya looked at Temwani, who nodded in agreement. She went on. 'What the job losses have done is to completely change things around. Now the woman's supplementary income has become the only one. The woman selling fruit and vegetables, trading in fish, mending clothes, or raising chickens has now become the main breadwinner. Nobody is talking about how this is affecting the dynamics of family relationships. I think journalists should chronicle these stories.'

'Preach, sister, preach!' Temwani raised her hand in a high five.

'How do we do that, Maya?' Hamoonga leaned forward attentively.

'I say we need to have more female journalists. Right now men are reporting with a distinctly masculine point of view. I feel women are better able to focus in on the human story and bring it to life. Besides, in my view, we would have been able to broker much better deals for our people if women had been leading the negotiations in privatising our mining assets!' Maya could not resist scoring a point in favour of the female sex.

'Yes,' Maya continued, 'the Chinese takeover story is multifaceted. It is also a story of women's empowerment and the reversal of some traditional gender roles just as much as it is a story of job losses, resource plundering, and government incompetence.'

'What about all the roads, stadiums, and bridges that the Chinese are building?' Ken asked, turning his head to look at Temwani.

'That's a good point, Ken!' Hamoonga said. 'One cannot deny all the impressive infrastructure projects that the Chinese are executing in the country and across the continent. Many towns are receiving a face-lift, and it's becoming much easier to travel thanks to the great road network the Chinese are building.'

'True,' Temwani added. 'We cannot deny that the Chinese build really awesome structures. How many state-of-the-art football stadiums has the Zambian government built since 1964?' Temwani asked rhetorically making a large zero with her fingers. The others chuckled.

'But at what cost?' Brave asked in frustration. 'Are we to sell our country's soul for a few nice stadiums? Who has the short end of the straw here?'

Hamoonga nodded, 'I think Brave raises another good point. The Chinese are getting away with a deal lopsided in their favour by oiling the hands of our politicians. China's own house is not clean either, so unlike Western nations, they enter into deals with despots without, for example, asking questions or demanding democratic reform.'

The group discussion continued in the same vein for the better part of two hours with no definitive conclusion. In the end, everyone left with a lot of ideas to use in writing their papers. They continued to meet over the remaining three weeks of the semester, and with each session they grew more familiar with one another, developing a warm friendship of peers. Ken was kept at arms' length by Temwani, but he continued to harbour hopes of 'turning her around'. He believed, or at least he said he believed, that she would eventually succumb to his charms. Hamoonga and Maya continued to flirt with each other without really talking outside of the group. Hamoonga being a gentleman, hesitated for fear of misreading the signs.

Evelyn Hone – year two, first semester

June 2006

It was the end of examination season and the relief in The Hone campus air was palpable, like the sudden popping of a wax-filled ear. A cacophony of sounds emanated from the open windows of the dormitory rooms. Students were chatting away loudly, shuffling through corridors, packing, and playing music at full blast. Bob Marley roots-reggae tunes intertwined clumsily with fast-hopping South African kwaito sounds from radios. Piles of trash had suddenly appeared overnight across the campus like tiny anthills dotting the landscape. Most students were excited to be leaving campus the next day. There would be no books, study groups, lectures, or tutorials for six weeks until the next semester. It was a chance for students to return to their families and be sons and daughters again in the safe bosom of their parents' homes.

In Hamoonga's case, he would be staying on campus as he had done for the year and a half he had been a student at Evelyn Hone. He could not afford the bus fare to Kitwe. Besides, going home would mean that he would lose the opportunity to make a little extra cash assisting Professor Ndlovu with his research work on '*Developing Internet platforms for news media in Sub-Saharan Africa.*' It was cutting-edge work, for the Internet was a new phenomenon in Zambia, something that had the promise of changing how news was delivered and consumed across the entire country. The research work was funded by a grant from the Norwegian government. Professor Ndlovu had secured funding for the project when he was on political asylum in Norway a few years prior to coming to Zambia. While living in Zimbabwe several years earlier, Professor Ndlovu had been an outspoken critic of President Robert Mugabe's land-resettlement programme. This had seen a number of white settlers killed and thousands forcibly removed from their farmland. His articles criticising the government had made it increasingly dangerous for the good professor to remain in Zimbabwe. So, when invited to attend an academic conference in Norway, he refused to return and sought asylum.

It was eight o'clock in the evening and Hamoonga was alone in his room, lying on his narrow bed, reading Chinua Achebe's *Things Fall Apart* for the umpteenth time. Ken had already left that afternoon and would be away for the duration of the six-week break. Hamoonga flipped through the pages of the novel, absorbed in its prose as if for the very first time. As he lay there reading he heard an almost inaudible knock on the door that made him look up and pause. There it was again, another faint knock.

'Hello, who's there?' he called out. Background noise from the other rooms could still be heard in the distance. 'Please give me a minute.' Hamoonga folded the corner of the page, laid the book next to him, and rolled out of bed. He was naked above the waist but had on a pair of faded counterfeit Chelsea Football Club shorts. This Club was his favourite soccer team in the English Premier League. He had followed the team religiously since he was a boy playing on the dusty open fields in Kitwe. He walked the few steps to the door and reached to open it.

'Maya!' he exclaimed, surprised to find her standing alone at his doorstep. 'Hey, what a pleasant surprise. What brings you here?'

Maya wore a *chitenge* with an intricate red and black floral design. She had the cloth neatly tucked underneath her armpits and it extended below her knees. Avoiding eye contact she responded softly, 'Are you busy?'

'Uh, no, no, no, please come in.' He opened the door wider to usher her in. She hurriedly walked in and scoped the room like a cat looking to mark its territory.

'Are you sure I'm not interrupting?' she asked.

'No, no I wasn't doing much, please sit down.' Hamoonga signalled for her to take a seat on his bed as he closed the door behind him. Maya sat down on his bed and picked up the Achebe book he'd been reading.

'Are you reading this?'

'Yes,' Hamoonga replied. 'I must admit this is perhaps the hundredth time. It's such a classic that I find myself going back to read parts of it again and again. Have you read it?'

Maya nodded. 'Yes, I did once in school, but it took me ages. I struggled through it. I just got bogged down by all the details. I mean, Achebe goes on and on describing the seasons, bare-chested men wrestling and so on. It just wasn't my cup of tea. But I do recognise that he's an iconic African writer.'

Hamoonga chuckled nervously as he sat down next to her. 'I get what you mean. I can see why some people might not like the novel, but for me it's not only a seminal book, but it also has sentimental value. It was the very first book that I ever read by an African writer, so it will always be something special.'

'You read a lot, don't you?' she asked.

'I try to, it's good for the soul,' Hamoonga replied.

'I can tell. You always have such intelligent things to say. I like that.' Maya looked down at the floor.

Hamoonga smiled at the compliment but said nothing. There was an awkward silence for a few seconds then Hamoonga asked, 'I'm sorry, can I offer you anything – water or juice?'

Maya shook her head. After another awkward silence, Maya looked up at him and said, 'Hamoonga is there anyone special in your life? I mean, what kind of woman do you like?'

Wrong-footed by her forwardness, the young man fumbled for a response. 'Uh, no, I don't have anyone… I mean I have many friends, but not like that.'

'Why is that?' she asked, cornering him.

'Well, I don't know, I guess I've just been focussed on school, busy studying. You know how hectic it gets.' He didn't expect that a girl could be so straightforward about such matters.

'So what kind of woman are you looking for?' she asked again.

Hamoonga hesitated, not knowing how best to answer her. He looked up at Maya. She was now staring directly at him, watching and waiting for his answer. He thought, perhaps, the look in her eyes was that of supplication – a woman ready to give of her most sacred fruit if only he would ask. 'Well, I guess I'm looking for a person that I can get along with, a person for whom I have a special feeling.'

'So, do you feel something special for me?' It was such a direct question that Hamoonga was dumbfounded. She paused momentarily and then moved closer to him. He could feel the warmth of her body through her *chitenge*. Without saying another word she reached to untie the knot in the wrap. It loosened and fell to her waist revealing two perfectly formed breasts. Hamoonga was transfixed, unable to resist her overtures. He kissed her tenderly on the lips, and as he did so he could feel the warmth of her breath pulling him towards her. With each pulsating motion of their lips, he could feel her pace quickening. He sensed her confidence growing and her inhibitions melting away. Finally, he embraced her and laid her prostrate on the bed.

❖

Maya left early the next morning as she'd told Hamoonga she needed to catch a bus to her elder sister's home in Livingstone. He felt it rather cowardly of her to slip out so early just to avoid the awkward dance that first-time lovers are compelled to have the morning after. As he lay in bed, he could still smell Maya's sweet feminine musk. He reminisced that it had been only his third time with a woman. Actually his second, because the first time had been back in the day playing childish games in the bushes with a local girl named Mukosha. They were both about ten years old at the time, so that didn't count. The only other time was just after high school when he had slept with Mwansa, his sister Beatrice's friend. She had been much more experienced than him. He recalled fumbling his way for all of two minutes and then wondering what all the fuss was about. But Maya had been tender and responsive to his caresses, she had clung to him, and he had felt the tension and relaxation of her every muscle in their embrace.

When the new semester finally started, Maya and Hamoonga began to spend more time with each other. He stopped by her room in the mornings to walk with her to lectures. They would spend afternoons studying in the library and take evening strolls around the campus buildings, just talking with the openness of youth, willing to indulge in the infinite possibilities that lay in the distant horizon too far away to be constrained by the laws of nature. Without making any formal commitments or grandiose promises, there was a sort of tacit agreement between the two of them that they were in a relationship. He cared for her and she cared for him; it needed no formality.

Maya had experienced a challenging time growing up. She was an AIDS orphan, as her parents had both passed away within a year of each other when she was only fourteen. She then moved to Livingstone to live with her elder sister. Ten years her senior, her sister was married with three little children of her own. When she was sixteen and living with her sister, Maya was sexually abused by her brother-in-law. It left a scar harboured deeply hidden within her, like a murdered body stashed away in a dark cellar – out of sight but forever present. The abuse had lasted for several months before her sister found out and divorced her husband. With him gone, Maya's sister was left to support her three children and her sixteen-year-old sister. It was a squalid episode that not only stretched their finances but perforated the relationship between the sisters, leaving it vulnerable to bitterness and disdain.

As the weeks progressed, Ken gained a newfound respect for his understated roommate. 'You Kopala Boys got some mad skills, *exsay!*' Ken would say, proceeding to interrogate his roommate for intimate details, which Hamoonga never fully shared. Ken himself continued to struggle with winning the affections of Maya's friend Temwani, but like a stubborn cold sore he persisted.

Chapter 4

Meet Lulu

Evelyn Hone - year two, final semester

October 2006

Three weeks into the final semester of Hamoonga's sophomore year, he and Ken were returning to the town centre from Northmead. Hamoonga could still feel a tingling sensation on the shaven skin behind his ears and on the back of his neck. He caught a whiff of the spirit that the barber had doused him with after his shave.

It was a clear Saturday morning, the hot sub-Saharan sun was beaming down and the two men were returning from Momo's Barbershop. Ken had suggested the excursion, as he placed great stock on appearance. Influenced as he was by American hip-hop music videos, it was his credo to dress in fashionable jeans and jackets, don the latest sneakers, and get a *shape-up* at the barbershop every fortnight. Despite his protestations earlier that morning, Hamoonga had reluctantly tagged along with his roommate. He generally didn't opt for frivolous expenditure on fancy clothes and hairstyles.

Going to the barber was eventful because it meant riding on the local minibuses which were always packed to the hilt: meant for twelve, they were typically filled with twenty-plus passengers, not counting the driver and conductor. Indeed, being a passenger in a minibus on the streets of Lusaka felt like being a contortionist, as one had to skillfully adjust or deform one's body to fit into an improbable space. Additionally, the buses seemed to be perpetually in disrepair with faulty brake pedals that needed repeated pumping, rusted bodies, and noisy, punctured exhaust pipes that spewed blue smoke. The interiors of the buses were frequently decked with makeshift seats and cheap synthetic upholstery. The conductor, or *kaponya*, was usually a rude teenage boy, high on weed, barking obscenities at passengers and passersby alike. He would insist, 'Five, five *ku* last!' Regardless of heft, there had to be five people on the back seat.

At the behest of the conductor, the bus came to a halt in the town centre at the intersection between Cairo Road and Church Road. The two young men hurriedly grabbed their change from the conductor and clambered out over the limbs and seats of other passengers.

'*Aba leya, aba leya!*' the *kaponya* shouted, showering those closest to him with spittle and waving his arms demonstratively to passers-by in a bid to solicit new passengers.

'*Exsay*, I tell you, I hate those buses, it's like you're sitting on top of each other the whole time! And I gotta tell you, some people need to take showers and use some deodorant, for real, *brah!*' Ken lamented as they began to walk down Cairo Road. 'I mean some people's armpits be kicking like karate, you know what I'm sayin'? You know some of those smelly pits could kill a fly, it ain't right!'

Hamoonga laughed. Ken knew how to use the most colourful language to express himself. 'I hear you, man. The thing that bothers me is that it's not safe to pack people into a tiny bus like that. If we got into an accident – man, I don't even wanna think about it!'

'*Brah*, I swear, *exsay,* when I make my millions, I ain't never using public transportation again, I swear, *exsay!*' Ken shook his head in disgust. As he saw it, using public transportation was an indignity that he had to suffer, a slight to his debonair self-image.

'Ha, ha! I hear you, yeah, that's the spirit, work hard and make those millions, brother!' The two walked down the busy sidewalk teeming with street vendors selling their wares. Ever since President Chibompo had put a stop to the city mayor's drive to clear the streets of illegal panhandlers, the sidewalks had become overwhelmed by vendors. The president had weighed in because the mayor's initiative had caused a political stir. The street vendors were being forcibly removed by the police and this had angered the powerful Marketeers

Union. Sensing a political backlash, President Chibompo had issued an edict to stop the removals. The president's intervention was more out of self-preservation than concern for the vendors. Nonetheless, his edict had resulted in even more street vendors selling their wares on the sidewalks and pavements; overflowing onto the roads, they created an unsightly shambles.

Dodging their way through the sea of bodies, Ken and Hamoonga spotted a familiar face; it was Ben, from their Journalistic Ethics discussion group. He seemed to be engaged in an intense price negotiation with one of the female street peddlers.

'Ben!' Ken shouted as they drew nearer.

He looked up at the sound of his name, and seeing Ken and Hamoonga approaching through the crowd, grinned in recognition. 'Hey guys! *Whassup, ma bros*, what brings you to town?' he asked. 'I was just trying to load up on some *tute* and groundnuts for the dorm. What's good with you boys?'

'Ah, that's the real deal, dude!' Ken responded. 'I think I found you at the right time, *brah*, I need some grub. I swear this heat is making me wanna *nosh* so bad!' Ken chuckled as he extended his arm. The two friends pulled each other in for a manly half hug and perfunctory pat on the back. Ben then turned to Hamoonga and the two exchanged a similar embrace.

'Where are you *owns* coming from? You look like *owns* on a mission. I'm sure there's either *cheddar* or *goozers* involved.' Ben laughed.

'Ha ha! You know it, *exsay*, you know how we players play!' Ken responded with an arrogant smile. 'We just came back from Momo's, *exsay*, we *rocked* there to tighten our fades, *exsay*; you know how it go, *exsay*?' He stroked his head to show off his new clean-shaven look with its raised tuft of hair on the top. 'There's gonna be a mad jam tonight by Zenon and I, for one, wanna look tight for the chicks, you understand?'

'Ah I hear you, *ma brah*, a man's always gotta look sharp – sharp to get the best *goozers!*' Ben chuckled. 'I gotta take *ma* lessons from you, *brah, fo' sho!*' The two slapped each other's hands in agreement.

Hamoonga always felt a little out of place in conversations like this. He couldn't quite speak the hip Lusaka lingo, and the whole overt bravado of it all usually put him off. Most times he simply listened, smiled and laughed tepidly at their jokes – most of which he did not really get.

Ken and Ben continued to make small talk for a while, oblivious to the frustrated pedestrians that were forced to manoeuvre their way around them. Having waited on the periphery for a few minutes, Hamoonga turned to excuse himself. 'Hey guys, let me just shoot over to Shoprite for a second to grab some milk. Do either of you need anything?'

'Nah, you go ahead. You'll find us here. We have to wait on the grub. I ain't leaving without it, *brah*!' Ben replied. Ken reached out and slapped Ben's palm.

'Me neither, I'm straight, *brah*, you go ahead. You'll find us here,' Ken added with a check of his head.

'Okay, cool, I'll see you in a few minutes then.' Hamoonga hurried off to the supermarket a few blocks down Cairo Road, melding into the bustling crowd.

Shoprite was always a stuffy place, teeming with customers. The atmosphere in the store was usually dense with hot body odour mixed with smells of soap, raw meat and fruit. The lines at the counter were perpetually long and the checkout personnel seemed perennially rude and disinterested. Still, Hamoonga frequented the store for its broad selection of fresh food. It went against the grain to spend money in a big, foreign-owned chain store, but there weren't too many other good options.

He made his way to the back of the store and pulled out a half-litre container of milk from the open refrigerator. The surrounding air was frigid, a welcome reprieve from the heat outside. He promptly brushed through the thicket of bodies to the nearest checkout line which, surprisingly, was not very long for a weekend. There was a small boy ahead of him with two loaves of freshly baked bread, and a tall gentleman in a navy suit in the process of paying for his basket of assorted goods. Waiting, Hamoonga saw a small refrigerator with neatly stacked Coca-Cola on the top shelf, Fanta on the middle shelf, and Sprite at the bottom. Indulging an impulse – he leant over, opened the display door, and took out a Coke. The bottle felt cold, droplets of moisture covered the surface like morning dew. It was at that moment that he heard a sultry but confident female voice from behind him.

'You know that drinking that stuff will kill you, right?'

He glanced over his left shoulder with a quizzical expression. An expensively dressed woman was standing behind an overflowing shopping cart, her hands, nails sculpted, resting on her trolley; she was surely too elegant to be pushing a cart, doing her own shopping!

'Drinking that stuff will kill you,' she repeated with the confidence of a woman fully aware of her own charisma.

Hamoonga, momentarily tongue-tied, glanced down at the bottle in his hand and then back at her and was smitten.

'Sorry?' Hamoonga stuttered.

'Are you hard of hearing?'

'I, I, *uhm*, well it's just a drink,' Hamoonga didn't have an answer. How could he explain that he drank so little Coke, it was always a treat.

'Do you know how much sugar is in those soft drinks? You'll be suffering from diabetes and goodness knows what else by the time you're fifty.' The woman smiled, revealing a perfect set of white teeth. 'Besides, you don't want to lose that figure. I'm sure it would be a shame for the ladies,' she said teasingly.

Hamoonga searched for a clever response, but couldn't find one.

'So what do you suggest I drink?'

'Oh, you can't go wrong with water. It's zero calories and it cleanses your system. You look like an educated guy, you should know that.'

'That's good advice,' Hamoonga began to enjoy himself, 'but my mother always told me not to listen to strangers.'

'I believe it's "never *talk*" to strangers, but I guess you already broke that rule,' she smiled. 'I'm Lulu, and who are you?'

'I'm Hamoonga, pleased to meet you.'

'And pleased to meet you,' Lulu smiled confidently revealing two perfect dimples in her cheeks.

'Next please!' The rude voice of the cashier prompted Hamoonga to quickly give his Coke and milk to the teller who scanned the items and punched a series of keys. 'Three pin five,' she announced unenthusiastically, without making eye contact. The young man rummaged through his pockets and produced some crumpled kwacha notes. He counted the money, two, three, three thousand one, three thousand two... He was short. Conscious of all within earshot – especially Lulu behind him – his chest tightened as he searched his pockets again. *Oh God, don't embarrass me in front of her, not now, not now!* He thought to himself. He was sure he'd had just enough change: the bus conductor must have stiffed him. Bastard! Tail between his legs, Hamoonga reached out to remove the Coke but was stopped by Lulu behind him.

'Here you go,' she said, handing the cashier a crisp five-thousand-kwacha note. Like a live chicken stuffed in a wet sack, Hamoonga could not look at her directly.

'No, you don't have to, I… ' Hamoonga began.

'I know,' Lulu interrupted. 'You'll pay me back some time.' She smiled as the cashier processed the transaction.

'Thank you so much, this is so embarrassing. I must have left my wallet. I promise I will pay you back – I promise,' Hamoonga tried to save face.

'Don't worry about it, you'll pay me back, I'm sure; you look trustworthy. Here's my card.' She lifted a business card from her purse. Hamoonga meekly accepted it, almost too embarrassed to face her. 'Call me sometime next week, I'll be back from Jo'burg and you can pay me back then.'

◆

By the time Lulu was fourteen, her mother had decided to send her off to an all-girls' Catholic boarding school to curb the plethora of male advances Lulu was receiving. Lulu had always been the prettiest girl among her friends and she knew it. She was used to pimple-faced boys with cracking voices declaring their undying love. Once, Peter, who lived two streets down in Mungwi Close, compiled an entire ninety-minute TDK cassette full of R&B love songs, which he dedicated to her. Peter wrote a four-page letter in which he professed his 'endless love' and that he would follow her 'to the moon and stars above': phrases he had expertly plagiarised from the popular American ballads that all the girls loved. Peter delivered his cassette tape and letter one evening after school when Lulu had separated from the giggling bevy of schoolgirls on their walk home.

'Awww, you're so sweet, Peter,' she told him, extending her lower lip in a cute but mocking expression. 'But you're like a brother to me. How can I date my brother?' And so Peter was relegated to the line of hopelessly expectant boys who pandered to Lulu's every whim but fell short of receiving her romantic ministrations.

Sent away to boarding school, Lulu loathed it. She resented her mother for sending her away from her fiefdom to languish in the confined spaces of an austere school and chafed at all the rules. Our Lady of Africa Catholic Boarding School for Girls was located on the outskirts of Ndola, an old industrial town about three hundred and fifty miles north of her city, Lusaka. The school was surrounded by a wooded area that could be accessed only by a meandering, narrow, dusty road. It doubled as both a school and a nunnery, and the nuns ran the place with remarkable efficiency. They grew their own vegetables, reared poultry and pigs, and even had a borehole installed to supply water for the school. They used their limited resources to great effect. Most meals were prepared using local produce. Nothing was ever wasted; even the corn husks were used as feed for the livestock.

The classroom buildings were arranged in the form of a square with a patchy lawn in the central quadrangle. The classrooms were basic: concrete walls with a painted wooden blackboard at one end and plain glass louvered windows on adjacent sides. The floors were of smooth concrete stained with a burgundy polish that needed to be refreshed every few days, a chore the students detested. Each classroom was packed with close to forty rickety wooden desks and chairs. Fluorescent lighting tubes layered the exposed asbestos ceilings in each classroom, many of them in need of replacing.

Dormitories at the school were nestled roughly thirty metres behind the eastern side of the classroom square, with the principal's office directly facing the wide gravel driveway. Sister Rose Polenta was the principal, an Italian nun who'd come to Zambia as a missionary when she was twenty-one and never left. Sister Rose was a firm disciplinarian, quick to chide students and staff alike; she did not suffer fools lightly. There were rumours that she had once interrupted Archbishop Milingo during his Easter homily to publicly chastise two nuns who were whispering.

No one was allowed to leave the campus for any reason without the express permission of Sister Rose. She knew everything and everyone. Nothing escaped her. Needless to say, Lulu struggled to fit in. The regimented, communal life did not suit her and she longed for her old life in the city.

One warm Sunday evening, Lulu decided to stroll among the orange trees in the orchard at the southern end of the campus. She did this sometimes just to escape the confined spaces of the dormitory walls. It was always quiet at this time of day, for many of the girls chose to take a nap or catch up on their reading. Lulu relished these moments and imagined herself living freely away from the nuns, the claustrophobic buildings, the chores, and all the rules. As she made her way through the citrus trees, she savoured the peace. So, she was startled when she heard a voice from behind.

'I didn't know you were the type to appreciate nature?'

Lulu opened her eyes. 'Mr Chanda! I'm sorry, I didn't see you there!'

'That's okay, what are you doing out here all by yourself?'

'Nothing, sir, I was just taking a walk, trying to enjoy the quietness.'

Mr Chanda was one of two chemistry teachers and one of only four male teachers in the entire faculty. Sister Rose had recruited him as a last resort, due to an acute shortage of qualified chemistry teachers and because so few good teachers wanted a posting at a remote Catholic school. Mr Chanda had an impressive résumé. He had graduated from the University of Zambia with distinction and taught physics and chemistry at two of the best technical government secondary schools in the country. Despite this, Sister Rose had dithered, aware, firstly, that he was only twenty-eight, male, and unmarried. Young men and flirtatious teenage girls formed an unholy mix. Secondly, Sister Rose did not really believe Mr Chanda's reasons for wanting to work so far from the city. He had ventured that he simply needed a change and that city life was too fast for him.

'I would not have imagined you to be one for taking walks and appreciating nature,' Mr Chanda looked quizzically at the pretty teenager.

Coquettishly rubbing her index finger along her exposed collarbone, Lulu retaliated, 'Well, I come out here most Sunday evenings just to get away from those dormitory walls. Why is that so strange to you?'

The young man cleared his throat, 'Oh no… I get it. I take a walk around the grounds most evenings; it helps me relax. I just didn't think you were the contemplative type.'

'Oh, I see. Well, that kind of hurts my feelings, sir,' Lulu teased him, 'What kind of girl did you think I was?'

Visibly unsettled, the chemistry teacher pulled nervously at his sleeve. 'Oh, oh, no, I didn't mean it like that, I meant…' He choked as he struggled to find the right words like a confidence trickster suddenly exposed. She noticed that he had begun to blush. 'No, I mean, I didn't think you'd be someone to enjoy nature that much. I thought you were rather a city girl.'

Lulu smiled. Mr Chanda had an unexpectedly boyish quality, as he struggled to avoid eye contact and fidgeted with embarrassment. It was all too familiar. Many boys, and men, had behaved this way towards her. It was as if she possessed a certain force field that put a hex on men that drew too near. She basked in the knowledge that she was able to disrupt a man's thoughts just by her sheer presence. Looking at her new victim, she enjoyed the unexpected moment of power.

'Well, I do love the city but I also enjoy getting away, and the peace that nature offers. I guess you and me are very alike. Am I right?' Lulu gathered confidence as Mr Chanda seemed to lose it.

'Wha... what do you mean?'

'I mean are you for the city or the country?'

'Oh, oh of course, I... I love the country for sure, but I like the convenience of the city too.'

'So, what brought you here?'

'I grew tired of the pace of the city. I spent three years teaching in Lusaka, but it wore me out. I needed to get away.' He stared past her.

'Are you happy here then? No regrets?'

'Yes, I'm happy, it was a good move. No regrets, no regrets at all.' His tone was unconvincing.

'That's good, because regrets are like bad habits. You're better off without them!' Lulu raised her right eyebrow.

'Well, that's pretty profound for a teenage girl!' Mr Chanda's voice expressed surprise and patronage in equal measure.

'Yes, we teenage girls do come up with some pretty good insights sometimes!' Lulu said ironically as they both laughed, and the tension eased.

'Well, I'd better finish my walk before it gets too dark. Maybe I'll bump into you again. I might have some more profound insights, you never know!' Lulu smiled mischievously and walked away before the man could respond.

And so began a regular private rendezvous. And after the third *faux* serendipitous meeting, they shed all pretense, meeting every Sunday underneath the lemon tree away from the footpath and prying eyes.

Their friendship strengthened through each encounter. Mr Chanda spoke about his past life, a single-parent home, and his love of poetry, classical literature, and jazz. On a few occasions, he even brought his portable CD player and they sat side by side each with one end of an earphone listening to Miles Davis and Jonny Coltrane. Buoyed by her youthful enthusiasm, the teacher shared some of his own poetry with her, reading from a tattered notebook, ideas and feelings he had not shared with anyone before. Lulu listened as yet untainted by cynicism and the man felt she understood him in ways others could not. Lulu too looked forward to their encounters.

She was drawn to Mr Chanda's worldly knowledge, his ability to talk about European artists she'd never heard of such Picasso and Van Gogh or famous architects such as Frank Lloyd Wright. Lulu shared her music, Celine Dion, Aliyah, Whitney Houston, and Mariah Carey. She talked about her dreams: to travel, to write, to fall in love, and to champion the rights of African women.

The feeling that they were breaking the rules – rebelling from Sister Rose's ironclad hold – added a thrill to their trysts and the months passed. No one caught them out, and they became confident as they became careless.

Their Sunday evenings in the orchard continued from February of Lulu's final year until one Sunday in August of that same year.

'I know you'll love this song by Luther Vandross,' Lulu said excitedly. 'My cousin brought the CD for me when she visited my parents last weekend. It's amazing!' She placed a silver disk into the portable CD player with the enthusiasm of a little girl. The disk had the words, '*Chi Chi's Love Jamz*' written across one face in black ink. She scooted over to Mr Chanda's side as she navigated her index finger across the miniscule buttons on the the player.

He felt the warmth of her body and could smell her clean, flowery scent; excitement triggered a lucid image of him caressing her silky skin. He tried to arrest his thoughts by fiddling with the loose button on his cotton shirt.

'I think it's called – *So Amazing*. I fell in love with the song the moment I heard it!' Lulu placed one of the earphones in her right ear and the other in his left ear. She scrolled to song number five and pressed the play button.

Unable to control the torrent of thoughts flooding his mind, Mr Chanda stole a glance at her exposed shoulder. She began to sing along to the Luther Vandross song, 'Love has, truly, been good to me . . .'

Mr Chanda could feel his mouth going dry. He looked at Lulu's lower leg, smooth without blemish. His eyes followed her exposed limbs and foraged shamelessly up from her ankles to the nexus between her mocha-coloured thighs. He watched her as she continued to sing, her eyes closed. He drew closer with each accentuated movement of her lips until they were but inches apart.

Lulu opened her eyes and immediately stopped singing. Unsure, she hesitated. Mr Chanda could feel the cadence of her breathing. He slowly tilted his head and moved to kiss her softly. As he touched her lips, she pulled back. Her heart was racing laps in her chest. The man felt an amalgam of fear and excitement. If he had known months previously that meeting a young student was wrong, that he could be fired and dismissed from the teaching service, it was too late, he craved her. The teacher moved his right hand slowly up Lulu's inner left thigh, erasing her innocence with every inch. He kissed her again, parting his lips to feel the wetness of her mouth. This time she lingered a few seconds before pulling back again, perhaps conflicted by the angel on her right shoulder and the devil on her left. Mr Chanda kissed her again as his hand inched further up her thigh. The girl closed her eyes and succumbed to his advances.

This was not Mr Chanda's first rodeo. He had always had a weakness for underage girls, a perversion that had gone undetected for a few years in his early teaching career until he was caught in an uncompromising situation with a fifteen-year-old student. Each time the incident had been hushed up, for his uncle was the National Commissioner of Schools and each time he was merely transferred to a different school.

♋

Lulu and Mr Chanda stopped meeting after that Sunday in August. She could not talk to anyone about what had happened. Her teacher had stolen her virginity, her innocence, she felt it as a violation but she knew too that she had flirted with him and enjoyed his admiration. Confused, she avoided him at every turn and he did the same.

Lulu withdrew into a shell. Her friends and the nuns noticed her sudden disengagement but no one could figure it out. She studied alone, and even waited for the others to have their showers before she did so, as if she was afraid of something. She stopped participating in class discussions and was engulfed in a self-loathing that ate away at her like a tumour. A number of weeks passed with Lulu sinking deeper into a depression, until one morning she vomited in the dining hall and was taken to see the nurse. It didn't take long for the results to come in. She was pregnant!

Sister Rose was livid. She took it as a personal insult, an affront to the values she had worked so tirelessly to instill in her students. How could this have happened right beneath her nose? Like a woman confronting her husband about the perfume on his person, she demanded answers.

'My dear girl, you know what you've done,' Sister Rose said sternly as Lulu sat in her office and stared at the floor. 'And you know all too well that when we make decisions in life, we should be prepared to suffer the consequences of those decisions. How far along are you?'

Lulu remained silent.

'Are you deaf as well as stupid? Don't let me repeat myself!'

'Two… two months, I think,' the girl replied timidly, still facing the floor.

'Whose is it?' Sister demanded.

Lulu shrugged.

Sister raised her voice. 'I asked you, whose child is it?'

'I… I…'

'Don't tell me you don't know! Whose is it!'

'Mr Chanda,' Lulu surrendered almost inaudibly as she began to cry.

Sister Rose drew back, wincing in disbelief. 'What did you say?'

'It was Mr Chanda, the chemistry teacher.'

'What in heaven's name…' Sister Rose failed to complete her sentence. Her mind filled with thoughts about the repercussions and what should be done. She looked at the dejected figure curled before her, and was overwhelmed with pity. Lulu was after all a child, a child in her care who had been violated by a man in a position of authority, a 'degenerate' in her book. She leaned back silently in her chair. The silence broken only by the girl's sobbing.

Mr Chanda was summoned to Sister Rose's office and dismissed. Against her first impulse the nun had stopped short of calling the police. Mr Chanda might go to jail, but the publicity of the trial would take a terrible toll. Instead the young man was given an unequivocal warning that if he ever laid foot in another school in Zambia, she would personally report him to the authorities and expose him as a predator and rapist.

Lulu was sent back home to Lusaka, to the huge disappointment of her mother. Unwilling to stain the reputation of their family in their community, her mother decided not to pursue the matter of Mr Chanda. In her view, admitting that a mere secondary school teacher had impregnated her daughter was more shame than she could bear.

Sister Rose did, however, allow Lulu to return in December to sit for her national examinations. She passed and gave birth to a healthy baby girl in April of the following year. She named her daughter Misozi, a reminder of the hardships she'd had to endure as a frightened, pregnant teenage girl.

Lulu, though, had fighting spirit and like a flower blossoming between the cracks of a concrete pavement, she survived against the odds. With the support of her mother she enrolled in university and impossibly balanced her studies with the ever-demanding duties of motherhood. Determination bore her through the gruelling semesters and five years later, she graduated with a degree in Business Administration from the University of Zambia.

Chapter 5

Your Day

Hamoonga picked up the business card lying on his desk, a smooth white card with gold embossed lettering. '*Your Day-Event Planners*', and immediately below, '*We will make Your Day a day to remember.*' Then in smaller, plain typeface this was followed by Louise 'Lulu' Daka, Managing Director, and her contact details.

Hamoonga deliberated on whether or not to call, though the truth was that he had been thinking about Lulu ever since they'd met, repeatedly replaying their conversation. Of course, there was the question of returning the money he owed her, but he knew that could only be an excuse. She didn't need the money – it was but loose change to her. No, he knew that she'd been flirting with him and he'd enjoyed it. He also knew that if he picked up the phone to call her, there would be no turning back. Hamoonga sensed that Lulu was a woman who got whatever she wanted, and that once in her web, resistance would indeed be futile.

He thought about Maya. She was a sweet girl and maybe he loved her; certainly, he would never do anything to hurt her. But he could not put the encounter with Lulu behind him, and, finally, he rationalised that he was only doing the honourable thing, and returning the money he'd borrowed.

The phone rang twice before a cheery female voice answered, 'Your Day Event Planners, can I help you?'

Hamoonga cleared his throat, 'Good morning, madam, could I… please speak to a Mrs Daka?'

'You mean *Ms* Lulu Daka? Sure. May I know who's calling?'

'Oh yes, sorry, I mean, '*Ms*' Daka. My name is Hamoonga. I called because I owe…' Before he could finish his sentence, the voice on the line interrupted him saying, 'Please hold on as I connect you.' He stopped, cleared his voice nervously, his cell phone pressed tightly against his ear. He was standing in a corner of his room where the cell phone reception was strongest, all the while thinking about his 'air time'.

'So, I see you're a man of your word.' He heard a sultry female voice on the line after almost a minute.

'Hello, Lulu, it is me, Hamoonga. Do you remember me? You helped me out two weeks ago in Shoprite. I believe I owe you some money.' He hoped she couldn't hear his voice quavering.

'Yes, of course I remember you, and yes, I believe you do owe me,' she replied.

'I have the money now. What's the best way for me to return it to you?'

'Well, you can stop by my shop at Arcades Mall around four today. Ask for me when you get here.'

'Okay. I can do that. What's the name of your store?'

'*Your Day*, of course!' With that she hung up, leaving Hamoonga to replay the conversation in his head. He felt a little stupid. The name of her shop was written on her business card!

That afternoon, he headed towards Arcades Shopping Mall, the latest in a string of malls springing up in the city. It was an outdoor strip mall set behind Great East Road, and had an elegant frontage lined with palm trees and about thirty assorted shops. A few of them were small, privately owned boutiques with merchandise imported from China and Dubai, but the bulk of them were large South African-owned chain stores. There was a bookstore, a few coffee shops, bars, restaurants, a multi-screen cinema, and a bowling alley. Like most of such amenities in Zambia, Arcades was only accessible to the elite of society, and the expats from the US and Europe.

Hamoonga disembarked from the blue-and-white minibus at the stop across from the large outdoor parking lot. The minibus rattled away in its rusty metallic body as if whining to be put to rest. He opened his wallet and counted the crispy kwacha bills in his possession. He was not going to embarrass himself again. As he traversed the parking lot, he could not help but notice how full it was of expensive vehicles: Mitsubishi Pajero SUVs, Lexus sedans, Mercedes Benzes, Audis, and BMW convertibles. To his left, he could even see a bright yellow Hummer, an arrogant-looking teenage boy in dark shades behind the wheel.

This was certainly a world apart from Kwacha East Township in Kitwe where life was always a struggle just to get by. Here one could smell the opulence, here money flowed freely. It was as if these people had acquired the elixir that staved off all want. Straight ahead was a black 500-Series Mercedes Benz in immaculate condition, gleaming in the sunlight. As he drew closer he could make out the license plate, 'GRZ 1881' and two miniature Zambian flags set erect to the left and right over the bumper. This could only mean that the car belonged to a government minister, and he wondered which one. His eye ran over the stores in the u-shaped plaza as he looked for 'Your Day'. He passed a bookstore on his left which was empty of customers. He chuckled at the thought that rich people did not spend much time reading. He then passed two bustling shoe stores and a pretty courtyard with some outdoor chairs and tables before he noticed the gold sign ahead: *Your Day.*

The exterior of the shop was painted in white and gold, and had two large windows with mannequins dressed in elegant bridal gowns. A neon sign above the entrance flashed the name of the store. He looked at his watch – it was 3:42. He was a little early. He decided it wouldn't hurt to look around until Lulu was ready to see him. As Hamoonga approached the entrance, three people emerged, two men in suits, followed by a woman a few steps behind. The first, younger man had a muscular frame, a clean-shaven head and wore dark sunglasses. His black suit seemed a size too small for him. He appeared uneasy, looking left and right, behind and before him as if he was being chased by some invisible foe. The second man was shorter and stockier, with a head of salt and pepper hair groomed into a small afro. He wore a beige safari suit with a silky cream scarf draped elegantly around his neck. His generous waistline was further evidence of a comfortable existence. The woman seemed older than both of them and was dressed in a blue African *chitenge* and several heavy gold necklaces. Hamoonga made way for the trio as they briskly exited the store without acknowledging his presence. Breezing through the parking lot, they made a beeline towards the black Mercedes Benz where the older couple got into the back, and the younger man acted as the chauffeur.

Hamoonga slowly entered the boutique which had a spacious modern feel despite the several models ostentatiously draped and jewelled. Towards the back of the shop there were two high counters with stools for customers to browse through catalogues displaying their expensive products. Pretty young attendants in trendy hairstyles stood poised to answer every request. The store was relatively busy with women gathered around the catalogues and clothing racks twittering among themselves. Hamoonga felt awkward and out of place, conscious that he was both the wrong gender and the wrong class.

'Do you need some help, sir?' a young attendant with glossy red lips enquired. Hamoonga gave the girl his name and asked to see Lulu. She told him to wait and disappeared through the door marked 'Staff Only'.

Hamoonga fidgeted uncomfortably until she returned, saying cheerfully, 'She says you should come through to her office now,' and she signalled for him to follow her.

Lulu sat behind a large desk made of dark wood empty of everything but a slim silver Apple laptop and three photographs. A row of framed posters of beautiful African women in expensive wedding dresses or colourful traditional clothing lined the walls. The spacious room also had a lounge area with a black leather love seat, two matching armchairs and a coffee table on which sat an ornate carved bowl filled with aromatic potpourri. Facing the lounge area, was a large flat-screen LCD Samsung TV.

Lulu was pacing the floor behind her desk as she talked on her cell phone. She turned to face Hamoonga offered a welcoming smile and gestured for the young man to take a seat. The girl left quickly closing the door behind her as Lulu mouthed, 'Just give me a minute.'

Hamoonga smiled, nodded, and sat down. Then, leaning forward he tried to make out the faces in the photographs on her desk. Two, in black and white, were, he guessed, of her parents. The colour photograph was of a little girl of about five years old in red shorts and a T-shirt. It had to be a daughter or a favourite niece.

Lulu was wearing a single-piece bright yellow dress and carved wooden bracelets on both wrists which matched the pendant around her neck.

'Ba Mwape, I need you to go down to Kazungula border post tomorrow and sort out this mess with the paperwork,' Lulu's voice was clipped. 'I can't have my merchandise sitting waiting to be cleared. You know how things grow legs over there. Time is money. We need to have our new inventory in before the Christmas season. Can you do that for me?' There was a pause and then she continued, 'That's my man – I know I can rely on you to come through for me. Pass by the office tomorrow and I'll make sure you have enough for expenses. Okay, Ba Mwape, until tomorrow. Bye-bye!' She hung up and turned towards Hamoonga.

'I'm sorry about that. It was rude of me to keep you waiting. How are you, Mr Hamoonga?' She smiled brightly.

'Oh, I'm fine, no need to apologise.' He held out his hands. 'I've come to say thank you again for saving me from embarrassment at the grocery store – and,' he smiled sheepishly , 'to return the loan.'

'Can I offer you a drink?' Lulu asked, ignoring his words. 'I only have healthy drinks, none of those sugary soft ones.' She smiled as she got up to open the little refrigerator to the side of her desk. 'Let's see, I have bottled water, fresh fruit juice, or I can get Linda to make us some tea?'

'Um, I was not really going to stay long, I was just going to…'

'Mmh…' Lulu raised an eyebrow, 'Culturally it's rude to refuse to eat or drink when your host offers you something? I know we live in modern times, but we have to remain true to our culture, right?' She looked him in the eye and gave a mischievous smile.

'Okay, since you put it that way, I'll have some tea, please.'

'Good.' Lifting the phone she made the order and then turned her attention back to her guest.

'So tell me about yourself, Hamoonga – where are you from what do you do? My guess is you're not from around here and that you're a student of some sort.'

'You're right on both counts. I'm from Kitwe and I'm a journalism student at Evelyn Hone College.'

'That's interesting. I spent some years in the Copperbelt Province not too far from Kitwe at a boarding school. It seems a lifetime ago.' Hamoonga enjoyed the link, even though it was a small one. 'What did you think about that part of the country?'

'It was okay at the time but it was a little too isolated for me. I missed the hustle and bustle of the capital. You know, I'm a city girl, always have been, always will be. How long have you been in Lusaka?'

'Coming close to two years now. I like it but I miss home. I miss my family. I haven't been able to make it back yet since I arrived in Lusaka. I hope to go home this Christmas season.'

'Yes, family is really important. You must keep a connection with them. It's said, "never forget where you come from". Right?'

Hamoonga nodded, and pointed to the photographs on her desk. 'Is that your family?'

'Yes, that's my mother and father. My dad passed away many years ago and my mum died last year.' He could feel the pain in her voice and he was sorry he had asked.

'They were great people,' Lulu continued, 'both civil servants: mum was a nurse and dad a lawyer. They worked hard to provide for my sister and me, and we never lacked for anything. My father died in a bus accident on his way to the Eastern Province. His passing devastated us. Mum died of breast cancer.' She paused, her expression turned inward.

'I'm sorry, I didn't mean to bring up painful memories.'

After a moment's silence, Lulu began to talk more cheerfully about the little girl in the picture. 'That's my daughter, Misozi; she's everything that's good about me, and she means the world to me!'

Hamoonga resisted the impulse to ask about the father of the child. 'She's beautiful, takes after her mother,' he said, a compliment, which did not go unnoticed, judging from Lulu's smile. 'How old is she?'

'She will be turning eight next April,' she responded.

'And your husband, what does he do?' Hamoonga cleared his throat.

Lulu shook her head. He noticed a hint of displeasure in her eyes. 'No husband, it's just me and my little princess.'

'So, what do you do for...' Lulu was interrupted by a knock on the door. 'Who is it?' she shouted.

'It's me, *mah*, Linda. I have your tea,' the girl replied from behind the door.

'Come!'

Linda entered carrying a silver tray with white ceramic teacups, saucers, teapot, and silver cutlery. She walked a few steps into the room and asked, 'Where do you want it, *mah*?'

'On the coffee table would be fine.' Linda put the tray on the table and on her way back to the door, he caught her glancing at him with a small smile.

'Let's move to more comfortable chairs.'

Lulu sat down on the edge of the sofa facing him as he lowered himself into the armchair next to her. She placed a teacup and saucer near him and reached for the strainer. Straddling it over the mouth of his cup, she poured the tea.

'Milk and sugar?'

'I'm Zambian, milk and three teaspoons, please!' he laughed. She smiled and fulfilled his request.

Then she poured herself a cup. 'So, where were we? Ah yes, you were going to tell me what you journalism students do for fun.'

♋

Lulu and Hamoonga spent the rest of that afternoon engaged in flirtatious conversation. He learned that Lulu was a self-made businesswoman who was not afraid to push for what she wanted. She was twenty-six years old, four years older than he was, and had never been married. She balanced her life as a mother and business owner with the help of a live-in baby sitter and a driver who ran errands for her. When she was not away on business, she made sure that she saw Misozi before she left for school and in the evening before her bedtime.

Lulu travelled at least once or twice a month either to Jo'burg, Shanghai, Dubai, London or New York to purchase merchandise for her store and the event-planning business. She also had some impressive government connections, and this enabled her to bring in the goods without the usual harassment from customs officers at border points of entry and without paying tax. Lulu had also been awarded a lucrative contract to organise the African Union Heads of State banquet at the new Radisson Hotel. Despite her many accomplishments, Hamoonga sensed she was a woman who was still in search of fulfillment; she seemed restless and willing to take risks just for the thrill they provided.

Later that evening Hamoonga lay sprawled on his bed, thinking about his encounter with Lulu. Ken had the lamp on, and was studying, not something he did very often.

'Is it wrong to have female friends when you're dating a girl?' Hamoonga asked out of the blue.

Ken looked up with a huge grin, 'Player, player! My man, sounds like you have a love triangle going on! Damn, *exsay*, Mr Nice Guy, what happened to '*I only date one girl at a time*'?'

'No, no, no, I didn't say I was dating someone else! No, I said having a female friend, there's a difference you know. Maya is still the woman for me, I'm just asking if there's anything wrong with, you know, meeting other people, other women, that's all.'

'Yo, *Kopala*, you can tell me, *brah*. I ain't mad at yah. Who is she, *exsay*, spill the beans?' Ken had now moved to his bed across from Hamoonga.

'It's nothing,' Hamoonga tried to dismiss the subject.

'Spill the beans, *brah*! Come on. You know it's just me here. It doesn't leave this room *fo'* sure!' Ken prodded.

'Okay, okay, okay. A couple of weeks ago I met this nice lady in the grocery store,' Hamoonga downplayed the encounter.

'Which one?' Ken asked.

'Does it matter?'

'Hey, *exsay*, I gotta know the details man. So, which one, which grocery store?' Ken insisted as he leaned forward with eager anticipation.

'Shoprite,' Hamoonga replied impatiently.

'The one on Cairo Road?'

'Yes, the one on Cairo Road. Do you want me to continue or what?'

'Okay, uh huh, go on!' Ken was in his element. 'What did she look like?'

'Okay, yeah, so she was hot. The kind you don't expect to get a chance to talk to, she looked really established and all. You know, really wealthy – owns her own business… you know, that kind of woman. And she's four years older than me.'

'Oh, oh, oh, you *dawg*! Wow, an older rich chick! Damn, *Kopala*, *exsay*. I didn't know you rolled like that!' Ken exclaimed with great admiration. 'So what happened?'

'So, I was in the checkout line and she started up a conversation with me. I was able to get her business card and I linked up with her this afternoon at her shop at Arcades Mall. It was cool, we just talked a lot, that's all – nothing happened, just talk.'

'I swear you're now officially my hero, *exsay*! I will worship you from now on, *brah*!' Ken held up his hands in mock worship. 'Wow, so what are you gonna do now?'

'I don't know, she wants us to meet again this weekend at O'Hagan's Sports Bar over at Manda Hill.'

'Oh yeah? What did you say?'

'Well, I said yes, but it's not a date, we're just friends meeting up for a drink – that's all.' Hamoonga knew he was really trying to convince himself.

'Ha ha ha! That's the funniest thing I've heard all year, *exsay*! *Ati* we're just friends?' Ken was beside himself. 'Man I gotta tell you, women like that don't just do friendship. You, *brah*, are officially involved in a love triangle. *Exsay*, more power to you, *brah*! You done *done* it, my man. All I can say to you is: be careful, *brah*! Play the game but don't let the game play you, player!' Ken leaned back and folded his hands behind his head as he lay on his bed. 'Man, and to think I underestimated you when we first met!'

⌘

O'Hagan's Sports Bar was a popular hangout for many young professionals in Lusaka. Located at the western corner of Manda Hill Mall, it was a convenient place for people to meet, share a drink, and catch up on the week's events. The bar had an Irish theme, with green banners, solid wood furniture and assorted beer on tap. The waiters and waitresses were smartly dressed in black trousers and white shirts and the service was polite and quick, very different from that offered by many establishments in the capital.

Hamoonga sat across from Lulu as they waited for two Mosi beers.

'So, do you come here often?' he asked.

'I wouldn't say often,' Lulu replied, 'but I do make it once in a while when I'm in town.'

As usual, she looked stunning. She wore a short sleeveless shocking blue dress, and a gold necklace, and earrings.

'You haven't been here before?'

'Yes, a couple of times,' Hamoonga lied to save face. And, quickly changing the subject, 'When is your next trip? Will you be going somewhere exotic?'

'I'm going to London in two weeks. I wouldn't call that exotic. It's not my favourite place. I hate the congestion at Heathrow, and you wouldn't believe the hassle on Oxford Street, especially during the Christmas season.'

He smiled. 'I'd love to go to London. I'll go one day, I'm sure of it. I plan to visit all the major cities someday!'

'You're ambitious, I like that,' Lulu smiled. 'It'll happen; I'm certain. Keep dreaming. Everything begins with a dream and then you work at it.'

The waiter brought the two brown bottles of beer and set them down on coasters with two half-pint glasses asking if there was anything else they wanted.

'No, thank you, this is fine,' Lulu answered graciously as he hurried back to the bar.

Lulu and Hamoonga sipped their smooth cold beer as they chatted.

'So, Mr Journalist, what story would you write about me?' Lulu lifted her glass with a flirtatious smile but Hamoonga took her seriously.

'Well, I could write a biography or do an editorial feature column detailing your impressive accomplishments.'

'And what are those may I ask?' She seemed to be angling for compliments and the young man didn't mind indulging her.

'Let's see.' Hamoonga counted with his fingers: 'You're a self-made woman; you started your own business, which seems very successful; you have a lovely daughter; you are confident.' He paused, and added, 'And you're attractive.' He smiled.

'So you think I'm attractive, do you? I bet you pull that line on all the girls at The Hone!' Lulu raised a questioning eyebrow.

Hamoonga adjusted the lapel on his jacket as he thought about Maya. He'd lied to her earlier in the day, saying he would be out with Ken and the boys for a drink.

Just then, Lulu's cell phone began to ring. She placed her glass on the table and reached for her handbag. Pulling the phone out, she stared at the blue ID display screen for a moment with an apprehensive expression before she pressed the button and placed the phone against her ear.

'Hello,' she answered in a toneless voice. She listened intently as the person on the other end spoke and then said, 'Okay, I'll be there shortly.' Then she hung up.

❖

They hardly spoke after leaving O'Hagan's Bar. Hamoonga sitting anxiously in the passenger seat of Lulu's car, his thoughts whirling, as she careered through the streets towards Makeni, an area with large wealthy estates on the southern outskirts of the city. Hamoonga replayed the conversation they'd been having when she'd seemed so relaxed. Everything had changed with that one phone call. What was going on? As a man, he wanted to protect her; as an innocent, he wanted out.

Lulu had told him an urgent business matter had arisen which she needed to attend to immediately. She apologised, asked him to accompany her, and promised the whole matter would not take more than an hour. Hamoonga had agreed, not wanting the evening to end so quickly.

Their silver Toyota Hilux left the main road down a narrow dirt road. Lulu put her headlights on full beam. She looked deep in thought. They reached an imposing rusty iron gate with a high brick fence on either side of it. On top of both the gate and the fence were parallel rows of thin electric wires providing security against intruders. Lulu stopped and waited for a few seconds, the engine running. The gate opened and an armed security guard walked to Lulu's window, which she drew down. From his vantage point, Hamoonga could not make out the man's face. The security guard looked closely at Lulu. 'Ah, it's you, good evening, madam. Who is with you?' He strained to see who was in the passenger seat.

'He's a friend of mine,' Lulu replied.

'Your ID,' he demanded.

Lulu turned to Hamoonga, 'Do you have an ID on you?'

Hamoonga pulled out his wallet and offered his student card which Lulu passed to the guard. He looked at it, walked back to the gate and disappeared behind it, returning a few seconds later to return the card.

Then he opened the gate to let them in.

Lulu drove slowly up the wide, winding driveway, past the opulent three-story brick house on the left, and on to an isolated outbuilding in the back yard. A black Mercedes was parked beside it. Placing the gear in neutral, Lulu pulled on the hand brake, and turning to Hamoonga said, 'Wait here. I'll only be a minute.' She then stepped out of the car, leaving the lights on and the engine running.

As Lulu walked towards the Mercedes, a large man with a clean-shaven scalp stepped out of it. Hamoonga immediately recognised him as one of the men he'd seen leaving Lulu's store a few days previously. They stood facing each other, illuminated in the car's headlights. Lulu was clearly agitated and gesticulating rapidly but he could not make out what they were saying.

After about five minutes, Lulu followed the man to the outbuilding. Hamoonga waited nervously, unable to make sense of it all. After about five minutes, she emerged carrying a small green rucksack. She proceeded to the trunk of her car, opened it, and placed the bag inside. She then got back in the car.

'Sorry about that. We're done here, let's go!' she said coldly transposing the hostility she felt towards her guest.

The drive back was uncomfortable. It was as if Lulu had received some very bad news that she was loath to share. As they approached the downtown lights, she turned to Hamoonga and said, 'I'm sorry about tonight, but I think it's best I drop you off at the college. I forgot that I needed to prepare a few things at home tonight.' Hamoonga nodded, staring at the road in front of them not knowing what to say.

When they arrived inside the campus gates, Hamoonga directed Lulu to the parking space closest to his dormitory block. It was after 9:00 p.m. and many of the students were either in their rooms or out at bars and clubs in the city.

Lulu switched off the engine. 'Hey listen, Hamoonga, I'm really sorry about tonight, I have to make it up to you. Something's come up and I have to leave for Jo'burg tomorrow. I'll be back in a couple of days and we can do something when I get back.'

He remained silent.

'Hey,' she said touching his arm. 'I'm really sorry.'

He turned to face her. She was beautiful.

She leaned forward, and they kissed softly. 'I'll see you when I get back, all right? Think about me while I'm away.' Placated, Hamoonga got out of the car and Lulu drove off into the night.

Chapter 6

Sawubona!

Lulu loathed it when Minister Zulu and his wife made impromptu demands on her. Sure, she owed them a lot, after all they'd put up the seed money for her business. And yes, she had benefitted handsomely from their clout and influence, but she was the one taking all the risks. It was her neck on the line!

She entered her plush two-story Ibex Hill home holding the green rucksack, walked up the stairs and entered her master suite. Everything was neat and tidy, just the way she liked it. The bed was expertly made with gold satin sheets. She threw the rucksack on top of the bed and sat down, slipping off her high heels, she sighed, as she thought about the evening's events.

Putting on her slippers, she made her way down the long corridor to Misozi's room. The door was ajar. She pushed it open a little and peered into the room. Her daughter was sleeping peacefully nestled among an array of cuddly toys.

Lulu returned to her room and prepared for a shower. She was soon standing underneath a steady stream letting the warm tingling water ease away her anxieties.

♋

Fackson Zulu was the current Minister of Mines, a lifelong politician, he had served in various ministerial portfolios for over thirty-five years, and was President Chibompo's right-hand man. The two had worked together as freedom fighters during the struggle for Zambia's independence from the British. Both had served as cabinet ministers in Zambia's first indigenous government of 1964.

Zulu had been Deputy Minister for Agriculture and Chibompo had
served as Minister of Foreign Affairs in the first cabinet. Over the
years their friendship had grown and was further strengthened when
Zulu married Elizabeth Banda, Chibompo's second cousin. As Chibompo's influence in the ruling Freedom Party grew, Zulu's fortunes
also improved; he had also proved to be a critical ally in 1985 when
Chibompo made his bid to assume the top leadership position in the
Party, subsequently becoming President of the Republic. Rumour
was that Zulu was the one who had finally convinced the ailing incumbent and first president, Joshua Lupupa, to step down and hand
the reins of power over to Chibompo. Minister Zulu and President
Chibompo's bond was unshakable, like the trunk of a firmly rooted
baobab tree, and over the years, Minister Zulu had become one of
the most powerful government ministers in the land.

Lulu had first been introduced to Mama Elizabeth Zulu, Minister
Zulu's wife, at a dinner at their opulent residence in Makeni. Lulu
had been working as a member of the event-planning team at the
Pamodzi Hotel, one of the few four-star hotels in the city. The Zulus
had hired the services of the hotel to plan and cater a dinner for
the wives of foreign dignitaries during an AIDS summit in Lusaka.
Mama Zulu had been impressed by how 'take-charge' and resource-
ful Lulu had shown herself to be and began to specifically request
the young woman to arrange her events. As their relationship developed, Mama Zulu introduced Lulu to her husband, the minister.

In conversations with the Zulus, Lulu had alluded to her desire
to begin an event-planning business of her own as well as a desire
to travel the world. They saw in her the perfect asset for their nefarious ends and offered Lulu seed money to start her business in
return for a 'one time' favour. In exchange for $250,000, the Zulus
asked Lulu to carry a package to Jo'burg when she went to purchase
merchandise for her new business. 'It will be fine, my dear, just carry
this little parcel in your check-in luggage. There will be a gentleman
waiting to collect it on the other side. It's simple, there's no risk, we
have our people planted at customs on that side but we need someone we can trust to carry the parcel,' the Zulus had said. Ultimately,

Lulu's ambition got the best of her. The temptation to finally have the money to live out her dreams and to provide for her daughter was overwhelming. She had done what the Zulus had asked, but like greedy shylocks coming for their pound of flesh, they kept asking for more favours. Would the cycle ever stop? Was there no end to their greed?

⌘

Lulu shuffled uncomfortably in her aisle seat; she was tense and her throat stung in the cold, dry air. She always slept very badly every time she had to carry a package for the Zulus, an errand, she had run five times over the previous two years; this would be the sixth occasion. It never got easier. They promised her that after the fifth time, they would not ask again, but here she was headed for Jo'burg yet again.

The flight from Lusaka to Jo'burg was short, just under two hours. She was on a South African Airways flight scheduled to land at 2:35 p.m. local time. She knew the drill. She would say she was 'Visiting family in Sandton for two days.' She would pick up her checked-in bag at the carousel, and walk casually through customs with nothing to declare. The key was to walk not too fast and not too slowly. Also, contrary to one's intuition, it was important to make eye contact with the customs officers, just not to stare too long or dart one's eyes, a cool suave glance always did the trick. One last thing was to always have one's skimpy, dirty underwear packed at the top of the luggage, just in case one was pulled aside and searched. Dirty thongs were almost sure to deter even the most ardent customs officer.

Ding, ding! The bells sounded over the microphone as a prelude to the captain's announcement. 'Good afternoon, ladies and gentlemen, this is your Captain, Abraham Zuma, speaking. Please take your seats, fasten your seatbelts, fold your trays, and pull up your chairs. We are beginning our descent into Oliver Tambo International Airport. The weather is sunny and clear, local temperature is twenty-four degrees Celsius. We should be arriving ten minutes ahead of schedule, local time 2:25 p.m.'

Lulu looked at the little Customs Declaration form in her hand.

She had checked the box asserting that she had '*nothing to declare*'. She closed her eyes and focused her mind on her daughter in a bid to steady herself for what lay ahead.

Ten minutes later the plane touched down and taxied into the terminal. The captain delivered his parting address. '*Sawubona*, ladies and gentlemen, welcome to Oliver Tambo International Airport in Johannesburg, South Africa. Thank you for flying South African Airways…'

The overhead lights switched off and many of the passengers began to stand up. There was an Indian family in the row in front of Lulu. The couple and their child looked around to make sure they had collected all their personal items. Although they looked of Indian descent, they spoke English with a clipped South African accent. Their child, a little boy, was about Misozi's age, and he seemed quiet and well behaved as he followed his mother's instructions to pack up his comic books. She imagined herself married and having a good father around for Misozi. Despite her best efforts to provide a stable home full of love and all the material things Misozi needed, she always felt that she'd failed to provide her daughter with a positive male influence.

The passengers began to move out of the plane in single file like cattle in a livestock pen. The captain and crew stood near the exit of the plane offering their perfunctory *Goodbyes* and *Thank Yous*. Lulu clasped her brown Gucci handbag underneath her right arm and made her way down the long carpeted concourse. Oliver Tambo Airport was beautiful, she thought, with its with neon lights and designer shops – Coach, Gucci, Calvin Klein – it reminded her of being in London, New York, and Paris.

The end of the concourse opened up to the main immigration checkpoint. There were five booths but only two of them were manned. One of them had a black male immigration officer and the other had a mixed-race female. Both were dressed in their uniforms: navy blue trousers with a sky blue shirt and navy blue hat. When travelling, Lulu always joined the line with the male officer. It was simple logic: a male officer was on average less detail-oriented than a female one. Furthermore, she knew that her smile was like kryptonite to most men she encountered. She knew that this checkpoint would not be an issue though there was always a chance an officer could question why she was making yet another trip to visit family, so soon after the last one.

Lulu moved into line and with the queue until she was standing behind the yellow line. She sized up the immigration officer as she waited for his call. He was chubby, in his mid-thirties and had an incongruously bushy moustache. He signalled her to come forward.

'Good afternoon,' Lulu said with a smile.

The man nodded in acknowledgement and asked, 'Passport and landing card?'

Lulu promptly handed over her green Zambian passport with her Customs Declaration form nestled in the centre. The officer took the documents and opened the passport to the front. 'Coming from where?' he asked in poor English.

'Lusaka,' she responded. He looked at the photograph, and back at her. She smiled, he showed no emotion.

'Purpose of visit?' he asked.

'Visiting family in Sandton.'

'How long are you here for?'

'Just for three days,'

'Anything to declare?'

'No, nothing,' she replied.

The man seemed neither impressed nor suspicious. He scanned her passport on an electronic reader, peering over at the results on his computer screen. Again without emotion, he read the Customs Declaration form, appended his signature, stamped one of the inside pages of Lulu's passport and handed it back with a nod for her to proceed on her way.

'One minor hurdle over,' Lulu thought to herself. She proceeded to look for carousel five as she followed the signs to luggage claim. She recognised some of the passengers who'd been on the flight with her.

After waiting for about ten minutes the carousel conveyor began to turn and the wall in the back began to spit out a colourful assortment of bags. Lulu waited anxiously as they streamed by. She knew she would not miss her bag as it was distinct – red with a black stripe across the top.

After about twenty minutes, the crowd at the carousel had thinned to just three people, Lulu, and an elderly white couple. After turning empty for five minutes, the conveyor stopped and the noisy hum of the motor ceased. She felt anxiety stabbing the pit of her stomach. She looked at the couple next to her who were also agitated.

'Walter, where is our bag, have they lost it? I think we should call someone!' The woman sounded frightened. The man looked at his wife and then looked around anxiously to see if there was anyone around to assist.

'Sir, they've lost our bag!' The lady called out to a young man who was walking hurriedly past the carousel. He wore dark blue trousers, a white shirt and a fluorescent orange vest that betrayed his identity as an airport attendant.

'Madam, can I help you?'

'Yes, they seem to have lost our bag.'

'Oh, let me see if I can help you. What flight were you on?'

'We came in from Maputo at 2:00 p.m. on South African Airways, we've been waiting here but we can't see our bag!'

'Oh no, madam,' the young man replied. 'This is the carousel for the 2:35 p.m. flight from Lusaka. Let me check which carousel the Maputo flight is on.' The young man took out his walky-talky and quickly confirmed that they were indeed at the wrong carousel. They needed to be at carousel ten a little further down. The couple thanked the young man profusely and headed off in the right direction.

Lulu was now in a panic. She turned to the young airport attendant for help. 'My bag is missing, I was on the 2:35 p.m. flight from Lusaka but it's not here!' she said with a note of desperation. The man calmly reassured her, saying that it was not uncommon for bags to get misplaced. They usually turn up after about a day or so. He helped Lulu file a claim at the lost-and-found luggage desk and left to continue his shift.

Lulu waited until she had reached her hotel room in Sandton before calling Babu, the Zulus' henchman back in Lusaka. She was trembling.

The phone rang a couple of times before he answered.

'Hello,' Babu said in his booming voice.

Closing her eyes, Lulu responded timidly, 'It's me. I have a problem. The airport lost the bag.'

'What?' he said in disbelief.

'They… they, misplaced the bag but I'm sure it will turn up today or tomorrow.' She cleared her voice as she spoke.

'How did this happen?' his voice boomed through the telephone.

'I…I don't know, it just happened. I waited and waited, they searched everywhere, nothing…'

He interrupted her. 'Lulu, don't play with me, *eh*!'

'Someone maybe took it by accident and will bring it back,' she volunteered.

Babu fell silent for a few seconds. She could hear him breathing heavily on the line. Then he said in a slow, menacing voice, 'Don't come back here until you find it, and pray to God that you do!' With that he hung up. Lulu began to sob as she thought about Misozi and how reckless she'd been to gamble with her child's safety like this. If there was one thing she knew for certain, the Zulus were not people to be played with.

❖

Lulu could not sleep a wink that night. At nine o'clock in the morning she called the airport's lost-and-found luggage hotline to check if anything had turned up: nothing! She began a ritual of calling the airport every four hours, but the result was always the same. She did the same over the following day before finally calling Babu again.

'Hello,' Babu answered.

'Babu, it's me, Lulu. Nothing has turned up yet,' she said with deep regret.

Babu listened silently and then responded, 'This is a big consignment worth over half a million dollars. Don't play with me, Lulu! If I find out you are playing games, by God you will regret it!' He cut the line and sent a shudder down her spine. Lulu feared what Babu and the Zulus might do. She thought about her daughter. 'Please don't hurt my daughter!' she thought. 'Please God, not Misozi!' The idea of anything happening to Misozi sickened her. She would not be able to bear it if something happened to her only daughter – the thought turned her stomach. She ran to the bathroom and emptied the contents of her gut in wrenching heaves down the sink. A bitter taste of bile filled her mouth. She wiped away her tears with the back of her hands; she had to think straight and she had to act fast. She knew at this point that the chances of the bag turning up in one piece were next to nil, given how long it had been missing. She could not take the chance of Babu and the Zulus harming Misozi. She steeled herself and began to consider a plan to get her daughter to safety. That was the only thing that mattered now!

That afternoon Lulu called her assistant, Linda, at her store and instructed her to purchase a return ticket for her daughter Misozi to Jo'burg. Lulu always left a couple of signed cheques with her assistant in case of an emergeny or urgent expense. Linda was then to pick up Misozi after school, pack a few essentials and collect the passport from the back shelf of the closet in her bedroom. Linda would then text Lulu so that she would know when to call to speak to her daughter. All this was to be kept absolutely secret, as it was a surprise for her daughter.

Linda did as instructed. When Lulu received the text message, she called and assured her daughter that it was okay for her to go with Auntie Linda to the airport to board a plane. Misozi was excited. Lulu continued to pray for her daughter's safety. Her heart would not be at ease until she could hold her in her arms.

◆

That evening Misozi made it safely to Oliver Tambo Airport and walked into the embrace of her tearful mother. 'Thank God you're here', she whispered again and again.

Babu was growing suspicious. Lulu had not called for four days. Had she truly lost her bag, or had she devised a scheme to run away with the contraband? He brushed aside the thought like an irritating housefly. She'd always come through for them in the past. Besides, she knew not to cross him or the Zulus – she would not dare do that. He contemplated the idea once again. 'She has a daughter and she's intelligent enough to know that her daughter would not be safe if she tried any funny business!' he said to himself. He then stepped into his car and drove over to Lulu's residence in Ibex Hill.

'I'll kill her!' he yelled in front of Lulu's terrified maid. He was furious, out of control like a rabid animal.

'I swear, *bwana*,' the maid said, 'I have not seen madam or her daughter for three days now! Her assistant, Linda, told me madam had taken her daughter on vacation for a few days!'

Babu punched the wall. Two large framed family portraits fell to the floor. The maid screamed as she covered her face fearing the worst.

'I'll find her and I'll kill her!' he shouted at the top of his voice. 'If it takes me to the end of the earth, I'll find her and I'll kill her!' He stormed out of the house and drove off.

Fifteen minutes later, he stormed into Lulu's store knocking over one of the mannequins closest to the door. His footsteps were hurried and determined.

'You! Where the hell is she?' he shouted as he grabbed Linda furiously by the arm as if it were a flimsy twig. The few customers that were in the store scampered out like roaches suddenly exposed to light. Before Linda could say a word he struck her fiercely across the face, his ring drawing blood. Linda cried out in pain.

'Your boss, Lulu, where is she? Tell me now!' he demanded.

'She… she went to Jo'burg with her daughter. She was supposed to be back yesterday but I've not heard from her, I swear!'

He struck her again 'I swear to you that's all I know,'

'Call her now, now!'

Her fingers trembling, Linda placed a long distance call to Lulu's cell phone as Babu towered over her, eyeing her every move like a king cobra ready to pounce. There was a delay and then there was a loud feminine automated message stating that the number was no longer in service. That message was the proverbial final straw that broke the camel's back.

Babu lost it. He savagely struck Linda across the face so hard that she tumbled over the desk in front of her, sending papers and pens flying. He bent down next to her, and continued to unload his frustration with repeated blows to her body until she lost consciousness.

When Babu finally entered his car again he clenched his bloodied fists in anger. He was fuming with rage. He breathed heavily and then leant back in his seat as he began to cast his mind back to remember any detail that would lead him to Lulu's whereabouts. 'That night!' he thought to himself. 'When she got the rucksack. She was not alone. There was someone else in the car with her!'

Chapter 7

Cha-Cha-Cha

The door flung open with a force that shook both Hamoonga and Ken out of their sleep. Three men burst into the room. Two of them were wielding AK-47 assault rifles across their chests. The third man was holding a torch in one hand and a large wooden baton in the other.

'Get up, get up, come on, up, up, up!' the men shouted. One of the rifle-wielding hooligans descended on Ken; the other one on Hamoonga, slamming the butt of his rifle into Hamoonga's midriff, and grabbing him by the throat. Hamoonga gasped for air, pain pierced his chest. Overwhelmed by the unexpected assault, Hamoonga failed to muster the strength to yell for help. 'Which one of you maggots is Hamoonga? Tell me now or I'll kill you both!' the man yelled as he tightened his grip on Hamoonga's throat.

Ken was not faring any better. His assailant had laid a fist directly into his mouth cutting his upper lip and dislocating one of his incisors. His mouth began to bleed. His attacker proceeded to pull Ken out of his bed by ferociously grabbing his shoulder. '*Ni we ndani iwe?*' he shouted pushing his face against his victim's. Ken felt the man's spit shower his cheeks. He had foul breath, a caustic concoction of a cheap alcohol, mixed with weed and a lifelong absence of dental hygiene. '*Ni we ndani iwe?*' the man repeated at the top of his voice.

Hamoonga was still gasping for air when his tormentor head butted him. Blood poured from Hamoonga's nose. '*Ndiwe* Hamoonga? *Nati ndiwe* Hamoonga?'

'Yes, yes, please!' Hamoonga finally managed to blurt, his voice choked as he tried to release the man's hand from his neck, a basic survival instinct. His legs were frantically kicking as he felt life slowly draining out of his body like a wet towel being wrung dry. From the corner of his eye, he could see that Ken was in terrible shape. He had been thrown to the floor and two of the men were kicking him as hard as they could. Hamoonga's last memory was of the man who was throttling him. He had a boney face with a shrivelled goatee, and his look was that of brutal rage.

♋

Hamoonga opened his eyes to a dark room. He was lying naked on a cold concrete floor. He had a throbbing pain in his head, and he felt weak and nauseous. Where was he, and how long had he been there? Where was Ken? Had those thugs killed his friend?

He remembered the awful assault like a distant nightmare. The last thing he could recall was being strangled by a man with a steely determination to end his life. He remembered thinking he was surely going to die. He looked up trying to see if he could recognise anything; but it was too dark; then he attempted to get up off the concrete floor but his body couldn't move. He felt dizzy and disoriented by pain. He thought again about Ken and the last moments he could remember of the assault. He recalled his friend being kicked around on the floor by two men. Was he alive? Was he somewhere here in this cold darkness? Hamoonga shifted his weight to alleviate his discomfort. He breathed deeply and with the little strength he could muster and attempted to shout, 'Ken, Ken, Ken, are you there?'

'*Sssshhh*! They don't like it when you make noise,' a male voice sounded from the shadows.

'Who is that? Who are you? Where am I and what have you done to Ken?' Hamoonga asked. Though he feared the response.

'You're in Cha-Cha-Cha prison camp, the place of the forgotten,' the voice responded.

'What have you done with Ken?'

'I don't know of any Ken in here. You were brought here alone,' the voice answered.

'Ken, my roommate – we are students at Evelyn Hone College.

He was with me when we were attacked by bandits.'

'You were brought here alone two nights ago. You were in an awful condition. You were unconscious and had trouble breathing. I didn't think you'd make it, but I guess you're a fighter.'

'Someone please call the police. I was attacked; we were attacked in our dorm room by bandits!'

'I'm afraid to tell you, young man, they were not bandits.'

'What do you mean; you mean you know who tried to kill me?'

A dishevelled old man emerged from the shadows. He was shirt-less and, as he drew closer, Hamoonga could see that his face had been unshaven for a long time. He crouched down close to Hamoonga, 'You must've pissed off a powerful politician, that's the only reason why we're all in here!'

'What do mean, I'm not into politics, nor is Ken. It's just not possible. There must be some terrible mistake!' Hamoonga protested. 'I'm a student at Evelyn Hone College, I have no interest in politics. I must have been mistaken for someone else. I just need to talk to the police and all this can be explained!'

'Young man, I do not know your story nor how you came to find yourself here but what I can tell you is that this is a place for political prisoners, enemies of the state, if you will. No one makes it into this prison without having angered a politician or posed a threat to the state, real or perceived. My advice to you is to keep your head down, make a full recovery, and do as you are told. There are not many things we can control in here, but I can tell you now that your chances of survival hinge on your ability to do as you are told and not get noticed!'

'But I've done nothing wrong! I was assaulted, I'm the victim. I need to speak to somebody to explain.' Hamoonga began to cough uncontrollably and he struggled to breathe. The old man cradled the young man's head in his arms as he lost consciousness again.

When Hamoonga opened his eyes, the old man was hovering over him with a concerned expression on his face like a father anx-iously nursing a sick child. 'You passed out again. You mustn't exert yourself. You are still very weak. I know you've many questions but be patient, give yourself time to heal.' Hamoonga managed a weak nod and lay his head back down.

In the ensuing hours Hamoonga discovered that there were six other men in the dark prison room. The only light came was from a six- by twelve-inch hole in the wall about ten feet above ground, and traversed by strong metal bars. The prisoners each introduced themselves to Hamoonga. One man had been there for eighteen months, locked up without trial for helping to organise a student protest at the University of Zambia. After all their appeals had failed, they were demonstrating against the chronic delays in issuing government bursaries to students. Two men had been in prison for six months. Their crime, trespassing. They had entered the Arakan soldiers' barracks in a bid to buy subsidised alcohol, and caught after boasting of their exploits, which were unfortunately overheard by the Deputy Minister of Defense. The three remaining men – Mr Chokwe, Mr Banda and Mr Miti – had each been in prison for seven and a half years for treason, conspiring to overthrow the government, or so it was said, and they each expected to hang.

The old man, Mr Miti, had been the ringleader. Story had it that one October morning in 1997, Mr Miti, an air-force commander, and fifteen armed soldiers had taken over the government broadcasting station in Lusaka where Mr Miti, the leader, had made an announcement: 'Brothers and Sisters of this great Republic of Zambia, my name is Air Force Commander Joseph Emmanuel Miti. Due to the gross incompetence, mismanagement, corruption, and greed of the Chibompo government, I am forced to declare its dissolution and to assume power as interim leader until we usher in free and fair elections for a new government to better serve the people. I urge you to stay calm and stay in your homes until further direction is given by this interim regime. May God bless our beloved nation of Zambia.'

They had then proceeded to the airport, which they planned to commandeer. Another truck of armed men had made for State House. They were to calmly approach the western gate and ask for Sergeant Bwalya, a co-conspirator, who would ensure safe entry of the soldiers into the State House grounds.

In a twist of fate, Sergeant Bwalya had a terribly upset stomach and was unavoidably indisposed. So, when the driver asked for him, his subordinate was hesitant to call his boss. Moreover, not recognising the men in the vehicle, and knowing nothing of their intended mission, the soldier had sounded the alarm. A gunfight had ensued. The men in the truck were captured and tortured along with Sergeant Bwalya, and the coup attempt failed; all because Bwalya's wife had served him some bad fish.

In a bid to show the world that he was a man who adhered to the rule of law, President Chibompo held a trial, but to all in the know, it was a farce. The court found the three surviving conspirators, Mr Miti, Mr Banda, and Mr Chokwe, guilty of treason and sentenced them 'To hang by the throat until you're dead.' However the mock trial did not pass unnoticed. Certain western countries threatened to pull the plug on a number of lucrative contracts and withdraw donor funds if the political prisoners were executed. So, reluctantly, President Chibompo's government had simply imprisoned their enemies indefinitely.

⌘

Back at Evelyn Hone College, Maya and Temwani were in tears, their clothes covered in Ken's blood. It was Maya who'd found him lying on the floor of his room when she went to check on Hamoonga, after he'd failed to pick her up for their newly established, early morning fitness routine. The young men's room was set apart from the rest of the dormitories having been converted from an outhouse to accommodate the ever-increasing student population. Separated from the dormitories by a long concrete passageway, most people would not venture that way unless they were specifically going to see Ken or Hamoonga. When Maya arrived, she found the door broken and ajar, the handle forced. Tentatively peering into the room, she saw Ken lying face down in a pool of blood. Hamoonga was nowhere to be seen.

She gasped in horror and oblivious to the blood that drenched her track suit leaned close to Ken's damaged face and felt the feeble pulsations of his breath – as faint, as the soft purring of a cat, and knew he was still alive, albeit barely.

'Oh my God, Ken. What happened?' she asked rhetorically. 'I'm going to call for help. You'll be okay, I promise.' She pulled out her phone and first dialed her roommate, Temwani, who came quickly. But who to call, what to do next? 'We have to get him to the hospital quickly. I can't find Hamoonga, I've been calling and calling but there's no answer!' Maya said trembling.

'Jesus! *Iyee imwe shuwa*, what's going on?' Temwani's voice expressed the horror she felt. 'Let me call Ben, we'll need his help! We must get him to a hospital fast, fast *manje*. There's no time to waste! Have you called a cab?'

'Yes, the cab is on its way now!'

Ben, similarly appalled by the scene, was sensible. 'You've called a cab, but you know strictly speaking we shouldn't move him. First, we could do more damage if he has internal injuries, he needs an ambulance. Second, we should call the authorities and have them call the police.'

'It's too late,' said Maya, 'by the time the police and the ambulance come, Ken could be dead. He's unconscious, and look, he's lost so much blood. Our only chance is to get him to hospital in a cab.'

Afterwards, Ben and Temwani were to comment on how firm and collected Maya was, how good in a crisis, but then Maya had said, 'I don't know.' Tears broke her voice. 'Supposing he dies, and it's our fault. And what will the authorities say?'

Ben wiped his brow with his forearm and turned to face Temwani, 'Look, I think Maya's right. We don't have time to lose. It's still early. Most people are not up yet. Ken could die any minute, so it's a risk we have to take, yes?'

The girls nodded.

Ben moved quickly to put his arms underneath Ken's flaccid body. 'Okay, let's lift his legs gently and take him outside!' Ben instructed Maya and Temwani. Ben put his arms underneath Ken's armpits as Maya and Temwani lifted his legs. Together they managed to carry him out to the tiny Toyota Camry cab waiting outside.

Cholwe, the cab driver, exclaimed at the sight of Ken's helpless, bloodstained body and the pale distraught faces of his friends. '*Mah mah mah mah, eh,* what happened?'

'We need to go to UTH now, please, please, fast!' Temwani said, her voice tense, as they lifted Ken onto the back seat. Temwani squeezed carefully in beside him and put his legs across her lap while Maya, getting in on the opposite side put his head, still leaking blood, onto her lap. She bent her head over his, 'I think he's still breathing,' she said, her voice taut. She prayed that by moving him in this way, they were not making matters worse.

Ben got into the front passenger seat and Cholwe immediately stepped on the accelerator and sped off south down Dushambe Road, past Independence Avenue, and onto Burma Road. Fortunately, the roads were clear as it was still so early in the morning. The cab was silent. They all feared the worst but no one dared voice what they were thinking.

When they arrived at UTH, Ben and Cholwe leapt out and Temwani put Ken's legs cautiously down on the seat. Then they began the difficult process of lifting Ken out. Once this was done, they moved as fast as they dared with the inert body of their friend and reaching the hospital pushed through the double doors, where they found two nurses in the reception area. Having just arrived on duty, the two nurses, moved quickly into action. They pulled up a creaky old stretcher covered with a thin white bed sheet and directed the group to place Ken face-up on top of it. The two nurses methodically felt Ken's pulse and examined his wounds as they peppered the group with questions about the circumstances leading to his current state.

'What happened to him? How long ago did you find him? Do you know if he was taking any medication? Is he allergic to anything?' the nurses asked in quick succession. Maya, Temwani, and Ben answered the questions as best they could.

The nurses paged the doctor on duty as they hurriedly wheeled Ken away behind another set of double doors. Maya and Temwani moved to follow the stretcher but were sharply rebuffed by the heftier of the two nurses.

'You cannot go beyond this point. Leave it with us. We'll take care of your friend now. You must wait in the waiting area. We will inform you once the doctor has seen him!' She spoke with authority – a mother hen protecting her young. Maya and Temwani stepped back and watched her disappear behind the double doors.

Cholwe, Maya, Ben, and Temwani all walked back to the tiny waiting area in silence. They were the only people in the room. Its emptiness and the faint smell of antiseptic added to their sense of bleak unreality and shock, now that the immediate urgency of the situation was over.

After several minutes of silence, Ben turned to Cholwe and asked, 'Can you take me to the Central Police Station? We need to file a police report.'

'Yes,' Maya said, 'and please report that Hamoonga is missing. I'm so worried, I still can't reach him. I can't imagine what has happened to him!' Tears streamed down her face. Temwani put her arm around Maya's shoulders.

'I'm sure they'll find him, it'll be fine, you'll see,' Temwani said unconvincingly.

At the Lusaka Central Police Station, Ben and Cholwe went straight to the reception counter which was manned by two police officers, a woman and a man. The old grey Formica surface was worn by years of tactility by countless anxious, greasy fingers. The two officers were deep in conversation. There were already five people sitting humbly or resignedly on wooden benches in the waiting area. It was not clear whether they had already been attended to, it seemed not.

Ben spoke up first, 'Excuse me, please, we're here to report an assault and a missing person!'

But the two officers ignored Ben and Cholwe and continued with their conversation.

'Yes, I told my wife that when I come home I must find the food ready, I don't want to sit around waiting for her to start cooking. That's not the way to run a home, you know!' the officer said to his female colleague, his index finger raised.

'*Aaahhh*, Ba Shi Bwalya, are you living in the nineteen fifties?

These days even the women are working, your wife sells at the market during the day. What time does she have to prepare food for you before you come home?' She laughed.

'No, but it's tradition, when we got married...'

'Excuse me, officers!' Ben said his voice tight with anxiety and impatience, 'We've come to report an important case!'

The officers turned to face the person who had dared disturb them. Agitated, the female police officer barked, 'Are you mad, do you have any sense?' She sucked her teeth and continued, 'Can't you see two police officers are talking? Disturb us again and you'll see what I'll do to you!'

With a dismissive shrug, the male officer picked up where he'd left off, 'I tell you, it's tradition, a woman must take care of her husband, eh! I can't be waiting for two hours to eat when I get home! It's her duty to make sure that everything is ready for me when I get back from work!'

Ben and Cholwe looked at each other. Ben was visibly upset. He leant across the counter determined to try again.

'Hmmmm, Ba Shi Bwalya, I'm also a woman, I have a husband and two children. My husband does not wait for me when I'm late coming home or on night shift. If he wanted to wait for me to cook for him after I get home, he'll surely starve!' She laughed. 'A marriage is a partnership, a couple has to work together to make things work, you cannot be so rigid, Ba Shi Bwalya!'

Ben felt frantic. The long tense early morning hours were taking their toll. Ken was in the hospital fighting for his life, Hamoonga missing and perhaps in danger. These civil servants were paid with his taxes. How could they be so negligent and arrogant!

'Officers! Please, I beg of you, we have an urgent matter we need to report!' Ben's loud voice was cracked with pent-up emotion. Cholwe intuitively stepped back away from the counter as if to distance himself from the culprit.

Both officers rose from their chairs.

The female officer was in her mid-twenties. Her braided hair was tucked into a bun underneath her police hat. She had a stern, slender face. Her khaki uniform was sharply creased with a hot pressing iron. Her partner was in his forties. His belly protruded over his tightly pulled belt. *'Koma ni o pusa iwe!'* the male officer's voice was threatening.

'Didn't I tell you not to disturb police officers when they are talking?' the female officer shouted. Ben was silent. 'What's the matter, eh?' she asked rhetorically. 'Do you think that you're more important than these people who are waiting and have been waiting a long time?' Her eyes narrowed. Ben knew better than to respond.

'Do you want to sleep in the cells tonight?' the male officer continued. 'Eh, answer me! Do you want to sleep in the cells tonight?'

'No, no, no, sir, it's just that my friend is…' Ben began but before he could finish his sentence, the female officer struck him with her open hand across his left cheek.

'What? You're even talking back?' She breathed heavily, *'Koma ni o pusa* too much!'

Ben staggered back from the counter, a stinging sensation in his jaw. He was now shaking, fearing what the officers might do next.

The female officer continued to hurl obscenities; cursing Ben's parents and insulting his manhood before stepping back behind the counter to continue her conversation with her colleague. Ben and Cholwe humbly retreated to the waiting area and joined the forlorn group of people who were too scared to voice their displeasure at the abysmal service they were receiving from the officers.

It took a total of three hours before Ben and Cholwe were able to successfully enter a police case to initiate an investigation into Ken's assault and Hamoonga's disappearance. The officers grudgingly entered the details in a large handwritten notebook on a page full of smudges. After the details were collected, the officers curtly dismissed the two men, promising that they would investigate the matter.

❖

Back at UTH, Maya and Temwani succeeded in contacting Ken's parents, who, fortunately, were both medical doctors in the hospital. Once everyone knew that Ken was the son of the beloved Simutowe doctors, all of the best personnel and equipment were deployed to care for him. Surgeons and nurses milled around, equipment was pulled in from adjoining operating rooms, no effort was spared for the son of the Simutowes.

Ken was in the intensive care unit for almost eight hours. Later that day the hospital staff informed Maya, Temwani, and Ben that Ken was stable but his injuries were severe. He had suffered damage to his spleen, lacerations to his legs and arms, a broken rib, and worst of all there was damage to his spinal cord. The surgeons said that it would be some time before they could determine if Ken would regain the use of his legs. The news was very grim, but at least Ken was alive.

The three students returned to the college campus after dark in a sombre mood. They still had to talk to the authorities.

Chapter 8

What a Little Loyalty Will Do

It took several days before Hamoonga was taken out of his bleak prison cell at Cha-Cha-Cha and thrown into a smaller but brighter room. Two prison guards ushered him into the room and pushed him onto a lonely wooden chair in the middle of the floor.

'Sit and wait here!' one of the guards barked as they left the room and locked the door behind them.

The room had no windows but had a central fluorescent lamp mounted underneath the concrete ceiling directly above Hamoonga's head. The lamp illuminated the room with a brightness that hurt his eyes. The rest of the room was empty but for a metal bucket in the corner in front of him. The room was damp and musty but at least it lacked the putrid smell of urine and excreta that marred his previous cell. The smooth cement floor beneath his bare feet was hard and cold. Hamoonga's naked body shivered as he struggled to get accustomed to his new environment.

Waiting nervously on his lone chair, Hamoonga listened for sounds. He could hear the rhythmic dripping of fluid, which he imagined to be water coming from a damaged pipe in a nearby room. In the distance he could hear the echo of footsteps and muffled voices too far away for him to comprehend. His breathing grew heavier as he waited, not knowing what to expect. After what seemed like an eternity, he turned his head to the clanging sound of a metal latch as the door behind him opened. In walked the tall silhouette of a well-built man. The man shut the door behind him and walked up to Hamoonga with slow, heavy footsteps. Towering over him like a cumulus cloud, the man cast a shadow that allowed Hamoonga to make out his face. Immediately, he recognised him as the same hefty man that he'd seen coming out of Lulu's store. The same man he'd seen arguing with her outside the tiny outbuilding in Makeni that night.

'Let's make this very simple, my friend. You and your girlfriend have something of mine. Tell me where it is and I'll let you go,' Babu said very slowly and sternly in a tone that left no room for compromise. His use of the word 'friend' somehow had the effect of emphasising his malevolent intent.

Hamoonga felt his heart racing like a runaway train accelerating down a track. He became oblivious to the cold floor beneath his feet. He could tell from the inflection in the man's voice that he had no time for niceties – the man wanted answers and he wanted them now, or else!

'I… I swear to you, I don't know what you mean, sir. Please. I have not stolen anything, there must be a very big mistake. You have the wrong person, I swear to you!' Tears welled up in Hamoonga's eyes.

Babu narrowed his gaze and said again, 'My *friend*, I am not one to play games. You were in the car the night your girlfriend took something that belongs to me and disappeared with it. I saw you with my own eyes. I want it back!'

Hamoonga's mind travelled back to that night with Lulu. He burrowed through the reaches of his memory to try to find something – anything– that would appease his interrogator. He drew a blank. There had been a terrible mistake; he knew nothing about her dealings and he certainly knew nothing about the bag that she took from this man.

'No, no, no, sir, please believe me, I have nothing to do with that. Lulu is not my girlfriend, I… I just met her that evening and she asked me to ride along with her because she needed to attend to something. I sat in the car and afterwards she… she dropped me back at school. I haven't seen or heard from her since! I swear on my mother's life that is the truth, the God's honest truth. I know nothing about what she took from you!' Tears began to roll down Hamoonga's cheeks. 'I swear to you!'

Babu gritted his teeth like a mad hound ready to attack. He clenched his fists into large steely balls and lashed out at Hamoonga, punching him in the side with the ferocity of a raging bull unleashed from its pen. Hamoonga vomited, and fluid leaked from his nose, splattering over the concrete floor. He gasped for breath as he felt a piercing pain in his rib cage akin to a sharp lance puncturing his side. The acidic taste and the vile smell of vomit lined the walls of his mouth, and filled his nasal cavity.

'Do you take me for a fool?' Babu screamed. 'You and that girlfriend of yours think you can run away with my property and get away with it? Where is it?' he demanded.

Hamoonga fell to the floor and curled up like a foetus, and held his side. 'I swear to you, I swear on my mother's life I know nothing!'

Incensed, Babu picked up the wooden chair and slammed it on top of Hamoonga. The chair smashed into several pieces leaving him reeling in agony, 'I know nothing! I swear to you, I know nothing!' Babu pelted his defenseless victim with one blow after another until he had tired himself out. He then got up, pulled out a handkerchief from his inside jacket pocket to wipe his sweaty brow. He paused for a few seconds as if to admire his work and then meticulously wiped his fists of Hamoonga's blood before straightening himself up. Visibly frustrated, he spat on his victim and walked towards the door.

Eyes tightly shut, Hamoonga lay curled up, sodden in blood and vomit, fearfully awaiting further punishment before he heard the door opening again. He then heard Babu issuing a forceful command, 'He's not talking yet, but I want you to make him rot in here until he does! You understand me?' There was the metallic clanging sound of the door closing and then the hollow clacking of fading footsteps.

♋

Ken's condition began to improve. After a week he was able to ingest fluids through his mouth. On the tenth day he was able to muster a few words and was moved from the ICU to the main recovery ward.

It was on the twelfth day after his surgery that two detectives visited him to ask questions about the night he had been attacked.

'Mr Kenneth Simutowe, my name is Detective Jones Sakala and this is my partner, Detective Eli Mwansa. We are from Lusaka Central Police investigating the case of your attack on the night of Thursday the twenty-second as well as the disappearance of your roommate, a Mr Hamoonga Moya. Can we ask you a few questions?'

Ken was lying in his hospital bed propped up by two pillows. The two detectives were standing to his left next to the bed. Detective Sakala was slim, tall, and clean shaven. He also wore a pair of silver thin-rimmed glasses that rested halfway down his nose and he peered above them like a man older than his age. He wore a pale-blue, short-sleeved shirt, no tie, and a pair of black slacks. Next to Detective Sakala stood Detective Mwansa, who was short, stubby, and also clean shaven. Detective Mwansa seemed reserved and pensive, a man of few words. He held a blue Bic pen in hand and a small yellow ring-bound writing pad. His off-white shirt underneath a black bomber jacket and black slacks completed his understated look.

'We have been coming to the hospital for several days but you've not been in a condition to make a statement,' Detective Sakala continued and looked at Detective Mwansa who gave a slight nod of concurrence.

Ken smiled slowly in acknowledgement of his visitors. He looked down at the saline drip nestled in his left arm and then back up at the detectives. 'I'll do my best to answer your questions.'

'Okay, thank you,' Detective Sakala said as Detective Mwansa readied himself to take notes. 'So, tell me what happened the night of Thursday the twenty-second?'

The young man breathed deeply as he attempted to clear his throat. He turned his head to the plastic jug of water and cup at his side, unable to reach for them.

'I'm sorry,' Detective Sakala moved quickly to pour Ken some water. 'Here you are.' The detective proceeded to place a straw to Ken's mouth and watched him sip at the fluid. When he was done, the detective replaced the cup on the table next to the bed and waited for the patient to gather himself together before resuming his line of questions.

'So, Mr Simutowe, you were about to tell me about the night – the Thursday night you were attacked?'

'Well, *ahem*,' Ken cleared his voice. 'All I can recall is a loud noise, which must have been the door breaking open and then three dudes entering the room.' He paused and took another deep breath. 'They had guns. One of them grabbed me from my bed and started whacking me bad. The other man was attacking Hamoonga.'

'Can you remember anything about the men, what they wore, their faces or anything they said?' Detective Sakala probed.

'*Nah*, it was dark. Hamoonga and I had both been asleep. They had flashlights, I *skeem*. The guns looked like the rifles military people use and they kept asking which one of us was Hamoonga.'

Detective Mwansa scribbled down a few notes.

'I see. Anything else you can remember, anything at all?' Detective Sakala asked again.

Ken shook his head. '*Nah*, nothing, the next thing I knew – I woke up in hospital not able to speak or move my legs.' With that, Ken broke into a coughing fit. Detective Sakala reached for the water again but Ken waved him away. The detectives waited for Ken to catch his breath.

'What kind of man is Hamoonga? I mean do you know if he was involved in anything?' Detective Sakala asked, carefully assessing Ken's facial expression.

'*Ah*, what do you mean, *bali*?' Ken asked.

'I mean did Hamoonga hang around certain people, doing drugs or dealing in stolen goods, did he owe money? Was he involved with anybody who would want to see him harmed?' The detective paused. 'Did you see any traffic of people coming to see him, you know, suspicious types?'

Ken shook his head emphatically, 'Hamoonga is a saint– a straight *own* – everyone likes him. He wouldn't steal or do drugs or anything like that, *bali*. He's a stand-up guy.' Ken thought hard. The Hamoonga he knew was peace-loving and kind to everyone. There was no way he could be involved in anything nefarious. 'Detective, do you think someone was after him?'

Detective Sakala dodged the question. 'Okay, I think we have enough for now. The doctor told us to take it easy on you. We will stop by if we have any more questions. Please tell the doctor to call Central Police and ask for Detective Sakala or Detective Mwansa in the Violent Crimes Unit if you remember anything else.' With that, the two men left Ken to rest.

As they left Ken's ward, Detective Mwansa looked at his notes and said to Detective Sakala, 'Well that was a waste of time, the boy remembers nothing. He seemed to have been banged up very well!'

'Yah, he didn't offer much,' Detective Sakala mused out loud. 'Except I think that his assailants were military men and they were after his roommate. If the guy was as clean as everyone keeps saying he was, I wonder if this has political ties. I mean, who wants to rob a student? It's got to be something he must have said or something he knew that he was not supposed to know. We have to look into his associations. Did he mess with the wrong person?'

'I agree,' Detective Mwansa said. 'That seems like the most plausible theory, at least at this point – we'll have to dig deeper.'

⌘

Later that afternoon, Detective Sakala was shuffling through loose notes on his paper-riddled desk when he was summoned to go and meet with Police Chief Daka up in his third-floor office. It was extremely unusual; rarely was anyone called up to meet with the Chief of Police, 'in his office'. It was never good.

After fumbling with his shirt and tie for about a minute, Detective Sakala made his way up the broken parquet-tiled flooring of the staircase leading to the third floor. He walked down to the end of the dark hallway and knocked tentatively on the frosted glass door with the signage *Police Chief Evaristo H. Daka.*

'Come!' sounded a chirpy female voice from behind the door. It was the voice of Chief Daka's secretary, Imelda Nawa. Detective Sakala straightened himself one last time before opening the door.

'How can I help you?' she asked as Detective Sakala walked in.

She was sitting, back straight, behind a desk neatly lined with multi-colored folders and a typewriter. Imelda's voice matched her appearance; she was sunny and bright, every hair in place, with lipstick and nails matching the pink flowers on her flowery dress.

'I was called to see Chief Daka in his office,' Detective Sakala said almost apologetically.

'Oh, yes, you are Detective Sakala?' she said, keeping her eyes on a piece of paper in front of her. 'Yes, he's expecting you. Please go through.' She continued typing without waiting for him to respond. Detective Sakala hesitated momentarily before making his way towards the varnished wooden door that stood to the left behind the secretary. Reaching the second door, he knocked again. Imelda turned her head and nodded for the detective to go in. He slowly opened the door. It made a creaking sound indicating it needed some lubrication at the hinges.

'Detective Sakala!' Chief Daka boomed. 'Come in, young man, and take a seat!'

'Good afternoon, sir!'

Chief Daka stood up from his chair and extended his large hand in welcome. He was a decorated police officer with over thirty-five years in the force. He had strong political connections with the government, something one needed in order to rise to the rank of Chief of Police. He was a mountain of a man; six foot two in height and two hundred and ten pounds in weight. He had been extremely athletic in his younger days playing soccer, boxing, and joining an occasional game of basketball. He was also a man of insatiable appetites for food and women, evidence of which could be seen by his girth and his nine children by four different women.

'Take a seat, Sakala!' he said, patting the detective on his back. The young detective dropped uneasily into one of the two seats in front of Daka's desk.

'You wanted to speak with me, sir?'

'Yes, I sent for you,' Chief Daka said as he resumed his authoritative position behind the desk. 'I have heard great things about the work you have been doing in this police force. All the officers speak very highly of you!'

Detective Sakala smiled nervously, unused to flattery. 'Thank you sir, that means a great deal coming from you.'

'This department, no, this country needs more young officers like you! Yes, you can go far, very far with the right tutelage.' Daka leaned back in his chair and rubbed his pumpkin-sized jaw. 'Sakala, what is the greatest quality a police officer can have?' The chief's expression was suddenly stern, and the atmosphere changed to frosty.

Detective Sakala hesitated for a few seconds, unsure of whether or not the chief's question was rhetorical and then attempted a response. 'Aaahhhh, well, I…I'm not sure, sir. Honesty, integrity?'

Leaning forward, shortening the distance between them, Chief Daka proceeded to provide his well-thought-out retort. 'Sakala, you and I live in a harsh world full of sometimes ugly truths. You and I are exposed to a world that the ordinary citizenry cannot stomach. A nefarious world riddled with brigands, shylocks, charlatans, and thugs. A world that the average person chooses to ignore. They live in a world of make-believe, oblivious to the harsh truths. You and I, my friend, cannot afford the luxury of believing in a utopic world of clear black and white! No, my friend, you and I have to deal with the messy underworld so that law-abiding citizens of this country can live in their make-believe world of fairy tales and ice-cream castles in the sky!'

Detective Sakala listened intently, trying to understand where the winding monologue was leading.

'Sakala, in my thirty-five years on the force, there is one thing and only one thing that I have relied on time and time again. One thing that has guided me through all things; one thing that has frequently been the difference between life and death. The one thing that separates those who get killed on duty and those who make it home to their wife and children every night!' The chief paused for dramatic effect. 'That one thing is *loyalty*!' He lingered on the final word for emphasis.

Eyes firmly fixed upon the detective, Daka continued, 'The case of the two students who were attacked a few weeks ago. I want you to close the case. There is nothing more to be found. The two boys were attacked by unknown common bandits and the missing boy has run off with some loose woman somewhere and does not want to be found. Case closed. Do you understand me? Can I rely on your loyalty, Detective Sakala?'

Chafing around the neck, feeling his tie had been pulled too tightly, Detective Sakala nodded slowly, understanding clearly that he had been offered a choice. Essentially, comply – do as you are told, or you will be squashed like an ant beneath a boot. It was a false choice and he knew it, but there was nothing he could do about it.

'Good then, we understand each other!' Chief Daka said reverting back to his initial affable disposition. He leaned back into his chair with a beaming smile, tension in the room fully dissipated. 'I knew I could rely on your loyalty!'

❖

Back at Cha-Cha-Cha prison, Hamoonga had endured a torrid few days in his bright, solitary room with the cold, concrete floors. Prison guards would show up unannounced and take turns peppering him with blows as they tried to extract information out of him. Their erratic appearances were by design to inflict a heightened sense of terror, to strip him of any semblance of order in his existence. He was truly at their mercy, not even given the power to know when it was day or when it was night. Some days they would beat the bare soles of his feet with wooden batons. Other days they would unleash a torrent of blows and kicks to all parts of his body. He still had no answers that satisfied the guards. After what seemed an eternity to him, the guards returned Hamoonga to the darkened communal cell that he recognised from the offensive stench of urine and fecal matter. He was weak and badly broken, a man drifting fluidly between being consciousness and unconsciousness.

Once he was thrown back into the common cell it was again Mr Miti who tended to him. Like a fragile bird with a broken wing, Hamoonga was nursed to health by Mr Miti. The older man cleaned his open wounds with damp rags and made sure Hamoonga received a portion of the scraps of cold *nshima* and wild herbs that the inmates shared. It took about a week before he had the strength to recount the events of his days of torture in the brightly lit room. Mr Miti listened attentively, nodding his head and shaking his head at various points through the narrative. Hamoonga recounted the night he was attacked as well as the days before the attack. He described how he had met Lulu, her store, their date at O'Hagan's Bar. He described how he had recognised the hefty bald man when he was speaking to Lulu and how it was the same man that now had interrogated him so brutally. Mr Miti listened to it all in silence, collecting the disparate pieces of the jigsaw puzzle. Then with the air of a concerned parent, he whispered, 'My boy, I think you should be very careful, very careful indeed. I think that your friend, this Miss Lulu, was involved with some very powerful people. Be careful with what you say for there are very dangerous, powerful people in this country.'

'You think this has something to do with politics?' Hamoonga asked.

'Most definitely. The GRZ number plate, the nature of the attack, the interrogation, and the mere fact that you are here. I have no doubt in my mind that your friend has angered some extremely powerful people in government – I have heard of such things before. If you value your life, I suggest you tell them everything you know. People like this play for keeps; they are ruthless. Your friends, your family, they all could be in danger!'

'That's the thing, I know nothing, nothing at all,' Hamoonga lamented tearfully. 'It's all been a terrible mistake. I am just a student. It's all a terrible mistake, I tell you! A terrible mistake!'

Chapter 9

Don't Rock the Boat

'Hamoonga Moya, get up!' a high-pitched male voice called from behind the main cell door. 'Hamoonga Moya, come with me!' There was a murmur of unease in the communal cell as the other inmates began to scuttle away from Hamoonga, as if he was a leper. The clanging of the metal latches could be heard as the unknown person from outside the dark cell worked to unlock the door. The door pushed open, letting in a blinding light that made all the inmates squint. Hamoonga felt a sick, empty feeling in the pit of his stomach, as the memory of torment surged through his mind.

The tall, erect figure of a man stood in the light and asked again, 'Hamoonga Moya, where are you? I need you to come with me.' Hamoonga hesitated before raising both of his hands in surrender.

'Please, please, sir, I've told you before, I know nothing. It's been a terrible mistake, I swear to you!' he was almost in tears. 'Please, please don't hurt me, I beg of you!'

'Up, up, up, come on, let's go!' the man ordered coldly. 'I need you to come with me!'

Hamoonga slowly picked himself up and hesitantly began to walk towards the light like a man taking tentative steps to the gallows. He feared the worst. More torture, more questioning, bright lights, and more beatings. They might kill him this time.

When Hamoonga reached the doorway he shut his eyes, for the light was intense and blinding. The prison guard nudged him forward and then turned to lock the metallic cell door behind them.

'Where are we going?' Hamoonga asked, his voice shaking

'Move!' the man replied with a push to the prisoner's back. He yielded to the man's order and they began to walk slowly along the narrow corridor in front of them. The man remained silent and their footsteps sounded eerily along the bleak corridor. After about thirty paces the man pushed Hamoonga into another narrow passage and towards an unpainted wooden door. The man then picked out a small silver key from his clunky keyring and unlocked the door. Pushing it open, he pulled Hamoonga by the left wrist as they entered. The room was dark, in stark contrast to the brightly lit corridors they had just traversed. The man flipped a light switch and the darkness was illuminated by a comfortable amber glow. The room was only about fifty square feet, and the dim light made it feel smaller. There were two desks at a right angle to each other. Both were covered with dishevelled files and paperwork; it appeared to be an office of some sort. The man pulled a chair out from behind one of the desks, placed it in front of Hamoonga, and signalled to him to sit down. The man then manoeuvered his way behind one of the desks, a position that looked familiar to him, and sat down

'Sit!' the man ordered. Hamoonga was still standing in fearful anticipation of what was to happen next.

'Please, sit down,' the man said in a tone that was clearly more congenial than before. Hamoonga sat down slowly, his body still quaking with fear.

'So, you are a student at Evelyn Hone College?' the man asked.

Hamoonga nodded.

'Why is a poor student like you messing around with powerful politicians in Lusaka?' the man asked with a quizzical frown. He had thin eyebrows and narrow lips darkened by years of chain smoking.

'Why would a young student like you be foolish enough to mess with a politician, in fact a government minister? You must be either very bold or foolish beyond belief. Which one is it?'

Hamoonga hunched his back as he felt the weight of the world's problems. He shook his head and replied for what seemed to be the hundredth time, 'I don't know what you mean. I'm not involved with any politicians. It's been a terrible mistake. I was simply in the car with that woman... I have nothing to do with her or her dealings. I hardly even know her!'

The man sat silently for a while staring at him. He seemed to be searching for signs of sincerity in Hamoonga's face. Then he broke the silence. 'So, you did not know Lulu, Babu, or Minister Zulu and his wife?'

'Who is Babu and who is Minister Zulu?' Hamoonga asked. 'I swear by Almighty God, I do not know these people!'

'Well, until recently, your friend Lulu had been a close associate of Minister Zulu and his wife. It's known that they have done many things for her, helped her out with her business, opened doors, and basically treated her as their own daughter. But, things have changed now. She has taken something of theirs and disappeared with it. You can imagine that they feel betrayed and they, of course, want their property returned to them.'

'Lulu stole something from a minister and his wife?' Hamoonga asked. 'What is it that she stole?'

'Yes, she ran away with a very expensive package. Something they have to get back, and they will not stop until they do so!'

'You have to believe me,' Hamoonga pleaded, 'I have nothing to do with any of that. Nothing. I'm just a student that went out on a date with a woman I barely know, I swear to you!'

The man paused again, looked at Hamoonga, and replied, 'I believe you.'

Hamoonga looked up in disbelief. The man had his eyes squarely fixed on him.

'Thank you, sir. Can you... can you please tell them to release me? I beg of you!'

'Hmmm, well, it's not that simple. You see, Minister Zulu and his wife are very powerful people, people not to be messed with. They will stop at nothing to protect their interests. Right now they believe you and Lulu have conspired to steal from them. Their henchman, Babu, with whom you have been brutally acquainted, has given explicit orders for us to see that you remain here until he instructs otherwise.'

'What? But I'm innocent, I did nothing wrong!'

'At this point it is not a matter of guilt or innocence. At this point the Zulus view you as a threat to their public image and reputation. You see, many people in this country know the Zulus to be a powerful political family. They have great wealth and would like their legacy to continue. Rumour has it that they are grooming their eldest son, Ziyembe, for the presidency, and they do not want anything to come in the way of their role as king makers.'

'But how am I an impediment to their plans? How does a lowly student like me pose a threat to them, I don't understand?'

'Well,' the man leaned forward and lowered his voice into a whisper, 'How do you think the Zulus accumulated such immense wealth? They have created a vast empire of corruption, patronage and greed. They are involved in many things – kick-backs from foreign companies wanting government contracts, drug trafficking – you name it, they've done it. They have used their political connections to smuggle narcotics across borders in Africa, Europe and Asia. They operate with impunity in this country for they're above the law. However, they fear that their plans to install their son into the highest office of the land could suffer a huge blow if their drug-trafficking empire was to be exposed to the wider public. So you, my friend, are a threat that they cannot afford at this crucial time. In fact, the only reason you are still alive is that they believe you are their best hope of finding Lulu.'

Hamoonga's head was spinning; he had found himself in the eye of a perfect storm. One day he was a poor student, the next he was a threat to the machinations of a powerful political dynasty! His mind flashed back to an image of Lulu holding the green rucksack that night. His anger towards her stirred up inside of him like piping stew. If he had never met her, none of this would have happened!

'But what can I do? You have to help me, you have to tell them I know nothing and I will remain quiet. I… I have no intentions of talking to any one, I…'

The man interrupted. 'All I can tell you is, if you know anything about your girlfriend's whereabouts, tell them now and pray that she returns what she has stolen. If these people cannot get what they want, it will be bad for you. Very bad!'

❖

Letter from the Dean of Evelyn Hone College

Friday 27th October 2006

> *Dear Mrs Moya,*
>
> *I hope this letter finds you well. I am writing to inform you that two weeks ago your son, Hamoonga Moya, fell victim to a robbery incident at Evelyn Hone College. The police were called to investigate the case but it is with great regret that I have to inform you that at this time the where-abouts of your son remain undetermined.*
>
> *It is recommended that you travel to Lusaka as soon as you possibly can to enter a statement with the police and answer some questions. Your input could prove indispensable in assisting the police in locating your son.*
>
> *Time is of the essence.*
>
> *Yours sincerely,*
>
> *Maxwell Mulundika*
>
> *Dean of Evelyn Hone College, Lusaka*

The letter arrived a full three weeks after Hamoonga's disappearance. Mama Bupe was overcome with fear and anxiety. The news enveloped her like a cold fog. Her only son was missing; the son she was so proud of was missing. Was he hurt, was he alive? The unthinkable gripped her mind, she pushed against the thought: was he dead? She could not bear to lose her one and only son; that would be worse than death itself. Could God be so cruel as to take her husband and now her firstborn child?

Mama Bupe shared the letter with her daughters, Beatrice and Moonga who was similarly filled with despair and disbelief.

'Oh, Mama, what shall we do? This is terrible!' Beatrice said, tears in her eyes. 'Please, Lord, let him be safe!'

'I'll go with you, Mama!' Moonga offered. 'Surely the police must be able to find him!'

Mama Bupe took her daughter's hand and shook her head. 'No, I'll go myself. Your husbands and children need you here. I'll ask for a few days off …'

'But I don't like the idea of you travelling by yourself to the city. Lusaka is huge. Please let one of us accompany you!'

'Moonga's right, Mama, we don't know where Hamoonga is and my God, it would be terrible if something were to happen to you as well!' Beatrice said.

'Nonsense, I'll be fine. You two stay here with your families. I'll manage!' Mama Bupe was adamant. Having a plan gave her strength. 'I've already spoken with Father Banda. He's given me the name of a friend at Saint Ignatius Seminary. They'll have a room for me where I can stay for a few days.'

'But what about transportation? How will you get about in the city?' Beatrice asked.

'I'll walk and use the bus, same as here. I'm not helpless you know!' The older woman tried her best to force a smile.

'This is terrible, so terrible! If something has happened to him, I… I…' Beatrice burst into tears.

'Don't say that, don't say that!' Moonga clenched her hands as she too balled up in tears.

The three of them embraced, as they tried to comfort each other in Beatrice's tiny living room, a family devastated. Not knowing seemed almost worse than a knowledge of death.

❖

When Mama Bupe arrived in Lusaka the next day, she wasted no time. She caught a cab to the Lusaka Central Police Station. The cab driver was an older man also originally from Kitwe. He was moved by Mama Bupe's story. He felt pity for a mother searching for her missing son in the big city. The cab driver had heard too many stories of young men killed in dark alleys by drunken gangs of drug-crazed thugs. The cab driver would not accept Mama Bupe's money when they arrived at their destination. Instead, he simply bade her goodbye and promised to pray for the safe return of her son.

Mama Bupe was a diminutive lady; she always wore an African-print *chitenge* on top of her dress as most women her age did. She also covered her short grey hair with a matching *doek*. Her small frame contrasted with her strong, tenacious spirit. This was not the first time she had confronted adversity. She made the sign of the cross, said a silent prayer and then entered the police station.

'So you are Hamoonga Moya's mother.' Detective Sakala was sitting behind his file-laden desk, his hands in plain view.

'Yes, I am. I have come because of a letter I received stating that my son was missing. He has not been seen for several days,' Mama Bupe kept control of her emotions which trembled under her words.

'Where have you travelled from?' the detective asked perfunctorily

'I arrived today from the Copperbelt. Please. I'm very worried about my boy. He's a good son.'

'May I see your *reggie*?' Detective Sakala avoided her eyes.

Mama Bupe searched through the cloth handbag in her lap and produced her green National Registration Card. Detective Sakala examined the card for a few seconds, as if he was playing for time, and returned it without a word.

'Sir, do you know what has happened to my boy?' Mama Bupe was not unfamiliar with the arrogance of civil servants, and she knew no matter the provocation, patience was best.

'Its true…your son has been missing for close to three weeks now. There was a burglary and assault in his student hostel and he has not been seen since. We have reason to believe that he may have been involved with some shady characters, people to whom he may have owed money.'

'No, no, no, sir, my son would never ever borrow money! He's a good boy, a God-fearing, gentle soul. No!' she felt tears prickle her eyes. The police did not care. She took a deep breath.

'We have a first-hand account that your son was attacked by sophisticated criminals who could have kidnapped him,' Detective Sakala said impassively. 'We are currently investigating the case but there are no breakthroughs at this time.'

'Oh my Jesus, oh my Lord, why, why, why!' Mama Bupe lost her self-control and began to cry. 'What have they done to my son, where have they taken him? My only son, where is he?'

The detective paused allowing Mama Bupe's crying to subside a little, and when he spoke he sounded a little more humane. 'Madam, think carefully, is there anything you can tell us that would help us establish his whereabouts? Anything at all? Please, think hard.'

Mama Bupe mopped her eyes before shaking her head and answering, 'No, sir. He didn't know anyone in Lusaka, nor did he ever mention any particular friends or acquaintances in his letters. I have no idea where he could be.'

'Did any of your family talk to him recently or did he share any news or information with anyone other than you?'

'No, not that I know of. He's close to his sister Beatrice, but we discussed his absence yesterday and neither of his sisters had any idea what could have happened.'

Mama Bupe wept unrestrainedly. The anxiety since receiving the letter, the haste with which she had made arrangements, the long journey, had worn her out. Deep down, there had been a small, almost unconscious hope flickering, that the police would know something, or by the time she arrived, Hamoonga would have been found.

'Madam, we're doing all we can and we will continue to look for him. Please go home and take some rest, as you have had a long journey. We can talk more later.' The detective stood up from behind his desk. Mama Bupe nodded her head, clutched her bag, and got up slowly from her chair.

'I will speak with you tomorrow and believe me, if anything new comes up, you will be the first person to know,' Detective Sakala said, but his voice was hollow.

♋

Mama Bupe was determined to stand up for her son. She would not be placated by the police's false assurances. She decided to go to Evelyn Hone College to find out what she could for herself. She had, after all, the letter from Dean Maxwell Mulundika and she would follow up with him.

Dean Mulundika fidgeted with the papers on his desk. Stacks of yellow, blue and white forms lay before him. He settled on a single sheet of paper which he picked up and put down several times, as if he didn't know what to do with his hands. 'Yah, Mrs. Moya.' He sighed heavily before adjusting his thick-rimmed glasses. 'It's very sad, very, very sad. We have heard nothing more. It came as a complete shock. Hamoonga... he, he, is such a good student.'

Mama Bupe struggled to hold back her tears. She was not the tough resilient woman she had once been, age had softened her and news of a son's unaccountable disappearance had removed her sense of a future, and left her intensely vulnerable. 'But who could have done this to my son, Ba Mulundika? *Awe shuwa*, all I want is for him to return safely – I'm so worried.'

The dean picked up the piece of paper again and stared at it for a moment. 'This is a copy of the police report that the detectives shared with us. They are investigating the case thoroughly; they assured us that they would leave no stone unturned.'

'But I've been to see the police and they can't tell me anything about where my son is or what happened to him. I was there this morning.' The old woman's voice broke revealing her frustration and despair. 'Surely, there is somebody here, in the school. A friend, a teacher... perhaps someone who knows something?'

'Madam, I assure you that everything is being done. The police were here and they interviewed all his friends and many of his classmates but none of them knew anything. His closest friend, Ken, was attacked in the room with him and he is lying in hospital as we speak.

'*Iye imwe shuwa-shuwa!*' the woman cried out in anguish. The principal averted his eyes, embarrassed by her show of emotion.

'Sir, please let me speak to his friends. I need to speak to them, to ask them myself. Somebody must know something, anything...'

Dean Mulundika slowly rose from his seat and moved from behind his desk. He put his hand on her shoulder. 'Wait here a moment Mrs Moya. Let me see what I can do.'

Half an hour later he returned to the office. Mama Bupe, her purse nestled in her lap looked up anxiously. 'I managed to get in touch with one of his classmates, her name is Temwani. His friends are actually now at UTH visiting Ken – your son's roommate. Apparently, he's recovering slowly but is still unable to talk much.' He paused. 'If you're willing, I can drive you to the hospital now and you can speak with them yourself.'

'Oh praise be to God Ba Mulundika. You are a man of God!' The woman's hopeful sincerity was as transparent as the Dean's barely disguised fatalism.

When they reached the hospital, they found three young people sitting by the bedside of a frail young man. The two girls and the boy stood up at the sight of Mama Bupe and Dean Mulundika. The former introduced themselves as Temwani and Maya, their companion was Ben.

Mama Bupe moved to Ken's side and instinctively placed her hand gently on his forehead. '*Iye tata lesa aye*, what have they done to you my child?' Tears rolled down her cheeks as her fears for her son came to the fore. Was he lying alone in a ditch somewhere, brutally assaulted and helpless?

'*Mwebana*, what happened, who did this to you?'

Ken shook his head slowly. 'Don't know.' The words seemed to draw all his energy. His eyes fell back and he dropped his head to the side. Mama Bupe stroked his hair for a moment before turning to face the others.

'*Mwebana*, tell me, who did this to him and where is my son?' Sadness filled the room as Ken's friends failed to provide a response. 'Can you, his friends, tell me who he may have been involved with or who might want to do such a terrible thing?'

Maya broke down in tears. Temwani put her arms around her friend's shoulders before facing Mama Bupe. 'Mayo, what has happened is terrible. None of us can imagine who *would* or *could* do such a thing. We have spent hours trying to make sense of the attack but our minds are blank. Hamoonga and Ken were normal, hard-working students…'

Dean Mulundika removed his glasses and wiped his face with his handkerchief.

Mama Bupe's shoulder's slumped with a sense of defeat as her last hope left her.

A voice from behind them broke the moment of silence. 'Visiting time is over!' yelled a stern-faced nurse.

The next day yielded nothing more. This time it was Detective Sakala's proxies who gave Mama Bupe the run-around. 'Detective Sakala is in the field as we speak,' they assured her. 'There has been no development. Hang tight. You will be the first to know when there is a new development in the case.' But, one day turned into two and two days into a week. Finally, Mama Bupe had to return to Kitwe to resume her job. The police had made no discernable progress, Hamoonga was missing, and the longer his absence the less the authorities seemed to care. There was no justice for the poor. If Hamoonga had been a well-known politician or some rich man, the police would have done everything to find him.

Several weeks passed. Ken grew stronger but he remained bed-ridden as he had not regained the use of his legs. His parents, at first simply relieved that their son had survived, began to worry that he'd remain paralysed. As doctors, they deliberated over what they could do to help Ken. If they kept him at UTH, they would be able to keep a close eye on him and monitor his progress; but they were very aware that the hospital lacked the latest facilities which could help their son to walk again.

If they sent him abroad, he would get the best medical care, but they would be far away from him and unable to give him their personal attention. In addition, there was the cost of sending him overseas. A full regimen of physiotherapy and specialist treatment could easily cost thousands of pounds. Finally, after eight weeks, Ken's parents decided to send him to Manchester, where they had gone to medical school, and where their son could receive specialist care. Both doctors still had many personal and professional connections in this northern city.

It was hard for Ken to leave. He still had many unanswered questions about who had attacked them and he could not understand why there still was no word about what had happened to Hamoonga. Maya, Temwani, and Ben had all been frequent visitors to his bedside and they all said the same thing: the police had been investigating, but the trail had gone cold. Nobody knew who the assailants were and no one knew what had happened to Hamoonga.

Hamoonga's friends, Maya, Ben, and Temwani, did their best to keep following up with the police, but they were met by the same apathy and incompetence. After two months the case was all but forgotten. Lusaka police station was always inundated, and under-staffed. Once a police case entered its third month, it was as good as dead.

⌘

It had been a full three months since Hamoonga had had his one-on-one conversation with the sympathetic official. During that time he had been pulled into the bright interrogation room and beaten a total of four times. Each time he pleaded his innocence. After each beating, it took him several days to recover before being pulled into the torture cell again. It seemed like a cruel game. However, it was almost three-months to the day that the same official sat slouched in the small office looking directly at Hamoonga.

'So, my man, it seems as though there's been a development in your case.'

Hamoonga remained silent. The prison, the terrible beatings, the loss of hope had numbed his senses. Beyond the point of caring, death seemed the only way out. He knew he could not take one more beating. His body was broken.

'I said, there's been a development in your case,' the official repeated. Hamoonga did not even lift his head.

The guard continued, 'It seems your girlfriend, Lulu, is wanted by Interpol.'

Hamoonga slowly looked up.

'Aaahh, that got your attention! Yes, it seems a suitcase with packets of heroin was intercepted at Oliver Tambo International Airport some days ago. The drugs were valued at over US$600,000! It seems the suitcase was misplaced by baggage handlers and eventually made its way to lost and found. The bag lay there unclaimed for weeks and was eventually transported to a central holding location. During a routine check the canines from the narcotics squad raised an alarm and the suitcase was opened. When investigators traced their records, they found it led to one Louise Daka of Ibex Hill in Lusaka. Nobody has been able to find her yet, but her picture is all over the papers.'

'You see, I told you I had nothing to do with this!' Hamoonga's words were slurred. It was as if he had protested his innocence so often that they had lost their meaning.

Then, as the impact of the information the official had provided, broke through his misery, he looked up and said, 'That proves it, I'm innocent! Surely, you can see this.'

'Hold on, hold on, my friend. Life is never that simple. You're right, this information does seem to prove that you didn't conspire with Lulu to steal from the Zulus, but there's a problem.'

Hamoonga hung his head. He might have known it. For a moment he'd understood what it meant to hope, and allowing that moment to break through, somehow made reality even worse.

'I am merely an employee in the state machine. I only take orders and do what I'm told. I also have to feed my family. We have received explicit directions from above not to release you. You are to stay in custody until further direction.'

'Why?' Hamoonga's voice cracked, 'I'm innocent!'

'I cannot go against my orders, none of us can. In fact, I'm breaking protocol explaining this to you. Do you realise what trouble I would be in if they ever found out?'

Hamoonga's eyes welled with tears. He felt the brutality of an unjust system.

'I suspect that now there's an Interpol investigation leading to Lulu, the Zulus are playing it safe. They don't want the risk of there being anyone who can expose them. And to be honest, my friend, for the first time, I believe you're safer in here than out there on the streets. At least they know where you are and can be sure you're not talking to anyone.'

'I'll make sure you're treated decently in here... at least I can promise you that. There'll be no more beatings if you co-operate and lie low. Just bide your time; it will be over at some point. Don't rock the boat!'

Hamoonga, nodded, then he asked, 'Could you do something for me?' The officer's eyes met Hamoonga's but he did not answer. 'Sir, if I cannot be released, could you at least pass on a message to my poor mother? I need at least to let her know that I am still alive.'

The officer averted his eyes. It was clear he felt some sympathy for the broken figure sitting in front of him. After a long pause he replied, 'I can't promise you anything, but I'll see what I can do.'

❖

So it was that Hamoonga's life at Cha-Cha-Cha prison improved a little. The beatings stopped and he began to spend most days working in the massive agricultural field within the perimeter of the prison. The work was hard but it was refreshing to be out in the open air instead of being cooped up in the dingy communal cell. The field spread over four hectares of open land. A portion of the field was allocated to growing vegetables such as tomatoes, cabbage, cauliflower, and green beans, and this section demanded daily care – weeding, watering, and applying fertilizer. The remaining back portion of the land was allocated to cultivating maize, a tricky crop. Commercial seed from the pre-eminent Zambian grain seed company, Zamseed, was used. Planting was all about timing; one had to pay close attention to the rainy season, had it begun, or was it a false start, as well as when to apply fertiliser, and when to weed.

Hamoonga and the other prisoners – about a hundred men in all – worked ten-hour shifts six days a week. None of the men complained, for each of them cherished the opportunity to be free of their dark cell. To supplement the pittance of a budget received from the state, a bumper harvest was essential for the prison. Farming provided a vital source of income to help run it. The produce from the field also provided the food that fed the prisoners. A poor harvest meant the prisoners would go hungry. This imperative was not lost on the minds of the prisoners. They worked hard, each man giving of his best.

Hamoonga had now been imprisoned for eight months. He was bitter but he had resolved to focus on the present so as not to be driven mad. It was Mr Miti who had advised him to take one day at a time. 'Focus on the immediate, do not fill your mind with thoughts about the past, nor should you waste your energy imagining the future. One has to live in the present, one second at a time, one minute at a time, one hour, one day at a time; it is the only way to survive in here.' And, Hamoonga realised, the old man was right.

◆ ◆ ◆

One afternoon a guard pulled Hamoonga to the side as the prisoners were making their way in single file back to their cells having put in a full day's work in the field. 'Our boss needs to see you.' Fearing a return to the dark torturous days of incessant beatings, Hamoonga's heart began to do laps in his chest. Why did they want to see him?

The guard directed him down the corridors to the tiny office he had visited before. Recognising the office, Hamoonga's tension eased. He recalled the last conversation he'd had with the officer several weeks back. He had not heard from him since. The thought of hearing news of his family on the outside lifted his spirits. The guard knocked on the door, and saluted when it was opened. 'I've brought the prisoner, sir.'

Thanking the guard, the official ushered Hamoonga into the room. 'Sit down, my man.' Hamoonga was glad to see the officer with whom he had now developed something of a rapport.

As Hamoonga moved to take a seat, he noticed an uneasy expression on the officer's face. Something was bothering him.

'Sir, were you able to contact my family to tell them that I am alive and well?' Hamoonga asked expectantly. 'I know Mama must be worried sick. I can imagine the pain and anxiety she must have felt not knowing whether I was alive or dead. It must be killing her.'

'I placed the call to your family yesterday… It took me some time to find the right moment … but … I have some unfortunate news, Hamoonga. It's your mother. She… she died three days ago,' the prison official's voice was kind. 'When I called the number, it was your sister that answered and she informed me of the sad news.'

'What? No, no, no! It can't be!' Hamoonga shook his head from side to side as if to shake off some evil spirit or bad karma. 'What do you mean "dead"?'

'She was very ill. They said she had not been well since your disappearance. She had fallen into a deep depression. The doctor couldn't find anything physically wrong with her but she was bedridden, unable to walk. Then she stopped eating and, a few nights ago, she passed away in her sleep. I'm so sorry.' The guard's tone was low and apologetic. 'I confirmed the news with some contacts I have in the police force and it's true. I'm so sorry, my man.'

Hamoonga stood up and covered his face with both hands. He let out a guttural cry and then fell back into his chair as if the life had been sucked from his body. He tasted the salt from the tears that were streaming down his cheeks. 'Mama, oh, mama,' he cried bitterly. 'Don't leave me now, not now mama, you can't go like this, not like this!'

'I am so sorry, Hamoonga. So sorry for your loss.' The officer got up from his desk and made his way to the slumped figure. He gently patted Hamoonga on the back saying, 'I wish there was something I could do.'

The officer remained silent for a few minutes not knowing what to say or how to comfort the broken man in front of him. 'I need to bury her, I need to go and bury my mother! You have to let me out so that I can lay my mother to rest!'

The official straightened his posture, and then replied, 'I wish there was something I could do but you know I cannot let you out. There are explicit orders to keep you here until we are directed otherwise.' The officer's words had a finality to them which stung Hamoonga to the quick.

After the exhaustion of the last cruel months, the news of his mother's death, was too much. 'It's my mother we're talking about! I have to be able to bury my own mother!' Hamoonga shouted at the top of his voice, momentarily forgetting the imbalance of power that existed between the two men.

'Sit down! You will do well to control yourself - I've told you I cannot do anything about it. It's tragic but there is nothing I can do!' The warning in his tone was unmistakable – know your place!

'You need to help me. You are the only one who can help me. Please, I need to bury my mother! I must bury my mother!'

The officer narrowed his eyes. He had tried to help the prisoner, but now his own helplessness and Hamoonga's insubordination enraged him.

'You're a coward! How can you not allow a person to bury his own blood? It's inhumane! You must...' Before he could finish his sentence, Hamoonga was struck in the face. He had overstepped his bounds. A prisoner needed to know his place. Hamoonga had raised his voice and insulted a prison official. Much like a schoolyard, a prison operates hierarchically. Prison guards and officials must always assert their position before inmates or they lose their power.

'You will respect me, I don't care what has happened to you or who you have lost!' the official's voice was icy. 'If you know what's good for you, you will shut up now! I run things in here, remember that!' The officer grabbed him by the shoulder and pushed him to the floor.

'You are a coward, you are a coward!' Hamoonga yelled in defiance. With that the official unleashed a barrage of furious kicks on the prostrate man, who felt the full brunt of the officer's polished steel-toed leather boots in his sides. It was one kick after another, each kick adding to the numbing pain. The last thing Hamoonga recalled was the antiseptic smell of the office floor.

When he arose again he was back in the musky, dark communal cell. The right side of his face was swollen, his shirt was stained with crusted blood, and an excruciatingly sharp pain stabbed inside his rib cage. It took several weeks for him to recover to full physical health, but his spirit remained irreparably damaged by the loss of his mother. There were no more one-on-one meetings with the prison officer and it was several months before Hamoonga was allowed to rejoin the other inmates to work in the agricultural field outside. He could tell the prison guards were making a statement that was loud and clear: 'You are a prisoner, we are the guards; know your place, or else!'

After learning about the death of his mother, Hamoonga withdrew into a deep emotional stupor. He was bitter and cold. All that had been of value to him had been taken away – family, freedom, education, everything. Nothing remained but a cruel, empty existence where long days merged from one to the other. Hamoonga could feel his spirit withering each day like a plant left unattended. He distanced himself from the other prisoners including his friend Mr Miti who implored the young man not to dwell on the pain of the past or to think about the grave injustices he'd suffered. But still Hamoonga withdrew further and further into a deeper and deeper depression. He cared for nothing, lived for nothing, and that was how he would spend the next four years of his life in prison; a dead man walking.

♋

Zambia National Broadcasting Corporation (ZNBC) Presidential Independence Address

October 24th 2010

'We would like to interrupt this radio programme to deliver some breaking news. His Excellency, President Given Mwansa Chibompo, has issued a decree to close down Cha-Cha-Cha Prison within six months. The president has issued a pardon for the ninety-seven prisoners currently in Cha-Cha-Cha Prison as a gesture of his goodwill and a celebration of our nation's forty-sixth Independence Anniversary. May the almighty God bless this nation and may we be a beacon of light for Africa and the world at large.'

The scripted words of the heavily accented female radio announcer streamed through the airwaves. The news brought joy and relief to homes across the nation. Many fathers would be coming home to see their grown sons and daughters. Many husbands would return home to embrace their weary wives. And some would return to learn that family members had died or left the country. It was a pivotal moment. The President had finally relented to the international pressure to close the notorious prison and free his political rivals. President Chibompo was now old and frail; a second heart attack had left him in a wheelchair. The man clung on but his iron-clad grip on power was loosening. Faced with a rising discontent about the economy from both the poor and the rich, as well as the prospect of foreign donor countries withdrawing their largesse, the president had been forced to appease the West. Despite the growing presence of the Chinese, who kept their distance from the internal affairs of

African countries provided they were making money, President Chibompo knew that he could not survive without Western backing.

The news spread through the prison like wildfire. For the first time the atmosphere lifted with a feeling of joy, hope, and relief. The prisoners sang at the prospect of returning to their homes. Their ordeal was finally over. The prisoners were immediately allowed to send letters to their families to inform them of their impending release. For many, these letters were the first real sign that their long-lost family members were still alive. Hamoonga wrote to his sister Beatrice to tell her that he would be returning to Kitwe soon. He had been in Cha-Cha-Cha for four years.

Chapter 10

Who Says You Can Never Go Back Home?

When Hamoonga returned from prison, it had been over six years since he had last seen his sisters, after two years in college and four years in prison. Once he had left those dreaded walls, without money, he had hitchhiked the 250 miles from Lusaka to Kitwe. A Muslim Tanzanian driver named Salif Mohammed had allowed him to ride with him in the cab of his Volvo eighteen-wheeler freight truck to Kapiri Moshi where the two men had parted ways. Salif continued up the Great North Road to the border with Tanzania and Dar es Salaam. As they drove, Hamoonga had been content to let Salif ramble on about his plans to own his own commercial trucking company. He spoke of how he would be a better employer than the people he currently worked for. 'A man is only ever really free when he can work for himself. Own his own house, own his own business, *inshallah*, I will do that one day.' Salif had also spoken about his wife and two girls, about his faith and about how he had been saving up to go to the holy city of Mecca during Ramadan. He was a generous man, happy to share his food and drink with Hamoonga, saying it was his duty as a good Muslim to help a stranger on his journey. When the two parted ways, he gave his passenger a fistful of crumpled kwacha notes, certain that the man had very little.

Leaving Kapiri, Hamoonga hitched another much less comfortable ride in the back of a slow, heavily laden charcoal van. There were three other passengers, teenage boys, lying on top of the load. Grim-faced and blackened with charcoal dust, their bodies lean and taut, they were mute over the bumpy journey that took close to five hours, as if engaging in conversation would have sapped the last drops of their energy. Their thin bodies bounced up and down with every pothole on the road, while their expressions remained sullen and withdrawn. It was common to see youth like this, life already beaten out of them by hunger and affliction. They were probably orphans compelled to work on slave wages just to sustain a pitiful existence.

Arriving in Kitwe, Hamoonga disembarked and immediately began the back-breaking work of helping the three boys to offload the bags from the back of the van. This was his payment for the safe passage to Kitwe. The work was hard and unflattering, and by the time they were done Hamoonga was covered in black charcoal dust. Then, having bade farewell to the boys and the driver, he began the trek to his sister's home, walking for over an hour and a half to reach Kwacha East Township where he knew Beatrice and her husband lived. It was an easy decision to go there and not to Moonga's as Hamoonga had never been fond of her husband, Balam, whom he considered an illiterate, shiftless drunkard. He remembered how Balam would disappear for days until, eventually, she knocked on her mother's door weeping with anxiety about what fate may have befallen her husband. The family would then search for Balam, who they would inevitably find lying drunk in a ditch somewhere surrounded by mocking children. The man was an embarrassment. Moonga would always play the role of loyal wife; she would bring him back, bathe him like a helpless child, feed him and suture his wounds. He would swear never to get drunk again but the cycle always repeated itself.

Hamoonga arrived well after dusk at Beatrice's home, house number D1522 Musuku Road in Kwacha East Township. He made his way tentatively through the narrow passageways in between the indistinguishable township houses, finally arriving at his sister's front gate. This was made out of a rusted zinc corrugated-roofing sheet affixed to an unevenly welded metal frame by two twisted metallic wires that were unceremoniously strapped to the vulnerable frame. The white signage, 'D1522' was painted clumsily across the top of the gate and underneath it an unconvincing warning: *Beware of Dog.* On either side of the gate was a well-manicured hedge surrounding the tiny yard.

As the gate was ajar, Hamoonga hesitantly entered, walking up to the small concrete step polished red outside the front door. He was self-conscious about his appearance and apprehensive about the reception he would receive. He had written to his sister about his impending release, so she would be expecting him, but still, he was an ex-convict and so much had changed.

◆◆◆

Beatrice hugged him tightly, tears streaming down her cheeks, then stepped back to look at him. 'I can't believe it's you! You're back from the dead! Oh, Hamoonga, I've missed you so much. Look at you, you're as thin as a rake. Oh, what did they do to you?'

'I'm okay, sis, I'm fine, really there's no need to worry,' he smiled with the relief of years.

'Sit, sit, let me prepare something for you to eat.' Picking up his small bag, she ushered him into her tiny living room and removing a pile of clothing from one of the chairs, fluffed up some cushions and pressed him to sit down.

'Oh, I'm sorry for the mess, my brother. It's not always like this,' she lied. 'I've taken to embroidery to earn some extra cash. I sew badges onto school uniforms for primary and secondary school children. It's not much money, but it helps. Things are so expensive these days and we need everything we can get.'

Hamoonga sat down silently and looked around the room. The furniture was cheap and worn. The sofas were made from an olive-green fabric that was fraying along the edges of the armrests. The room was decorated with sentimental bric-a-brac and old family photographs in mismatching picture frames. Looking up from where he was seated, Hamoonga could see two floral curtains hanging languidly on a makeshift line covering two entrances – one to the kitchen and one to a solitary bedroom. Hamoonga recognised the plan of the house, so similar to many in Kwacha East. He knew, for instance, that a pit latrine and shower were located in an outhouse at the back of the yard and that there was a small verandah at the rear.

Beatrice spoke from behind the curtain leading to the kitchen. 'We were afraid we'd never see you again,' a clatter of metallic pots punctuating her words. 'We couldn't get any information,' she continued from behind the curtain. 'After an anonymous call we received years ago, I travelled to Lusaka several times, pleading with the officers to let us know how you were doing. They would never allow us to visit you. It was terrible.' She paused and returned to the living room. She shook her head. 'They would not let us in and they would not even tell us where exactly you were. It was horrible, I tell you. The not-knowing. We feared the worst. That is until we received your letter a month ago.' She sat down next to him and put her hand on his knee. He rested his hand on hers, silent. He didn't know what to say. So much time had passed, such a strange and terrible story, so many precious moments lost, never to be regained.

'I thank God,' his sister went on, 'that you're alive and that He has returned you to us.' She kissed his cheek, and disappeared behind the curtain again, still talking. 'You've another niece, you know, called Kangwa. She's six. She's at school right now. I've told both girls all about you. They'll be excited to see their uncle!'

'Yes, that'll be good, I'm looking forward to seeing them too,' he replied. He remembered Mr Miti's words, 'One day, one hour, one minute at a time, that's how the future begins.'

She returned and sat down on the sofa next to him. 'Food in just a few minutes. I've put the *nshima* on the fire on the verandah. So, how did you travel?'

'I got a ride from some good Samaritans, good people.'

'You should've called me and I could have sent you some money. You know you can send money using the phones nowadays?'

Hamoonga could tell things were not going so well for her. He could read the premature ageing lines on her face as well as her sunken eyes that she was barely getting by, that there was no money to spare and that the stresses of life were weighing on her like a heavy yoke.

'Oh, it's okay,' he said. 'I made it here just fine.'

She placed her hands on his right arm and stared at him with tearful eyes. 'Those evil men, they would not even let you come to your own mother's funeral. They're monsters! They deserve to rot in hell!'

Hamoonga sat silently for a moment. The pain of losing his mother and not being able to lay her to rest haunted him. It had been his worst night in prison; the beatings and humiliation paled in comparison to the deep emptiness he felt upon receiving the news of his mother's death, knowing that she did not even know he was alive. That night he had wished he were dead.

'You know Mama was not the same after you disappeared. She lost her desire to live. She tried many times to go to the police for any news concerning your disappearance. She even asked her employers to help but nothing worked. It seems when you're a nobody in this country, no one hears you!'

Beatrice wiped her tears away, got up, and went to the kitchen. When she returned fifteen minutes later, she brought out a tray with two covered metallic plates. She laid them on the coffee table in front of her brother and then disappeared again behind the curtain. She returned moments later with a plastic dish of water and a white tablet of soap. After washing his hands, Hamoonga uncovered the plates, finding a steaming mound of *nshima* on one plate and fried green pumpkin leaves on the other. He dug his fingers into the thick porridge and began to roll a ball of it in his hand.

'So you're not going to pray?' Beatrice interrupted. He paused for a second and then, lifting his eyes to meet hers, he said sadly, 'Where was He all those years I spent in prison?'

❖

Later that evening, Beatrice's daughters – Kangwa, six, and Mwamba, eight – barged into the living room in their charcoal-grey school uniforms with their blue-and-red school bags. Their excitement instantly transformed into an unsteady stare as they regarded the unexpected visitor in their living room.

'Girls, meet your Uncle Hamoonga,' Beatrice signalled for the girls to come closer. 'This is my older brother, your Uncle Hamoonga, the one I've told you about. He just came home from out of town. Come, come, greet him.'

The girls slowly moved closer, genuflected; each in turn giving their uncle a limp handshake, all the while averting their eyes as a sign of respect.

'Hello, girls, it's really nice to meet you. You know, Mwamba, you were a baby the last time I saw you. And Kangwa, you weren't even born. You are both such beautiful girls.' They smiled shyly, still unsure of their mother's guest.

'Go and get changed and then have your food in the kitchen,' Beatrice said.

'They're really beautiful children,' Hamoonga turned to face his sister.

'Yes, I know – but I fear for them. I want them to have a better life, you know.' Tears prickled her eyes again.

'What's the matter? Don't cry, sis, I know they'll be okay.' Beatrice put her hand across her mouth as tears journeyed down her cheeks.

'What's wrong?' he asked as she continued to sob. 'Beatrice, tell me what's wrong?'

She sniffled for a time before responding. 'It's… well, it's just that… their father. Their father, he left us a year ago. It's been so hard, Hamoonga. I feel like I'm sinking, it's so hard.'

'What do mean, where is he?'

Beatrice wiped her tears with the back of her hand. 'Well he, he found another woman, she gave him a son, and he's forgotten us. I prayed to God for him to return, but I will not beg for a man, you know. I've been trying. I do embroidery, I sell fertiliser, I sell vegetables at the market, fish, anything to bring in some extra money, but it's so hard. I need the girls to keep going to school. I've asked their father to help, but he will not. It's as if they are not his children. I get so mad sometimes. This society doesn't value women!'

Hamoonga reached out and hugged his sister. 'I am so sorry, I didn't know. This is terrible. I can only imagine what you've been going through. I'm here now, sis, I'm here now, we will do it together. They're my nieces and we will give them a better life – I promise you. We'll manage, somehow.'

The two spent the rest of the evening catching up, mostly reminiscing about their childhood days when their mother was alive and how she reigned with a hand as firm as the bark of a mukwa tree. That night Hamoonga attempted to sleep on the living room floor. Although he felt the tiredness in his body, he could not sleep, as so many memories raced through his mind. He mulled over Beatrice and his nieces; he recalled his dark days in prison; he thought about Lulu and that strange night that had severed his future from his past. His mind floated to Evelyn Hone, Maya and Ken, although he had not heard from them in years. He thought about finding a job and what the future held in store for an ex-convict with no college degree. Finally, he found comfort in the thought that for the first time in six years, he could dare to think about a future.

❖

Hamoonga awoke the next morning to the sound of a cockerel crowing in the distance. A soft amber light filtered through the thin, loosely strung curtains in the living room. He inhaled the homely ashy smell of his sister's house. The freedom to choose either to wake up or stay lying on the floor warmed him. As he lay there taking it all in, Beatrice emerged from the behind the curtain to the bedroom. Her face was solemn.

'*Mwashibukeni*, brother, how did you sleep?'

'I slept well, my *sisi*. How did you sleep?'

Shrugging her shoulders, Beatrice sat on the sofa in front of her brother. 'Huh, I couldn't sleep.'

'What was bothering you?' Hamoonga noticed a piece of paper in her hand.

'Beatrice shook her head. 'I just kept thinking about you and how those people have caused so much pain in our lives.' Hamoonga waited for his sister to get whatever it was off her chest.

'Last night, I couldn't stop thinking about this letter. I received it almost a year ago.' She took a deep breath and then continued. 'It came in the mail. It was addressed to you, so I opened it, hoping it contained news about you. It was from a woman who writes as if she knew you well. Her name is Maya.'

Hamoonga's heart began to pound. The thought of Maya and what might have been had never been far from his mind. Now his sister had a letter, and only a year old. He felt conflicted; on the one hand he longed to hear news of Maya, on the other, he feared what that news would be. Had she found someone else, did she have a family now? The thoughts gnawed at him like a dog clipping his heels.

'So it's true, the two of you were intimate?'

'Is she okay?' Hamoonga reached for the letter. Beatrice stared at him with sorrowful eyes.

Hamoonga unfolded the single sheet of paper and began to read the neatly curved, handwritten letter.

July 9th 2009

Dearest Hamoonga,

I don't know if you will ever read this letter but it is something I have to write.

The night you disappeared was the night I lost part of my very being. I have cried so many tears that my eyes have run dry. If ever you should read this, I hope that you will know that I love you and always will.

Someone once said that time heals all things. They lied. We do not heal with time, we can only choose to put the grieving aside and attempt to pick up the pieces of our lives.

As I write this, I am four months pregnant and about to get married to the father of my child. He is a good man and I love him but part of me longs for what could have been.

If you are wondering about our friend Ken; he has recovered from the tragic incident. He is in a wheelchair now but I hear he has made a good life for himself in the United Kingdom. Our old study group friends, Temwani, Brave, and Bernice all graduated and are working in Lusaka.

Hamoonga, I write this letter as much for me as for you. I would like to move on to the next chapter in my life but I needed to tell you that you will always have a special place in my heart.

Love always,

Maya

Hamoonga stared at the letter. Although he'd received answers to many of his questions, he felt that the tenuous threads, which had connected him to the more pleasant parts of his adult life, had just been severed. There was finality in his loss. He could not go back to relive the past, it was gone. Maya was departed into another life.

Chapter 11

A Good Samaritan

Three months after Hamoonga's return . . .

Kitwe, Copperbelt Province, Zambia

January 2011

There was a loud screeching sound followed by an almighty thud and the sputtering gasps of a dying engine. Hamoonga looked to his left across the narrow street. He could see the red rear lights of a car in the darkness like two beady eyes. He couldn't make out what kind of car it was, but he could tell it had run into a ditch. He heard the click of a switch followed by the wheezing of an engine as it struggled to start. The sputtering repeated several times before the driver abandoned all attempts to get it going again. As Hamoonga approached, he could make out the small thin figure of a man exiting the vehicle. It was a warm dusty evening and there were no other cars or pedestrians in sight along Nyerere Road close to Saint Anthony compound. Saint Anthony's was a small shantytown settlement on the outskirts of Kitwe close to the Chishimba copper mine processing plant. The compound was a ramshackle collection of tiny mud shacks with corrugated zinc metal roofing. The place was notorious for its nefarious characters and illicit activities, especially after nightfall. It was true that the trail of many burglaries, robberies, and violent crimes in the city led to this camp. It was imprudent to find oneself there after dark, and never alone, certainly not as an outsider.

Despite being aware of the risks, Hamoonga had few options, as three months of knocking on doors for work with no success had led him to search harder and walk longer distances to find a job. This morning, he'd walked all the way to the copper mining plant area on the outskirts of the city. He heard there were a few job openings for general labourers. Willing to pursue any lead, he made the long trek on foot and presented himself at the security booth just outside the front gate. The guards were characteristically rude and uncooperative. They turned him away and denied him audience with any of the mine supervisors. This, unfortunately, was an all too common story: many of the security guards purposefully blocked access to hiring supervisors within the plant. Aware of all vacancies, they filtered and channelled job openings to their friends and families, and to those willing to bribe their way in. Such was the depth of corruption in the entire system that even to get audience with a hiring supervisor was subject to patronage and cronyism.

Having tried unsuccessfully for many hours to make his way past the security guards, Hamoonga was on his way home, a dejected figure. It had been yet another frustrating day and he was desperate for someone to give him a break. He knew that he could not continue to be a burden on his sister.

As Hamoonga drew closer, he could clearly make out a navy blue Peugeot 504 sedan lodged at an angle with its front left tire wedged in a ditch by the roadside. As he drew closer still, he could see the lonely figure of a man standing akimbo looking intently at the wreck in front of him. He looked Asian – Chinese most likely. He had a full head of dark hair and thin, slanted eyes. In a chequered short-sleeved shirt with a pair of well-worn trousers, he seemed like someone accustomed to hard physical work.

'What happened? Are you okay?' Hamoonga approached the man.

'Aaaghhh, these damn roads, I hit pothole and lose control!' the man said as he looked at Hamoonga, sizing him up, unsure of whether the approaching stranger was friend or foe.

'Are you hurt?' Hamoonga asked. 'Everything okay?'

The man shook his head briskly, still mistrustful.

'Looks like you are having trouble getting out. I think you'll need a push,' Hamoonga said. 'You know it's not that safe around here.

There have been many incidents with bandits and robbers. I think we need to get you out of here as quickly as possible.'

'I try getting out but engine *won* start – I think I need push but I need to get out of ditch first.' the man said. Hamoonga noticed the man's minimal use of prepositions, a common trait among many Chinese in Kitwe.

Hamoonga circled the vehicle, assessing the car more closely. 'Okay, I think if we both get down to the front, we can lift and push the car out.'

The man still seemed unsure of whether or not to trust this Good Samaritan. Sensing his unease, Hamoonga reassured him. 'Look, if I was a criminal out to rob you, don't you think I would have done it already? Trust me, this is a bad area, a man like you should not be around here at this time of night, and if you leave the car here, I guarantee you that you'll be lucky to find an engine inside it by morning!'

The man ran his fingers through his hair as he thought for a second. He slowly got into the car and shifted it into neutral. Then he stepped out and the two men lowered themselves into the ditch. On the count of three they pushed up and sideways with all the strength they could muster. The car moved only slightly. They tried it again. The car shifted a little more but was still not out of the ditch. On the third attempt, the two men heaved forward finally succeeding in placing the left tire of the car onto the road. Crouched on the ground with their backs leaning against the front of the car, both men gathered their breath. Then the little man moved to the driver's side of the car and opened the door. Wedging his shoulder against the car while his left hand commandeered the steering wheel, he began to push. Hamoonga planted both his feet firmly on the ground, and pinned the full weight of his upper body against the rear end of the car. He then heaved himself forward. The car began to move forward, slowly at first and then picking up speed propelled by the force of the two men and the momentum from the slight incline in the road.

As they gathered into a trot, the little man jumped into the seat and began to turn the key in the ignition. The engine stuttered as he coaxed it with the accelerator. After moving several feet, the engine roared triumphantly to life. The man revved the engine before leaving it to idle in neutral. He then got out the car and walked towards Hamoonga. He pulled out a packet of Marlborough, placed a cigarette in his mouth and offered the packet to Hamoonga. He pulled on the stick for a second before handing it to Hamoonga. Hamoonga lit his cigarette and the two men stood there for a few seconds puffing in silence. Leaning his head forward in a bowing motion of respect, the man introduced himself. 'My name is Jinan Hu. Thank you for your help, you are good man.'

Hamoonga nodded his head in acknowledgement. 'You're welcome.'

'What your name?' Jinan asked. 'Why you walk so late alone here? It is bad area.'

'My name is Hamoonga' He paused and pulled on his cigarette. 'I came out here looking for work at the plant'.

'Do you find any?' Jinan asked with genuine interest.

'I couldn't get past the guards at the gate. They sent me away before I could even see anybody.'

'What type work you look for?'

Hamoonga pulled hard on his cigarette and puffed out a plume of smoke before responding. 'Well, at this point ... anything really, I need a job, any job. A man needs to work, you know?'

Jinan looked Hamoonga over again with a keen eye. Taking another draw of his cigarette, he nodded his head, 'You good man, you help me. Come see me at plant *tomollow*. Tell guard Jinan Hu send you. I have work but work is hard... You work hard?'

Hamoonga inched closer to Jinan; he towered over the little man. He nodded and extending his hand, the two men shook hands – Jinan had a firm assured grip and his calloused hands were proof of a man who never shied from hard manual work.

❖

Hamoonga arrived at the plant the next day, right before the closing of the first shift, nervous with anticipation. After mentioning the name – 'Jinan Hu'– he was grudgingly let through the security post. He felt the guards' disapproving looks as he walked past the post to the driveway that led directly to the tiny supervisors' office. He stood waiting for close to an hour as men in blue overalls trickled in and out of the office. The door was kept open and he could see Jinan behind one of the desks and three other Chinese men sitting opposite him in a U-shape.

Looking up from his desk, Jinan signalled for Hamoonga to enter the office. Without getting up from his seat, Jinan pointed to a small chair.

'Thank you for seeing me,' Hamoonga began nervously. 'I... I really appreciate you taking the time...'

'What experience you have?' Jinan interrupted, uninterested in small talk.

Hamoonga cleared his throat and shifted a little in his seat. The chair screeched against the concrete floor. 'Well, sir, I... I am willing to do anything that you have on offer, I'm a quick learner and a hard worker'

Jinan revealed no emotion. 'Have you work in mine before?'

'No, I have not, but I can work hard and I learn very quickly.'

'Work in mine very hard, I cannot have *razy* man, I need good hard-working man. Okay?'

Hamoonga nodded his head. 'Yes, I work very hard, anything you want done, any work you have I can do, I have no problem with that.'

Jinan shuffled through some oil-smudged papers on his desk and then looked up at Hamoonga again. 'I have job for mine worker in my team. I lose four workers in two month. They no work hard. I need hard worker, I need good man. You good man?' Again, Hamoonga nodded, eager to accept anything.

'You help me with car, you good man. I try you. But I warn you, work is hard and if you *razy* or you no show up for work, you gone, okay?' With that Jinan rose from his chair and handed Hamoonga a set of application forms to fill out.

○

The first days of work were backbreaking. Hamoonga woke up

at three in the morning to begin the hour-and-a-half-long walk to Chishimba Mine. At that ungodly hour only stray dogs, armed robbers, and prostitutes roamed the streets. He would make his way in the darkness, first through the pothole-ridden streets of Kwacha East, then down the dusty narrow footpath that formed the short-cut into Buchi Township, then past the Second Class Industrial Area onto Mindolo Road, Kalulushi Road, and finally to the plant.

In the initial days, walking alone to and from work was torturous; his feet would throb at the end of every long day. But he had to do it. Several months searching for any kind of work with no success gives a man a unique sense of gratitude for the few breaks he receives, no matter how small they might be.

He began by working the mind-numbing, labour-intensive tasks reserved for the illiterate contract works. He used a pickaxe and shovels to dig holes in the bedrock deep underground in search of copper ore. All the while, he never complained, always on time, never extending his breaks, hauling more rock than the others, and helping workmates struggling with their loads. Hamoonga was strong and humble; he endeared himself to his co-workers and his work ethic drew Jinan's notice.

At about the third month, Hamoonga showed a knack for operating many of the handheld excavation machinery such as jackhammers and drilling machines. Unlike the majority of the men in his crew, he had a level of college education and thus was able to read technical manuals and some of the mining charts. This was of great use to Jinan, who seized on the opportunity to nominate Hamoonga to take a series of on-the-job training classes at the mine. Again Hamoonga excelled, proving his ability to grasp the technical knowledge and the determination to improve himself. It was not long before he became an invaluable asset to Jinan and both a respected and admired colleague to his peers.

Chapter 12

There is Nothing Like Family

Beijing, China

October 2010

'There once lived a little boy, a boy just like you,' Nana said as she cuddled her little grandson, Tao, in her lap.

'Just like me, Nana?' little Tao asked, looking up at his grandma with shining hazelnut eyes.

'Yes, cute just like you,' she smiled as she tickled him on his exposed belly. He burst into a playful laughter, wriggling in the comfort of her lap.

'There once lived a little boy, in a far, faraway village in the countryside,' she continued. 'The boy lived with his mother and father in a tiny hut. They were very, very poor but they loved each other very much!' Nana held Tao even tighter. Little Tao, his eyes wide, were fixed on his grandma's wrinkled face as he listened eagerly.

'The family was so poor that they had nothing to eat. Many nights they would go hungry, no rice, no, fish, no pork, nothing at all.' She told the story with great drama. 'The boy's name was Hah-Shin.'

'Hah-Shin?' Tao echoed.

'Yes, Hah-Shin,' she confirmed. 'One day Hah-Shin went alone to the river with the fishing rod that his father had made for him. He wanted to catch some fish in the river to surprise his parents. He wanted to surprise them with fish they could eat for dinner. Hah-Shin sat on the banks of the river and cast his fishing line into the water. He waited and waited for a very long time but he caught no fish. He was very sad but he continued to wait. After a while, an old lady came to the river to draw some water for her home. She saw Hah-Shin sitting there with his rod and no fish.' Nana paused for a moment for dramatic effect.

Little Tao grabbed his grandma's arm and shook it. 'What happened, Nana?'

'Well, the old lady felt sorry for Hah-Shin. She said he looked very thin, as thin as his fishing rod. She felt that he needed some food so she invited him to her house. Hah-Shin accepted her invitation and they started on the journey to the old woman's house. Once they got to her house, she gave Hah-Shin a large bowl of rice to eat. Hah-Shin was so happy. He ate all the rice he could eat and thanked the old lady.' Nana lovingly stroked Tao's thick hair.

'After that day, the old lady would invite Hah-Shin to her home every day and offer him rice to eat. After many years, the boy grew to be a big, tall, strong, handsome man. Then one day Hah-Shin left his home village and went away to a faraway place to work in the rice fields of the east. Because he was big and strong and because he worked very hard, the people loved him. He worked very hard and helped many people, so one day they made him king!' Nana smiled. Tao was in heaven.

'When Hah-Shin became king he gave lots of poor people food to eat, and they all loved him very much. After many years Hah-Shin decided to go back and look for the old lady who gave him rice when he was a little boy. He looked and looked but she had moved from her old home and no one knew where she had gone. But he did not give up: he went from village to village in search of her for many years until one day he found her.' Nana placed her hand over her mouth in a gesture of mock amazement.

'Oh?' Tao mimicked Nana's gesture.

'Hah-Shin then filled the old lady's large bowl with a thousand pieces of gold to say thank you for all the times she had fed him! She was very very happy indeed!' Nana stretched out both of her arms in a fitting finale to her Chinese fable. She then pulled her hands back and began to tickle her tiny grandson on his sides sending him rolling around frantic with laughter. Just then there was the familiar sound of footsteps at the front door. The cast iron doorknob turned and the door began to creak open.

Looking up, little Tao raced into his mother's arms as she entered the room. It was a ritual that he performed every evening when his mother, Li Ming, returned from her long day at work. Li Ming embraced her son tightly, lifting him off the floor. It was getting harder to lift him these days; she could swear that he was getting heavier by the day. It seemed only yesterday that she had been cuddling Tao in her arms; her little angel. But Tao was now five years old and looking increasingly like his father.

Li Ming was thirty-eight years old. She had a tiny frame, small hands, and a pretty face with delicate features. Her lips were thin, her eyes were narrow and set slightly further apart than she would have liked. In keeping with her delicate features, Li Ming's eyebrows were faint, almost non-existent. Her thick locks of hair fell below her shoulders and were graying at the roots. She had the air of a woman who was tired and overworked. Her only source of joy these days was her little boy, Tao.

'Mama, mama, Nana says there was a king that looked just like me!' Tao reported to his mother in an excited tone.

'Is that so?' she asked her son as she placed him back on the floor.

'Yes, he was just like me, a little boy!'

'What was his name?' she asked glancing over at her mother-in-law who was sitting in her armchair in silence.

Little Tao was stumped, so he turned to his grandmother for help. 'Nana, what was the boy's name again?'

Grandma gave a broad smile and answered, 'Hah-Shin, his name was Hah-Shin'.

'Yes, Hah-Shin!' little Tao echoed.

'Aaahh, I see you've been listening to Nana's stories again?'

Tao giggled and nodded in agreement.

Tao loved spending afternoons and evenings with his grandma; Nana always told him fascinating stories about ancient Chinese emperors, explorers, philosophers, great warriors, and great dynasties.

Tao was captivated by stories about Confucius, Genghis Khan, the Ming and Qing Dynasties, the Opium Wars, and the Cultural Revolution. Some of it was hard for him to grasp, but Nana's colourful storytelling gave life to all the characters, enthralling little Tao.

'Have you washed up yet?' Li Ming asked. 'Remember, we will be getting up early tomorrow to take the train so you have to be ready.'

Tao gave a cheeky smile; he had not done as his mother had told him before she left for work that morning.

'Nana will heat up some water for you. Go and get ready,' Li Ming said. She pointed to his bedroom on the adjacent side of the tiny quadrangle of their old traditional Chinese home located in the densely populated *hutongs* of eastern Beijing.

Li Ming's husband, Jinan Hu, had been born and raised in Beijing; his family had owned and lived in their residence in Da Shi Lan for five generations. Li Ming came to live with Jinan and his family after they were married. At the time, Jinan's parents and grandparents were still alive. Jinan's father and his grandfather both passed away through illness within two years of the young couple's marriage. Now there were only four people living in the residence: Tao, Li Ming, her mother-in-law, and great-grandmother-in-law. With the death of Li Ming's father-in-law, money had become very tight. Even though both Li Ming and Jinan had jobs, it was difficult to buy enough food, clothes, and charcoal for cooking and heating during the cold winters. Li Ming had her assembly line job at a pharmaceutical company in Yizhuang southeast of the city. Jinan also worked in Yizhuang but as a welder for a metal fabrication company. The hours were long for both of them, typically twelve-hour shifts six days a week, and the pay was a mere pittance.

When Li Ming became pregnant with Tao, Jinan decided that he needed to find another opportunity that would pay more money to better support his family. It was then that he applied and was accepted to join the China Metals and Mining Company (CMMC). CMMC was a government-funded, multi-billion-dollar precious metals, mining, and exploration company with its tentacles all over the globe, most especially in countries in sub-Saharan Africa. CMMC had gold mines in Namibia and South Africa. They drilled for oil in South Sudan and Nigeria. They mined for diamonds in Sierra Leone and Botswana; for platinum and coltan in the Democratic Republic of Congo. Many of the locations making up CMMC's footprint were in troubled, war-torn locations; this worried Li Ming and Jinan. However, CMMC's latest frontier was mining in the recently acquired copper mines of a benign central African state called Zambia. Jinan and Li Ming knew nothing about Zambia, but officials at CMMC assured Jinan that Zambia was a peaceful place. Unlike many sub-Saharan African nations, Zambia had never experienced civil wars or coups. Zambia, he was told, was poor but peaceful.

It was now five years since Jinan had left to work in the Zambian copper mines. Over the years, he wrote Li Ming letters that would arrive about once a month. Li Ming wrote back with the same regularity. In her letters she described how Tao was growing up fast, and wrote of conversations with their son in great detail. She talked about how Tao was asking more and more questions about his father and when his father would return. She wrote about Tao's first day at school and how he had cried at the prospect of leaving his grandmother's side. Every year she sent Jinan a picture of Tao and every year Jinan marvelled at how rapidly his son was growing up.

Their money situation was a lot easier now that Jinan sent regular stipends back to home. Jinan made sure he lived a frugal life in Zambia – devoid of luxury or excess. Li Ming and Jinan's plan was for him to work for ten years at the copper mines in order for them to save enough money to send Tao to university when he came of age. Li Ming and Jinan were determined to give their son a better life than they'd had; they resolved that Tao would be the first in their family to get a tertiary education.

⌘

Early the next morning Li Ming awoke to the sound of her mother-in-law setting the fire for the morning meal in the central courtyard; it was 4:00 a.m. She gathered herself together and got up from her metal spring bed. She had taken a wash and packed her small bag the night before to save time. They would need to catch the 5:30 a.m.

speed train from Beijing South Railway Station in Fengtai. She was excited about the trip; it would be her first experience on the new speed trains that had been commissioned by the government in the past few years. It was also going to be her first trip with her son, to visit her relatives in Fuzhou in the southern part of China. Furthermore, it was going to be her first trip outside of Beijing in five years; it had all been made possible by the extra money that Jinan had been sending over the years. Finally, little Tao would get to see the countryside and visit the other side of his family. Fuzhou was where Li Ming had spent her childhood years. She always had fond memories of Fuzhou, the air was much cleaner than in Beijing, no smog or thunderous clouds spewing acid rain. The winters were milder and the food was prepared to a sweeter taste – food in China seemed to grow sweeter the farther south one went. It was exciting to go and see her parents and she knew they would be delighted to see their grandson again after so long.

The train took five hours to Shanghai, from there it would take two hours to Wenzhou, and three further hours to Fuzhou. Li Ming figured they would be at her parents' house just in time for the evening meal around sunset.

It was a warm July morning; Li Ming walked out of her room and stood next to her mother-in-law in the courtyard.

'Thank you, Mama, thank you for getting up so early to get the fire going!'

Nana laughed. 'You know we old people have trouble sleeping. I would have been up anyway.'

'You're so good to me, Mama, I don't know what Tao and I would do if you were not here,' Li Ming said with great love in her voice. 'You have been my rock since Jinan left, we owe you so much!'

'Nonsense, you are my daughter and Tao is my grandson, you mean the world to me. I wish I could do more for you. I know it has been hard with my son away, but the gods will take care of you, my child, and one day you will be together again!' With that Nana pointed ed her crooked index finger in the air.

Li Ming smiled softly. The time without Jinan had truly taken its toll; she was grateful for the extra income but she desperately missed her husband and she felt little Tao was growing up without a strong male figure in his life. 'Two more years,' Jinan had promised Li Ming. Two more years and he would return to them, they would be one family again, and they would have enough money to secure Tao's future.

'Thank you, Mama, you are such a strong woman. I hope one day I can be as strong as you. Sometimes I worry so much about Tao. I want him to grow up well, to be a good person, to be safe in this fast-changing world.'

'My dear, you are strong, and all will be well. When my husband and I were young we too worried about how we would make it and how we would provide for Jinan. Sometimes you just have to do all you can as a mother and a wife and trust that the gods will take care of the rest, as they have taken care of our people for centuries!' Nana stroked her daughter-in-law on the back and smiled.

'You must go wake up little Tao,' Nana said. 'I will prepare some rice for you to eat before you go. I'm glad you're taking a break. Tao is so excited. It will be good for him to see how large and beautiful China is.' Nana turned and walked away slowly to gather the rice and fish for their morning meal.

After the meal Li Ming strapped her grey satchel across her shoulder and secured little Tao's red Spiderman school bag on his back. They were not carrying much; she had packed one change of clothes, a single ankle-length frock for herself and a pair of grey shorts and a khaki shirt for Tao.

'I will miss you so much, my little prince!' Nana said to Tao. 'Who will I tell stories to now?' she said with a mocking sad face.

'I'll miss you too, Nana!' little Tao said to his grandma as he hugged her tightly.

'Bring me back something from the south!' Nana said. 'Bring me back something special!' Tao nodded and giggled, pleased with his new assignment.

Li Ming embraced her mother-in-law. 'Stay well, and we shall see you in five days' time.'

'I pray that you travel safely and return to us. Now go, go, you'll miss your train!' Nana let go and Li Ming and Tao walked through the front entrance of the square courtyard into the narrow street.

Daylight was just breaking as mother and child made their way in through the maze of narrow alleys, beside men and women dressed in dull-coloured clothing riding their bicycles to work. As they walked, Li Ming looked around in search of a pedicab operator to take them to their destination.

'Come on, let's cross the road,' Li Ming said as she pulled Tao by the hand. 'Let's catch a ride from that pedicab over there.' They walked quickly across the street to the alcove where five pedicab rickshaws were lined up awaiting customers. They approached the first one in line, it looked the same as all the others; a two-seater cab covered in black tarpaulin and attached to a bicycle with large, narrow tires and thin spokes. The pedicab driver was slender, all muscle and bones; he had sunken cheeks and yellow teeth – no doubt from smoking too many cheap cigarettes. He was a teenager but a harsh life seemed to have added several years to his appearance. He sparked into life at the sight of his two new customers.

'Zǎo ān,' said the pedicab driver as he ushered Li Ming and Tao into the two passenger seats. 'Where can I take you?' he asked politely.

'Zǎo ān,' Li Ming replied bowing slightly. 'We are headed to Beijing South Train Station. How much will that be?'

The pedicab driver named his price, and Li Ming nodded in agreement not having the stomach to haggle so early in the morning.

'Mama, how far away is the train station?' Tao asked.

Li Ming tucked Tao deeply into his seat and held their bags securely in her lap before responding, 'It will not be long, we'll be there in a few minutes and then you'll see the beautiful new train station!' She smiled and asked, 'Are you excited to ride the train today?'

Tao nodded with a big smile, 'Yes!'

'Good, it will not be long now, sit in your seat, don't move okay?'

The pedicab driver sped off into the Beijing streets, manoeuvered out of the winding *hutongs*, and turned west onto Zhushikou West

Street. He then drove the pedicab south down Taiping Street. Li Ming and Tao sat silently taking in the sight of increasing numbers of people moving hurriedly in the streets of the capital. They could already see the traffic building up as cars and buses alike began to stream into the streets as if responding to the call of daylight. Li Ming turned to Tao and stroked his hair. She was cherishing every moment of this rare mother-and-son excursion.

The pedicab driver peddled hard down the long Taiping Street. Li Ming could see his legs and arched back from her seat; he seemed to peddle with a relentless energy at odds with his slender frame. She looked to her right and observed the serene Tao Ranting Park with its manicured bushes; it seemed an incongruous oasis in the middle of the towering metropolis.

It was about 5:10 a.m. when they finally arrived at the South Railway train station. Li Ming handed the pedicab driver a fistful of renminbi notes and they parted ways with a reciprocal bow of respect. Mother and son proceeded to walk through the automatic glass sliding doors of the station. The inside of the station was breathtaking. It had a newly renovated interior with high glass ceilings in the atrium. There was a multitude of people buzzing purposefully around adding to the feel of modernity synonymous with the new bold ideals of the People's Republic of China. The floors were made out of smooth ceramic tiles, off-white in colour. The gigantic digital display boards mounted just below the ceiling left little Tao gazing overhead, speechless in amazement.

Li Ming pulled her awestruck son by the hand in the direction of the ticketing counter. There was a short line of early morning travellers looking to buy or redeem their previously purchased tickets. Li Ming and Tao made it to the counter in short order and requested two round-trip economy tickets to Fuzhou. Tickets in hand, they hurried off down the concourse in search of platform number twelve.

A sleek, aerodynamic, futuristic-looking train was waiting with doors open on platform twelve. Li Ming's spine tingled with excitement as they boarded it. The red seats were upholstered in faux leather that was smooth and soft to the touch. Each seat was essentially an armchair that could recline to position a passenger in an almost horizontal position with their feet up. The armrests were wide and retractable. Each seat had seatbelts for safety and there were spacious overhead bins to store luggage.

Tao did a tiny jig of excitement. 'Mama, mama!' he said, tugging at his mother's arm with both hands, 'Let's sit over there!' He pointed at two seats next to a huge window towards the middle of the carriage. The woman smiled and acquiesced. They moved to the seats; Li Ming lifted their two bags and placed them in the overhead bin that was closest to them and within view. Tao jumped into the widow seat and spread his arms out, clearly enjoying this rare foray into a world of luxury. Li Ming sat next to him and adjusted her chair for maximum comfort.

'What's that?' Tao asked, pointing to the black display panel on top of the central train carriage door. Li Ming followed the direction of Tao's little index finger and stared at the display for a second before responding.

'It's a screen to tell us how fast the train is moving. You'll see the numbers change as we start moving.' Tao seemed satisfied with the answer and turned his gaze out the window to look at the tracks and the other trains waiting at their platforms.

There was a muffled ding of a bell and an announcement on the overhead speakers to indicate that the train was now about to depart. The external doors slid shut and an almost imperceptible movement could be felt as the train left the station. As it gathered speed, the display above the central carriage door raced to rack up numbers. The display was in miles per hour; it moved rapidly from 60 to 75 to 100, 120, and then to 180 miles per hour at its top speed. As they flew through the city and shortly through the countryside, Li Ming and Tao could hardly feel the vibration of the train; so smooth was the ride. The trees and grass outside whisked past the window like a movie screen in fast forward. Li Ming stared outside as she thought about Tao, Jinan, her backbreaking factory work, Mama in Beijing, and her own family in Fuzhou. She looked back at Tao and noticed that he was beginning to doze off. She smiled and stroked his head. Five hours later the train pulled into Shanghai station. Li Ming and Tao were awoken by the sound of passengers exiting the train as others embarked.

'Have we arrived?' Tao asked his mother yawning.

Li Ming gathered herself for a second before responding. 'No, baby, we're now in Shanghai, halfway there.' She pulled her seat up and then stood to reach for her bag in the overhead bin. She brought it down and shuffled her hand through its contents. She pulled out two fist-sized parcels wrapped in newspaper and placed them on her chair before returning her bag to the overhead bin. Li Ming turned and handed one of the packages to Tao saying, 'Here's something to eat. Come on, sit up and eat.'

He sat up and clasped his mother's gift with both hands unwrapping the newspaper. Inside was a boiled sweet yam. Delighted, Tao began to eat, not quite realising in all the excitement how hungry he was.

'We have another five hours to go before we reach Fuzhou. Are you tired?'

Tao shook his head. 'Uh-uh,' He finished his yam and handed his mother the crumpled newspaper, she rolled it up into a ball and threw it into the receptacle behind her seat. The train was moving again, heading for Wenzhou.

About an hour and forty minutes after leaving Shanghai Station, Tao turned to his mother. 'Mama, can you tell me a story?'

Li Ming smiled, she could tell that her son was growing restless. 'Sure, move closer and I'll tell you a story.' She signalled for him to move into her arms. He quickly scooted over and leant into his mother's embrace. Li Ming wrapped her arms around him.

'There was once an ancient dragon that blew fire and smoke from its nose and mouth. It lived in the mountains far away from the village below. The dragon was large and fierce with scales and a long tail, everyone feared it! One day it flew down from the mountain into the village. Everyone was scared; they ran into their homes trembling in fear.' Tao hugged his mother tightly as he listened with excitement.

'Come out, come out, the Dragon shouted as it breathed fire. No one came out because they were all too frightened. Come out, come out! The dragon continued to shout louder and louder!' She did her best to mimic the deep baritone voice of the mythical creature.

Just as Li Ming was about to deliver the climax to her story, a tremendous bang shuddered through the train, followed by a deafening, tearing whining sound of metal being mangled out of shape. Before she could make sense of what was happening, she was flung from her seat. Little Tao flew out of his mother's protective arms and slammed his head into the overhead bins. In seconds it was over.

There was shrapnel everywhere; passengers could be heard wailing in shock and fear. The last thing Li Ming saw was their carriage falling to its side as it hurtled off a steep viaduct down into the river below.

〰

The train had been travelling at its upper limit, 172 miles per hour and all was well. Just fifteen minutes from Wenzhou, it slowed down to cross a steep viaduct, forty feet above the Ou River. Here, just a few minutes earlier, another train had experienced signal failure and was marooned at the centre. Once the speed train reached the viaduct, it was too late for the driver to stop it in time to avoid a collision. Instead it slammed headfirst into the back of the stationary train.

〰

Chishimba Mine, Copperbelt Province, Zambia
October 2010

It was Ping Li who broke the news to Jinan two days after the crash. Ping had received a call from the Beijing CMMC office that morning and he pulled Jinan into the small office shared by the supervisors. The office was empty but for the two of them.

'Please take a seat, Jinan.' Ping said somberly, his eyes already welling with tears as he braced himself to deliver the news that would surely break his colleague. Jinan could see the anguish in Ping's face and knew something terrible had happened.

'What is it, Ping?' Jinan asked, fearing the answer to his question.

'There has been a horrible accident.' Tears began to trickle down Ping's face as he touched his friend's shoulder. 'Something terrible has happened.' Ping swallowed hard trying to rid himself of the ball wedged in his throat. He took a deep breath and continued. 'There was a train crash near Wezhou; your wife and son were on the train.'

Jinan put his head in his hands, and Ping heard a deep moan. 'No. No. What do you mean – what are you saying?'

'They... they... they... were killed in the crash. Forty-four people died.' Ping let his tears fall.

Jinan burst into a bitter sob and sank deeper into his chair, his hands massaging his forehead as if to erase the news. Ping's few words had broken him. The sudden grief was like a vice. The moan came from the pit of his soul.

'No, no, no. No! Li Ming! Tao! It cannot be!' Jinan cried out again and again. Ping tightened his grip on his friend's shoulder and the two men wept unabashedly.

After some time, Ping explained further. 'I got the call from head office early this morning. They said your wife and son were on one of the new speed trains headed for Fuzhou.' Ping took several deep breaths, 'They said there was a problem with the track signals and the train collided with another on a bridge. That's all I know. That's all they could tell me. I'm so sorry, so sorry.'

Again Jinan sunk his head into his friend's chest and wept.

'I will make arrangements for you to fly home as soon as possible,' Ping said. 'Don't worry, we'll take care of your shifts. You must return to China. It's the right thing to do.'

So three years earlier than planned, Jinan flew back to Beijing to grieve for his wife and son and try to gather the pieces of his empty purposeless life.

◆ ◆ ◆

The company paid for his trip and even offered to repatriate him but Jinan refused, deciding instead to return to the Zambian copper mines. He could not imagine a life in China without his family. He was tormented by the thought that he had been away too long and not been able to protect his wife and his son.

The death of Li Ming and Tao was a tragedy that changed Jinan forever. His already shaky faith in the goodness of things was destroyed. How could such terrible things happen to good people; innocent people? It was he and not Tao nor Li Ming who had deserved to die. There was no fairness in life. No sense in living. These despairing thoughts ate at his core, devouring him like a malignant tumour.

Chapter 13

Into the Belly of the Beast

Chishimba Mine, Copperbelt Province, Zambia

September 2011

Jinan stretched out his arm and grabbed his old Nokia cell phone from the concrete floor. The screen's bright blue backlight momentarily blinded him. He blinked several times before reading the time. It was 3:28 a.m., time to get up. He pulled off the single cotton sheet covering his legs, and heaved himself off the folded blanket that provided a thin padding between his body and the cold floor. 'Yet another day in this wretched place,' he thought to himself. 'I'm tired of having to push and prod these lazy Africans, but I must. If I leave them to themselves, no work will be done! Only Chinese know hard work, Africans only want easy money!' He felt sour with bitterness.

Four o'clock starts were a daily routine. Being a shift supervisor, Jinan had to be at the site before all the mine workers. First, he would do a walk-through of the main changing room area that consisted of a row of grey steel lockers with an assortment of padlocks, one on each locker. There were four rows of wooden benches a few feet in front of the lockers. The communal toilets and showers adjoined the main changing area. The entire concrete ablution block had been painted dark blue and the rancid smell of urine, which lingered perpetually in the air, only contributed to the depressing atmosphere.

Today was no different. Jinan unlocked the front door of the changing room and walked through it; everything was in order. He unlocked his locker and took out his pair of navy blue overalls. They reeked of accumulated sweat, it was two weeks since their last wash. He grabbed his knee-length steel-toed rubber boots and dropped them onto the floor. From the back of the locker, he brought out his rubber gloves and a three-inch-wide fabric belt. Attached to the belt was a torch battery. Finally, he took the flashlight and a scratched white plastic helmet from the back of the locker, and he was dressed in his 'battle fatigues'. Then Jinan stepped outside to wait for the arrival of the African workers and the morning delivery of fresh *kampompo* and hot cocoa.

The African workers trickled in between 5:00 and 5:45 a.m.. There were eighteen men under him. Fifteen were Zambians, two were Congolese, and one was a mixed-race worker named Paul. No one referred to Paul by his given name, instead they called him 'Kalala,' derived from the word 'Coloured' – an old colonial term for mixed-race people. Kalala was half Zambian and half Norwegian. His mother had been a pretty young Zambian girl who had fallen pregnant by a Norwegian aid worker in the 1980s. Having indulged in the 'local fruits', Kalala's father had promised his naive Zambian girlfriend marriage but had left Zambia two months before the child's birth, never to be heard from again.

The two Congolese men in the crew were Kisanga and Kibongo, both refugees from the Congo-Rwandan border area who had fled the conflict and havoc that Joseph Kony's Lord's Resistance Army had caused. Kisanga and Kibongo were honest, hard-working young men with a sense of gratitude for their lot in life.

Now six months on the job and Hamoonga had become something of the unofficial leader of the fifteen Zambians and by default the leader of the entire crew under supervisor Jinan. The crew listened to Hamoonga, and Jinan knew and recognised this fact. The Zambian was not your typical larger-than-life firebrand of a leader. No, he was reserved and spoke with measured tones. He had a coolness about him that made him hard to read, a presence that demanded respect from the others. It was evident that Hamoonga was meant for greater things than the drudgery of the copper mines;

one could also tell that something had happened which had relegated him to this station in life. The crew knew little about his past but they refrained from asking probing questions. All the men knew was that Hamoonga had been hired by Jinan as a general mine labourer and had quickly distinguished himself as Jinan's favourite. He always arrived on time, never complained or engaged in aimless banter. He bothered no one and no one bothered him. Jinan admired Hamoonga's work ethic and his ability to learn on the job. It took but a few months for Jinan to rely on Hamoonga for the more critical tasks such as setting up the explosives line, checking safety harnesses, and doing preventative maintenance of key drilling equipment.

At 5:25 a.m. a white Toyota van stopped in front of Jinan who was waiting patiently as his crew trickled in one by one. Two wiry men in stained white catering aprons disembarked. From the back of the vehicle they unloaded a large steel vessel containing hot cocoa and set it on one of the empty wooden benches outside the workers' changing area. Then they returned to the van to offload a large steel tray heaped with *kampompo* and put it down next to the container of cocoa. Then, jumping back in the van, the two men drove off to repeat the process at their next stop in the plant area.

'Get buns one-one okay, *quickry, quickry* – no waste time!' Jinan shouted to his crew as he hovered over the mountain of rolls. The workers hurried out of the changing area, not needing to be asked twice. For many, this would be their only meal of the day. They needed every ounce of energy they could get before starting on their back-breaking ten-hour shift in the underground shaft.

'Foolish imperialist, who does he think he's talking to? Must he always scream at us?' Kalala murmured under his breath. 'I swear these Chinese people think they own us. This is not the 1960s, this is *our* country, and these are *our* minerals. The Chinks would be nothing without us!'

'Eh, *iwe*, come on now, stop your political freedom fighter nonsense. Nobody wants to hear it so early in the morning!' Kibongo replied with a dismissive wave of his hand. 'If you want to do your politics, go join those corrupt politicians; me, I want to eat, I have no time for your nonsense!'

'You see that's the problem with you Africans,' Kalala retorted. 'That's why you'll never succeed. You're too docile, too timid, you sell your souls for scraps and accept ill-treatment from imperialists. First it was the white explorer who dazzled your ancestors with cheap guns and cloth. They sold your birthright for paltry goods only to be enslaved and sold off in chains! Then there were the colonisers who promised you separate-but-equal opportunity and look where it took you? Now you look East. For just a few football stadiums you give away your mineral wealth and the future of your grandchildren?'

'What grandchildren? What nonsense? Eh, save your mad philosophy for your fellow madmen in the streets. No one cares here!' Kisanga took a large bite into his soft bun.

'Eh you stupid? I say fast, fast, *quickry, quickry*! You talk-oh too much!' Jinan yelled looking in the direction of Kalala and Kisanga. 'Shift start six *o'crock*! No waste time!' Jinan continued, 'You Africans too *razy*, every time you *wan* talk, come on, *quickry, quickry*!'

At 5:55 a.m. Jinan led the way to the underground shaft elevator entrance. The crew waited silently behind their shift supervisor. Pooohhh – pooohhh, pooohhh – pooohhh, pooohhh – pooohhh, the siren sounded three times. This signified the end of the night shift and the start of the day shift. The electric hum of the mine shaft elevator kicked into gear and steel wire cables could be seen moving through a huge pulley system that extended from the top of a thirty-foot control tower down to an underground elevator cage, a six-by-six-feet steel box, eight feet high. The cage slowly emerged out of the cavernous earth, spitting out twenty men in full mining gear stacked side by side like sardines in a can: the night shift with their grim, dirt-smudged faces. Worn out, they exited the cage in silence while Jinan's crew promptly took their places, packing themselves tightly into the cage. 'Ready!' Jinan shouted and down they went into the belly of the earth.

This underground mine shaft is one of the deepest in the world. At its deepest point, it extends more than 6,500 feet below the surface of the earth, where the mine contains some of the world's richest deposits of copper and cobalt. Mining operations continue 24/7 every day of the year. To say that mining is the lifeblood of the country would be an understatement; it is the lifeblood, the heart, the liver, the kidneys, and the brain of Zambia. Life begins and ends with copper, the red gold, the chalice that holds the dreams of a nation.

The elevator stopped at nine hundred feet and the men shuffled out into the darkness guided by their torches. They were soon busy at work.

'Kalala, must you always see things in terms of slave and slave master, subjects and their imperialist masters? Can't you see that we are working to put food on the table for our families? You see the problem with you is that you're confused, my brother. You're neither black nor white, and this provokes you to think the way you do,' Kisanga said, resurrecting the conversation that had begun above ground. He momentarily stopped digging and began to roll up the sleeves of his overalls.

'Eh, eh, but you haven't experienced war or real suffering in your life, that's clear. It makes you ungrateful for what you have,' Kibongo said as he pushed his shovel into a pile of dirt. 'Me and my brother Kisanga here have experienced civil war in the Congo. We saw death, child soldiers, and Ebola; so we are grateful for where we are!'

'Ebola, no, no, no! Speak for yourself, papa! Me, I saw no Ebola, God forbid, oh!' Kisanga responded laughing as those around him laughed.

Kalala shook his head and then brushed his forearm against his sweaty forehead. 'Ah, I pity you for you are ignorant, your mind is colonised and you cannot see the truth.' He put his helmet back on his head. 'My identity is clear. I am an African and as an African I will always fight for the economic and political freedoms of all Africans against all oppressors.' He wiped his brow as he rested his shovel. 'You see the key trick that imperialists use is to ensnare the mind by appealing to the greed of men. What the Chinese are doing today in this country and across the continent is to lure our political leaders into a state of passivity by buying them off with deals to build a few malls or stadiums for which our politicians make a handsome personal profit. The consequence is that politicians sell our people and enslave them into a life of poverty as they enrich the Chinese imperial master.'

'There you go again, it's always horse and rider,' Kisanga said in frustration. 'If you hate your job so much why don't you just quit and get into politics?'

'That's the thing, my brother, they have enslaved us so I cannot leave. What we need to do is to work within this corrupt system and find a way to get organised and get what is rightfully due to us. Look at him,' Kalala pointed to Jinan in the distance. 'He struts around screaming at us with an imperious air, yet we are the ones that do the work and this is our country, our land, our resources!'

Right on cue Jinan turned and shouted, 'Eh, eh, eh, you work, you work, no *razy*, no *razy*!' in the direction of Kalala, Kibongo, and Kisanga. Hamoonga had been listening silently to the conversation as he worked shovelling rocks into an adjacent wheelbarrow. He had never been one for politics, though he hated politicians given his past experiences, but he knew better than to engage in fruitless political discussion. Life was rigged in favour of those with money and power and that was the end of it. He remembered the class discussions at Evelyn Hone; how naïve and hopeful they'd all been – thinking they could change the country for the better. His feelings of bitterness towards people in power remained raw. Hamoonga was certain that no amount of organising, standing up to those in power, protesting, or lobbying – whatever they wanted to call it – would alter the status quo.

'Hamoonga! Watch your people! No time for talk, next time I no pay you for no work, understand?' Jinan yelled. 'Next time I fire your friends, *prenty* people need job, if you don't want job – I find someone else!'

Hamoonga turned to Kisanga, Kibongo, and Kalala. 'You heard the man. Get back to work!'

⌘

'We need you on our side, Hamoonga, we need your voice in this struggle,' Kalala said as he walked faster to keep pace with

Hamoonga's long purposeful strides. 'The Chinese supervisors listen to you. If you can just speak to them, I think our message will be brought home.'

Hamoonga remained silent, he didn't want to get involved in workplace politics.

'Hamoonga, the majority of the workers have little or no education,' Kalala went on. 'They can't express their grievances in a way that management will listen to them. I've been trying my best, but you know the Chinese have labelled me a troublemaker and my days here are numbered. If you speak up, both the workers and the management will listen. I know they will!'

Hamoonga stopped and turned to face the persistent Kalala. He was tired, it had been a long shift, and he could feel his lower back and shoulders aching. The last thing he wanted to do was to engage in a futile conversation about workers' rights and Chinese imperialists, so he sounded as cynical as he felt at that moment. 'Can't you get it into your head that nobody cares? No amount of discussion, lobbying or whatever you want to call it will make any difference. In this world you have the powerful and the weak; we, my friend, are the weak. That's the system that operates in this country, it's all about patronage; this is not a meritocracy, you rise and fall based on who you know not what you know!'

'You're right, but we can change that if we group together and present a united front!' Kalala ignored the bitterness that laced Hamoonga's words, happy to finally get a response out of him.

'A united front, a united front?' Hamoonga repeated mockingly. 'What power does a lowly mine worker have? How can a lowly mine worker stand up to the Chinese who are backed by big money and powerful politicians? Besides, what grievances or struggles are you talking about?'

'Ah, my brother, one or two lowly mine workers for sure cannot change anything. However, a few hundred … a thousand mine workers will surely turn some heads! You see, what we're fighting for is to have an equal seat at the table. Right now, you're correct in saying that powerful politicians and the Chinese management hold all the cards. Between these two camps they have shared the spoils. What we need to do is to ensure that we take what is owed to us; us the people!' Kalala clenched his fists as he made his point. 'Just as it was during the fight for independence from the British, we must rise up and claim what is rightfully ours!'

It was growing dark, an amber sunset was fading into the western horizon behind the large man-made hills of copper-processing waste. Hamoonga could see fellow mine workers hurrying towards the townships. His thoughts travelled back to Cha-Cha-Cha prison. The cold, damp cells, the beatings, the long empty days without news of family or friends. 'So you believe that we can just band together and demand higher wages from our Chinese bosses?' he asked in the full knowledge that he was oversimplifying things.

'In a nutshell, yes!' Kalala replied without hesitation. 'First, we need to bring the key people within our ranks together, those who can bring other workers with them. After that we can list our demands and put a plan of action together that will ensure we get what we want.'

'And what about the Mine Workers Union? I thought it was the forum to air mine workers' grievances?'

'Hamoonga, don't you know?! It's the worst kept secret that all the MWU leaders are in the pockets of the Chinese and the politicians. No, the MWU doesn't serve anyone but its own leadership.' Kalala's face expressed his contempt.

'But what specifically is it that we want as workers?'

'We want better conditions of service, we want to ensure that safety protocols are enhanced and followed. How many of our colleagues have died on the job just within the past year?' Kalala shook his head. 'We want livable wages. Mealie-meal has risen more than a hundred percent in the last two years but our wages have remained stagnant. We want good healthcare services for our families; ever since the mines were sold to foreigners, we've not been able to get good affordable healthcare!' Kalala was on a roll. He raised his palms above his shoulders like a preacher behind a lectern. 'We need and demand respect and better treatment from our management. How often do you hear our supervisors addressing us like bastard children or worse still like animals? This is not the nineteenth century or the pre-colonial time; we need to be treated with dignity and respect!'

Hamoonga listened quietly to Kalala who was like a human-rights activist on his soapbox. 'But why do you need me specifically?'

'Hamoonga, like I said, you're educated and articulate, the workers admire you, and the Chinese supervisors hold you in high regard. I'm certain that if you join us more workers will follow,' Kalala replied. 'I'm not asking you to decide now, but think about it and perhaps join us when a few of us meet after work next Thursday at the Insaka Bar. It's a friendly atmosphere, we'll be happy to have you. You can just listen and observe.' Hamoonga was non-committal, simply turning and resuming his brisk walk back home.

That evening, as he lay on the sunken sofa, Hamoonga stared up at the three wooden trusses and the thin corrugated roofing of his sister's house. It was raining and the drops pinged noisily against the metal. Kalala had made some good points. The miners' working conditions were deplorable and they were growing worse by the day. Gone were the days when a mine worker could provide his family with a decent living. Most workers were just grateful to be employed, but their existence was pitiful. On a mine worker's wages one could not afford to buy a month's groceries, school uniforms for the children, pay medical care, and rent. Nearly everyone was behind on one or all of these essentials.

But what could be done about it? The system was rigged in favour of the wealthy elite and their cronies. It was the greedy politicians who had neglected the plight of their people by selling off the country's heritage to foreigners.

❖

Insaka Bar was favoured by many mine workers being only a stone's throw away from the main plant as well as serving all the preferred commercial brews: Mosi, Rhino Lager, Hunters, and Amstel. Behind the main bar there was a large outdoor beer garden with five thatched areas where groups of men congregated in discrete parties sitting in circles on tiny wooden stools sharing a container of the illicit brew *katata*. A few small cups circulated so that each man could take a sip of the potent concoction which guaranteed a quick buzz at minimal cost.

It was Thursday night, two days after payday, and the place was alive with mine workers seeking a brief respite from their harsh circumstances. Hamoonga entered the beer garden and looked around for familiar faces. He could see Kisanga and Kibongo sitting next to each other in a circle of about twelve men. The other thatched gazebos were similarly full of animated men clearly under the influence of alcohol. Hamoonga worked his way towards Kisanga and Kibongo's party. As he drew nearer he spotted Kalala returning from the restrooms. His shirt was untucked and probably two sizes too big for his skinny frame but his square-jawed face broke into a broad smile when he saw Hamoonga approaching.

'Nice of you to make it, brother!' Kalala shouted a welcome above the general hubbub. 'Please, please, take a seat and make yourself comfortable, we are all family here!' He set aside a stool for his new visitor. Hamoonga nodded in appreciation and quietly took a seat next to a short bald man whose face he vaguely recognized.

'Brothers,' Kalala said, 'this is Hamoonga Moya. He works on our shift under that slave driver, Jinan!' We're all mine workers here, we're all brothers in the struggle, we all know what it's like to do backbreaking work for a pittance!' Kalala was very animated, he had been drinking for some time. 'Brothers, this man Hamoonga is a good man, he is what we need, with him on board we'll be able to stand strong and finally tell those bastards this is our country and they should respect us!' Kalala's voice rose to a shout.

The group of men were clamorous in their agreement. A light-skinned, muscular man spoke up and said, 'Things need to change for sure. Last week I went to my supervisor and asked for a day off to attend my uncle's burial but he refused to give me the time!'

There was a collective murmur of disapproval before the bald man next to Hamoonga spoke. 'Ah, ah, who is your supervisor?' he asked.

'It's that good-for-nothing idiot, Ping!'

'Ah, ah, that devil. They've no heart, I tell you!' the bald man sympathised.

'I was not permitted to attend the burial ceremony of my own uncle, the uncle who raised me when my father died. Supervisor Ping said that uncles are not part of the immediate family, so 'you cannot have a day off to attend his burial'. When I protested, he told me to choose between my job and my dead uncle! Is that the thanks I get for eight years' service in those blasted mines?' The group exchanged obscenities in disgust at the appalling treatment while continuing to pass around the little cups of alcohol. Hamoonga downed his first sip which burned its way down his throat.

'This country has been hijacked by blood-sucking vampires. They care nothing for the local people, all they want is to make money, pillage the nation, and then run away fast when they're done!' Kalala shouted, spit spraying out of his mouth. 'We need to organise ourselves and fight back!'

'Say we hold a protest and shut down the plant. They will listen to us then!' a youthful-looking man volunteered. 'If we interrupt the production of copper, we interrupt their flow of money and that will make them pay attention!'

'Don't be foolish – if you try to do that they will fire you and may even jail you. Then what will you have achieved?' Kisanga said, ridiculing the younger man.

'Yes, think of your families,' Kibongo added. 'Remember we're the lucky ones, we still have jobs. These guys can fire us one day and replace us the next. People are desperate for work.'

'You see,' Kalala interrupted, 'this is the problem with us Africans, we don't see strength in numbers. If we all band together and stick up for each other, they cannot fire us all. It becomes about the collective and not the individual.'

'Unh-huh!' The bald man nodded in agreement. 'You're right! Yes, we're strong in numbers.'

Another man, whose face was obscured from Hamoonga by the darkness, began to relay his personal grievance. 'Our shift supervisor calls us lazy all the time. He has no trust in our abilities and he hurls one insult after another. No respect at all, I could be his father's age and he calls me by my first name. No, no, no, that is not our culture. They must learn our ways and show respect for us elders!'

'Hmmm, Ba *shi* Harry, that's no cause for protest!' Kibongo chuckled. 'You cannot expect a foreigner to know everything about your culture, that's unrealistic. Surely calling you by your first name is not a crime!' Some of the other men laughed, lightening the mood a little.

'But there are real concerns, I admit,' Kibongo added. 'I think we must just be careful how we handle our approach. We don't want to let things to get violent and out of hand. I'm certain we all want to keep our jobs and feed our families!'

'Aaahhh, what do you Congolese know anyway?' Kalala said jokingly. At that moment the young man stood up and yelled, 'Zambia for Zambians! Africa for Africans!' The group in their inebriated state responded with a cheer, raising their fists in the air.

The evening went on in much the same way with back-and-forth political banter. Hamoonga took it all in. He empathised with the cause but was not convinced that organised protests against the Chinese employers would succeed. He simply could not believe that so-called 'strength in numbers' would be enough to sway the minds of the powerful. He knew how ruthless powerful people could be and to what lengths they would go to protect their interests and their assets.

Chapter 14

A Perfect Storm

'When you really want something, the world conspires to make a dream come true.'

The Alchemist, Paulo Coelho

Chishimba Mine, Copperbelt Province, Zambia

October 2011

Sometimes no matter what you do, the world conspires to create the perfect storm. Such was the case one early October morning at Chishimba Mine.

As every morning, Jinan was the first to arrive at the plant. He had already taken his customary walk through the locker room and showers. He had checked the equipment and read through the notes left by the supervisor from the previous shift. It was typically through shift notes that a supervisor would learn about any flashlight batteries that needed replacing, power tools that needed refurbishing or anything else that warranted attention. Everything was in order. The mine workers were beginning to trickle in with the breaking of the dawn sky as if drawn in by some mystical invocation to pay homage to the mining gods.

It was not an easy morning for Jinan, in fact it was a particularly difficult morning for it was a year to the day that he had lost his wife and son. Even after several shots of Black Label, he'd been unable to sleep the night before. Skin sticky with alcohol-induced sweat, he'd tossed and turned, plagued by thoughts of the crash, his imagination full of violent images. The terrible news had left him desolate. If only he'd not taken a job in Zambia, his wife and child would still be alive; if he'd brought his family to join him, they would have been spared. Jinan blamed himself and he blamed this godforsaken foreign land that had drawn him in as a mercenary chasing riches like all the other charlatans with an insatiable thirst for money. But, now, it was all for naught; he was a rudderless ship; a man robbed of his mission. His only relief was work, which for the duration took his mind away from the pain, the ceaseless regrets. Jinan came in earlier and earlier for his shifts, left later and later, and demanded more and more from his workers. Emotionally and physically exhausted, he was quick to lose his temper at the slightest provocation, real or imagined. His fellow supervisors felt it and stayed clear of him, but it was his men who bore the brunt of his bitterness. When he first came to Zambia, he had considered its people lethargic, now he loathed them. He hated their apparent dilatoriness. He was infuriated by their complaints about their shifts, their pay, the food, everything. He viewed them as laggards, a race of shiftless people who would rather engage in empty conversation or attend funerals than put in an honest day's work. The more his resentment grew, the more Jinan struggled to make it through each day but today, the pain and the desolation was especially piercing.

The *kampompo* truck arrived. Two men alighted from the vehicle and perfunctorily laid a heaped tray of buns and a large canister of hot cocoa on the nearby bench before proceeding to their next station. The mine workers promptly gathered around the tray to gobble down their day's pitiful ration.

'Ba Boss!' a voice from behind broke Jinan from his reverie. He'd not noticed that his team of men had gathered behind him with an expectant air. Startled, Jinan rose from his wooden stool. He felt the weight of their expectations. Mostly they clammed up whenever he was within earshot. They knew too well that he was prone to lash out at the slightest goading.

'Ba Boss, we need to talk with you,' Kalala said. To Jinan, Kalala was a dawdler and a troublemaker. He had already been reprimanded for distracting others from their work. Kalala himself had sensed Jinan's growing impatience with him and he was certain that his days were numbered.

Jinan inhaled deeply, straightened his back, and folded his arms defensively. 'What's it about? You know shift start in five minutes!' He gestured impatiently, looking down at an invisible watch on his wrist.

'Boss, it's important, we need to talk with you.' Kalala took a deep breath as his fellow workers stood to the side and behind him in a show of unconvincing solidarity. Hamoonga too hovered uneasily behind Kalala. Everyone but Kalala avoided making eye contact with their quick-tempered boss.

'It's about our wages, boss.' Kalala craned his neck to glance at his colleagues behind him before continuing. 'We would like to talk with you about increasing our pay.'

Jinan remained silent but his face betrayed his antipathy. His skin grew pale and his thin lips tightened, accentuating the age lines around his mouth. Undeterred, Kalala continued. 'Boss, we want a pay increase. Things in this country have become too expensive, boss. We are failing to stretch our money to the end of the month. We are suffering. We don't have enough to give to our wives to buy simple groceries to feed our children. We cannot afford uniforms or books for our children to go to school. Boss, none of us can even afford medicine for our families when they get sick. We just want to be able to afford a decent life for the work that we do.' Before Kalala could continue any further, Jinan erupted.

'Work, work? What work? What fuckin' work do you do?' His eyes narrowed as the scowl on his face hardened. 'You people do nothing and expect more money! You want more money for what? *Raziness?*'

The thin strand of solidarity tethering the men together weakened. The men lowered their heads as if to disappear from view, and escape the tension in the air. But not Kalala. He stepped forward bullishly and calmly restated his case; he was a man convinced of the righteousness of his plight.

'Boss, we're all simple men here, we all have families, we all have people who we look after and care about. A fair wage is all that we are seeking.'

'Fair? Fair?' Jinan was beside himself, he was fuming at the audacity of this man. 'You people!' He shook his head in disbelief. 'You people sit around talking and *compraining* every day and now you want more money? Now you want more money?' He paused and gave an icy chuckle, gritting his teeth. '*Rook* here, I will fire all of you, you hear me? Each and every one of you! There are many people out there who need job but all you do is *comprain!*'

Kalala would not back down; he simply took a step forward and continued, 'We don't want to cause you trouble, boss, we're just asking for what is fair. This company is making more profits than ever before, but we have not seen an increase in our pay. All we want, all we think is right is...'

Before he could finish his statement, there was a sonorous screech from outside followed by an almighty quake that shook the floor beneath them. In a moment of disorientation and panic, men scuttled to the floor, seeking refuge from an unknown foe.

'*Tata lesa aye!* What was that?' One of the men shouted, his voice trembling. Loud voices and rushing footsteps could be heard outside. They all waited a few seconds, uncertain what to do. Then, with instinctive curiosity, Jinan and his men tentatively made their way out into the open area to investigate. As they emerged they were accosted by a huge plume of dust obscuring what would have been a clear line of sight to the control tower for the underground elevator shaft. Voices of men in various states of panic and anxiety pierced the fog. It took a several minutes before the cloud of dust began to subside, and as it did so, about half a dozen men could be seen lying on the ground while others were dusting themselves off from the thick soot covering them. A crowd quickly built up. Mangled steel trusses were strewn across the ground in front of the elevator entrance. The steel cage of the elevator shaft was tilted at an angle and lodged in the earth. A deafening emergency alarm sounded from the elevator control tower.

A paramedic van appeared and four uniformed men hurried onto the scene. Two of them were carrying a stretcher. They went straight to the closest man lying on the ground. 'Are you okay? Are you hurt? Can you move your legs?' The two other men fanned out asking the same set of questions.

There were several cries for help as the paramedics attended to those that most needed assistance. But as time passed, and the panic died down, it became apparent that nobody was severely hurt; there were a few men with lacerations to their arms and legs, but not life-threatening injuries. Most of the men were merely very shocked, but they would survive.

It took another few minutes before a cohesive story could be pieced together. According to eyewitnesses, it was the elevator shaft that had malfunctioned. Apparently, as the elevator shaft was ascending with its full ballast of workers finishing their night shift, the steel cable hoist attached to the main cage had suddenly frayed. The overloaded cage had then tilted abruptly, violently jolting the metal framework of the elevator tower. Some of the metal trusses were ripped out of their joints and fell to the ground below. Fortuitously, the cage had jammed in a position that allowed just enough room for the men to clamber out to safety. A few of them had been thumped hard against the walls of the cage and had sustained flesh wounds. It was a miracle that no one was severely hurt and no one had died.

The scene had now drawn in a sizable crowd of several hundred mine workers. Many of them, like Jinan's group, had heard the commotion and felt the tremor before running out to see what had happened. The Chinese supervisors were also standing aghast next to each other absorbing the unfolding events.

'How could this have happened?' one of the Zambian men shouted angrily. 'The elevator shafts are supposed to be certified, preventive maintenance is supposed to be done every week, and engineering supervisors have to check and verify that everything is working as it should!' He was facing Jinan, Ping, and three other Chinese supervisors all huddled together.

'*Ehe*! How could this happen? In all my years working here I have never seen anything like this!' shouted an older worker, his face was etched with the wrinkles of a hard life.

'How could it happen? I'll tell you what happened!' another worker chimed in, also visibly upset. 'It's these bloody Chinese, always looking to cut corners, not caring about the workers, only caring about how much money they can make!'

A few of the men were now paying attention and their focus shifted from the chaos in front of them to the five Chinese supervisors standing to the side.

'You're right, they care nothing for us!' shouted one of the workers from Jinan's team. 'Just this morning we approached our supervisor to talk about a pay increase. He would not even discuss it, he responded with insults, calling us lazy and good for nothing!'

'How dare he call us lazy! How dare he insult us! This is our country, our land, our copper. You should go back where you came from!' a man yelled with pent up fury. 'We don't want colonisers again, enough is enough!'

Kalala standing near the front raised his fist in agreement, 'Yes, enough is enough, *twakana!*'

Years of resentment, ill-treatment and exploitation rose to the surface, stimulated by fear and the knowledge that their lives were at risk.

'Africa for Africans!' shouted yet another man. His chant was echoed by others; the crowd was coalescing behind their collective unhappiness. The accident had done more in minutes than hours of Kalala's rhetoric.

One of the younger mine workers, a white bandanna across his forehead, bounced up and down with clenched fists punching the air, his lean body revealing every sinew of muscle in his arms, stomach and back. 'Zambia for Zambians, Africa for Africans!' His torso gyrated as he geared himself up for a fight. Sweat trickled down his neck. 'Zambia for Zambians, Africa for Africans!' The crowd cheered. The young man punched the air savagely as if pummeling an invisible enemy. 'Zambia for Zambians, Africa for Africans!' He moved forward to the front of the pack revelling in the attention.

Then, like a man possessed, he leapt toward the Chinese supervisors and reached to grab Ping by throat. In an instinctive act of survival, Ping ducked and the young man lost his balance. Reorienting himself, he readied himself for another attack but before he could pounce, he was struck hard across the side of his head.

It all happened so quickly. The young miner lay sprawled on the dusty ground bleeding profusely. Fearing for their lives, the Chinese supervisors made a run for it, towards the guarded perimeter fence separating the offices from the main plant area. The altercation was fuel to the fire, and the crowd, incensed, were spoiling for a fight. Kalala was at the helm, his eyes shining with anger, '*Tiye, tiye!* .... Our demands were peaceful and they're responding as if we were the criminals. They're frightened of us, *tiyeni*, let's go!'

Jinan and his four colleagues ran for dear life, hearts racing, mouths dry – fuelled by fear. They made it to the guard post and through the gate, which was flanked by three guards armed with batons. On cue, the guards shut the gate behind them. The furious mine workers could be seen approaching, an angry mob moving in unison. They were now in full chorus, 'Africa for Africans, Zambia for Zambians! Africa for Africans, Zambia for Zambians!'

The Chinese entered their tiny one-room office and locked the door behind them. They moved one of the heaviest looking desks, to barricade the door and then they all dropped to the floor. Each of them had that sinking feeling, they knew they were as helpless as trapped animals in an abattoir.

Chapter 15

Murder at Chishimba Mine

'*Murder! – Chinaman Kills Mine Worker!*' That was the headline in the ubiquitous *National Post* the morning after the shooting incident at Chishimba Mine. The other tabloids carried a variant of the headline, all with visceral characterisations of 'evil' Chinese employers, pillaging the nation and murdering citizens. The papers railed against the new imperialism that was growing like a cancer sucking the lifeblood of the nation. 'How can our people be worked like slaves in appalling conditions within their own country and be murdered in cold blood for merely voicing their God-given right to a fair wage?' lamented the editor of the *Daily Mail*. The *Independent* blasted: 'What happened to government for the people, by the people? In whose interest is this government working? Certainly not in ours! Where is the protection of our human rights?'

The shooting incident had taken place shortly before 6:00 a.m. on Thursday, within an hour, the plant was barricaded by dozens of mine police officers, most of whom were loitering in the plant area, at pains to show that they knew what they were doing. Crowds of onlookers had gathered at a distance craning their necks and straining their eyes to see if they could catch a glimpse of the dead body. In true 'African time' it took a full three hours before a medical doctor arrived to pronounce the obvious. By this time rumours had already spread through the community like lice in the hair of a dirty child. Claims that five people had been shot dead by Chinese management; claims that there had been a fight among workers, which had led to a shooting. The newspapers had made the incident national news and with that came political reverberations. There were calls from opposition party members for the Minister of Mines to be sacked,

155

while others were on television and radio calling for a presidential inquiry and an overhaul of security protocols at all mining facilities. Still others wanted more radical changes such as the revocation of mining licenses given to Chinese companies and the expulsion of Chinese diplomats. All of this political grandstanding would ordinarily have been laughable and easily ignored or brushed aside by the government, but this was an election year and for the first time in a decade the incumbent government was vulnerable. Only two months before, the government had lost two important parliamentary seats through by-elections in areas considered to be safe. Times were changing. More youthful voters were siding with opposition parties with their message of hope and change. The ruling party itself had shown some internal cracks as the old guard struggled to maintain its iron-clad grip on power against the advances of 'Young Turks' from within. The pressure was building for action to be taken at the highest levels to address the crisis at the mines and with each day that passed, the chorus of dissenters grew louder. Something had to be done.

Jinan and his fellow supervisors had been taken into police custody a few hours following the shooting incident. It took the police three days to determine the sequence of events and to settle on Jinan as the leading perpetrator. The police continued to detain the five men in a holding cell awaiting instructions from headquarters. This turned out to be an inadvertent act of compassion because the Chinese men would not have been safe outside police custody; such was the vitriol and public outrage in the country over the incident.

☾

'Imbeciles! Complete idiots! These fools write whatever they want and feel they can get away with it!' Minister Zulu growled as he threw the folded tabloid newspaper across the length of his ornate hardwood desk.

'I'll squash them like ants! Remove me? Remove me? Do they know who I am and what I have done for this country? These rodents live under the freedom that I provide. Their insignificant lives would not exist but for my largesse! How dare they write filth like this… I will squash them like ants!'

Minister Zulu was clearly enraged. Despite being over forty years in politics, he still had a surprisingly thin skin when it came to criticism. Perhaps it was the vanity that accompanies the myth of one's own infallibility. During the freedom struggle against the British, Zulu had suffered. He had been detained countless times, beaten, forced to clean toilets and other demeaning tasks. None of this had diminished his fortitude; it was always the personal, psychological attacks, such as being called 'boy' or 'kaffir', that seemed to undermine him, and so it still was. The papers' depiction of him as old, incompetent, and out of touch with the needs of the common mine worker really ruffled his feathers.

Minister Zulu had assumed the position of Minister of Mines in the president's latest cabinet reshuffle. These were really only a game of musical chairs; the same faces changed positions every few years at the behest of the president. The reshuffles seemed to have no discernable pattern, no rhyme or reason other than the fact that a few of the most senior ministerial positions seemed to serve as rewards for the president's most ardent loyalists. Indeed, the position of Minister of Mines was one of the most coveted ministerial portfolios. Ascending to that office was akin to having access to a bottomless treasure trove. All mining licenses were issued by the Ministry of Mines and personally signed by the Minister. All the multi-million-dollar mining contracts given to foreign mining companies and contractors had to be personally underwritten by the Minister. '*Nchekelako*' was the unwritten process by which every person wanting a contract or deal in the mining industry had to pay the Minister of Mines. A well-known cost of doing business in Zambia, it was a practice that had slowly eroded any remnant of ethics within the entire industry. The graft was destructive, pervasive, and addictive. Taking bribes was similar to a drug addict who keeps injecting himself, knowing that the story could end tragically, but powerless to stop the addiction.

'"The president should sack the minister of mines?"– I should throw all of them in jail for uttering such nonsense!' the minister shouted. 'These imbeciles have the nerve to criticise me after all that I've done? I made this country!' He turned to his big bald henchman, Babu, 'Find everyone associated with these ludicrous papers and teach them a lesson. I want them all thrown in jail, the lot of them!'

Babu was seated, his back straight, in one of the studded leather armchairs that adorned the minister's expansive office. Seated four feet across from him was Mrs Zulu, calm as always and dressed in her multi-coloured traditional *chitenge* with matching headdress. Babu looked across at Mrs Zulu waiting for her to respond to her husband's rant. Having worked for the Zulus for over thirteen years, he knew the drill. First the hot-headed boss would mouth off and make huge demands, then, there would be a pause. Next, his more reflective wife would offer a well-considered strategic response. Mrs Zulu used her words sparingly, and every word was used efficiently to deliver the desired outcome. She was the brains behind their businesses, like the patient crocodile that swims beneath the waterline and strikes its prey with deadly force at precisely the right moment, she chose her moment for words or action.

'Bashi Z, you're a national treasure. History will show that without you this nation would not be what it is today,' Mrs Zulu began in her usual respectful tone. Clasping her hands in her lap, she straightened her back, and gently turned to face her husband. She knew when to stroke his ego, when to urge him on, and when to reel him in. 'Bashi Z, any sane person, who knows the history of this nation, knows your rightful place as a founding father – that is an unquestionable, unshakable fact.' She paused to allow her husband to soak in the accolades. 'Bashi Z, you're right, these people are troublemakers and should certainly be dealt with, but we need to be strategic.' She paused again like a painter stepping back to contemplate her artwork. 'Bashi Z, these are different times, news travels fast, and across the world, the media can be damaging or it can be used in our favour. We have to consider the broad picture – that is what a bad press, an overt, heavy-handed action would bring in its wake. Bashi Z, the main thing is that we do not want to lose the Chinese investors and we want to keep you in this ministerial position at all costs.' Her words resonated, the minister began to calm down.

'What are you thinking, Bana Z?' the minister asked.

'We need to change the conversation in the media, we need to drive the agenda. When a dog is fixated on a bone, one must not try to take the bone out of its mouth, one must simply offer it a more attractive bone to chew on and it will let go of the old one.'

Leaning forward the minister smiled and asked, 'And what is the new bone, Bana Z, what can we offer them?'

Just then the sharp electronic jingle of a phone ringing interrupted the conversation. Minister Zulu shifted in his seat and pressed the speaker.

'Sir, very sorry to interrupt you, but it is State House calling. Shall I put them through?' a timid female voice asked.

'Of course, Tandiwe, I will take the call now.'

Minister Zulu perked up, reached for the receiver and drew it against his right ear. 'Good afternoon, sir, *mulishani mwe mfumu?*' Protocol was everything: even though he and the president had known each other as friends for decades, the gravitas of the presidential office trumped all. In this hugely hierarchical society the president needed to be venerated in the manner as a child venerates his all-knowing father; everyone had to literally kneel in the presence of the president. One of the main reasons Minister Zulu had survived so long in politics was precisely because he understood this fact. Many young political aspirants in the past had made the fatal error of not knowing their place, not respecting their elders. If one wanted to have longevity in Zambian politics, one had to recognise that one existed at the whim of the president.

'Yes sir, yes sir.' Pause. 'Yes sir, yes sir, I understand, sir.' Another lengthy pause. 'Yes sir, understood, sir. I will take care of it, sir.' There was another long pause and then, 'Thank you, sir. Goodbye, sir,' and then the minister set the receiver carefully back in its cradle. Mrs Zulu and Babu sat anxiously waiting for the minister's debrief.

'The president wants us to go out there and sort it out. He wants us to take care of this mess before it goes any further. He says the Chinese government has threatened to pull the plug on all mining operations if the Chinese men are not released and absolved of all charges. We have to sort it out. But the public wants blood, and there will be disaster if those men go scot-free!' There was a silence before the minister's wife broke the ice.

'All will be well, Bashi Z, let's head to Kitwe. We will resolve this matter. Babu, make the arrangements, we will leave for Kitwe tonight.'

◆◆◆

The dead man was Kalala – as Hamoonga saw him prostrate and lifeless on the ground, he thought of his passion for justice, his refusal to be deterred by the apathy, fear or indifference of his colleagues. Kalala had been gunned down, the meagre cost of his life laid bare for all to see. Kalala had been right all along: no one cared for the indigenous mine worker, no one cared for the poor. If the people themselves did not stand up for justice and decency, no one would save them; the cavalry was not coming. Kalala's death marked a point of no return for Hamoonga; it brought back memories of all the injustices he had seen and suffered himself. The years in Cha-Cha-Cha Prison, starved, beaten, and denied access to family and friends. Denied even the basic human decency of being allowed to bury his own mother. And now this? Why should a man die for merely protesting against poor working conditions? Why should a person die on his own soil at the hands of foreigners simply for demanding a fair wage? A line had been crossed – the basic laws of what makes us human had been violated. Hamoonga recalled the words of Martin Luther King Jr., 'If a man cannot find something that he is willing to die for then he is not fit to live.' Justice had to be done, he had to take a stand. If not now, when? He had to take action: every fibre in his body was coalescing around one mission – *justice!*

◆◆◆

The men shuffled up to make room for each other as more and more of them streamed onto the dusty grounds in front of the District Governor's office building, an old colonial structure with tired blue paint peeling off its walls. Like so many such buildings it was exhausted from neglect and the lack of maintenance. A large central stairway led to the main entrance of the building.

A sea of men had built up and overflowed past the rusted wire fence, spilling onto the main city thoroughfare. Looking down from the stairway, Hamoonga estimated that there were over a thousand people, maybe even double that. An amorphous mass of human beings emitting a continuous humming noise of murmuring voices.

It had been a week since the assassination of Kalala. Since the incident, the mine workers had refused to return to work until their grievances were addressed. Each morning since the shooting the mine workers had gathered outside the governor's office and demanded:

- A swift prosecution of the five Chinese mine supervisors for the murder of Paul (Kalala) Berg to the fullest extent of the law.

- An immediate change in leadership at Chishimba Mine. The government should revoke the mining license of the Chinese and take interim ownership of the mine until a suitable buyer could be found.

- The resignation of the Minister of Mines for incompetence and failing to protect the interests of the indigenous mine workers.

- An immediate change in working conditions to include a 40-hour week and no less than a 50 per cent increase in wages across the board.

Kalala's death had been pivotal to Hamoonga's change of outlook. He had felt the imperative of action rather than discretion, or, as some might say, apathy. His latent leadership skills had ushered him into the forefront of the mine workers' rebellion. It was he who'd been able to articulate a clear direction for the disparate group to take. It was Hamoonga who had formulated the first draft of their demands and it was his idea to gather outside the municipal offices to gain maximum attention for their plight. It had been a masterstroke because the central location of the office drew the full attention of the media and the public. Furthermore, as the crowds began to increase in number, they blocked the main thoroughfare to the city causing major interruptions to commerce and the movement of traffic within the city. The loss of copper production at the mines also meant that the whole affair had become a national issue. The workers could not be ignored.

Megaphone in hand, Hamoonga signalled with his free hand for the crowd to quieten down. The crowd ignored him.

'*Bashi* mine!' he belted into the loudspeaker, his voice echoing in the quadrangle above the noise of the crowd. Hamoonga was repeatedly startled by how his voice carried over the din of the crowd.

'*Bashi* mine!' he repeated, this time getting the desired reaction though it took a few more seconds for silence to fully set in. A man tailor-made for the moment, Hamoonga began to address the crowd, punctuating each of his first few sentences with pauses as if to allow each word to sink in, just as a patient gardener slowly waters his plants, conscious of allowing the water to slowly seep into the soil.

'My brothers, *umuntu ngumuntu ngabantu*. A person is a person because of people. Indeed, it is because of you that I am and it is because I am that you are. My brothers, this is who we are, this is what we are; this is our essence as African people, without it we are lost!'

The crowd mumbled and shuffled in collective agreement. 'A week ago, as you all know, one of us was killed, one of us was murdered by a foreign hand. A week ago, one of our brothers, one of the sons of this earth, was gunned down, shamelessly killed in his own land for demanding a living wage!'

The crowd again shouted its anger and concurrence.

Hamoonga waited for what felt like an eternity before signalling for quiet. He continued, '*Umuntu ngumuntu ngabantu*, my brothers, these foreigners do not understand this concept. This creed is alien to them. They come to our land to pillage our natural resources, where is *umuntu ngumuntu ngabantu* in that? They come to our land and work us like slaves, where is *umuntu ngumuntu ngabantu* in that? They come to our land, to connive with our corrupt politicians to strip us of our inheritance, where is *umuntu ngumuntu ngabantu* in that?' The noise from the crowd ramped up with every rhetorical question

Hamoonga, a surprisingly natural orator, put to them.

'They come to this country and murder our people, where is *umuntu ngumuntu ngabantu* in that? My brothers, we do not seek anything extraordinary. No.' He paused. 'No, we are simply gathered here, as we have done all week, to seek justice for our murdered brother, for his family, for the common man. Brothers, what we simply seek is human decency, human respect from those who govern us and by those who are merely guests on our land!' The crowd cheered with chants of 'Justice now! Justice now!'

'In the sixties, Africans fought against the European colonial masters. We succeeded in gaining our independence but then we stopped being vigilant. My brothers, freedom and justice require constant attention, we should never be complacent, never sell our country, our inheritance, our children's inheritance to foreign powers. And we *must* keep those in power honest. Their duty is to serve us, we the electorate who put them into office. They are not put there to serve foreigners bearing gifts.'

Fists were raised as the miners and their supporters drank in Hamoonga's every word.

'If our leaders are not willing to serve our best interests, we should vote them out, replace them with people who will serve this country. Replace them with leaders who will ensure we achieve good deals with countries like China. Foreign investors need us as much as we need them and they must know that when they are here, in Zambia, they must abide by *our* laws, *our* way of doing things; they must respect the common man!'

Hamoonga, wiped his forehead, and concluded with the list of four specific demands they had previously drafted before leaving centre stage to a rapturous cheer from the crowd. Other speakers addressed the crowd as the day progressed. Local street traders in the streets with and without stalls brought in much needed fried dough, *nshima*, dried fish, vegetables, and water to sustain the men. The outnumbered policemen hovered at a safe distance unsure of how to deal with the movement that was gathering momentum. Newspaper reporters and television crews feasted on the images and sound bites;

Hamoonga, in particular, had captured media attention.

♋

Minister Zulu was in a foul mood. He had not had much sleep the previous night as he tossed and turned trying to find a solution to the intractable problem of the mine worker rebellion. Coupled with the fact that he hated travelling, especially to Kitwe, he was not a happy camper. He loathed the town with its dusty pothole-ridden roads, outdated buildings and polluted air. It felt to him as though every time he travelled to the mining town, it was to resolve some problem or another. Only three months before, he had been called to meet with civic leaders concerned about the apparent increase in cases of respiratory ailments due to air pollution. It had taken a full two days of meetings with church leaders, marketeers, and health workers to pacify them. Now he was back at the instigation of the president to put a stop to the mine worker's protest.

'Why can't you just fire the lot of them and then replace them? There are lots of unemployed men who would be happy to do the work these ingrates don't want to do.' Minister Zulu bristled in his armchair.

The three Chinese, all executives of CMMC, the proprietors of Chishimba Mine. Dressed in matching charcoal-grey suits and angel-white shirts, the only difference between then was their ties: the man in the middle wore a red tie, the men to his right and left a light blue and mauve one. They looked at each other as if determining whose turn it was to speak. 'Well, with all due respect, sir, we cannot fire fifteen hundred workers; and we would not be able to hire enough people to replace them,' said the man in the middle chair.

The minister focused his eyes on Mr red tie. 'Then why don't you just single out the troublemakers and fire them?' he asked. 'Surely that will send the message that you do not condone this reckless behaviour?' He peered over his left shoulder toward Mrs Zulu behind him.

The three executives exchanged a few words among themselves in Chinese. 'Sir, but if we fire the ringleaders, our people assure us that there will be a massive riot. Maybe even destruction of property.

We cannot have them destroy our investment,' replied Mr light blue tie.

'Yes, equipment very expensive,' added the man with the red tie. All three nodded.

'Governor, how did this happen on your watch? How did we reach this point?' the minister asked rhetorically looking at District Governor Mutale to his right. The governor shifted uncomfortably in his seat. He was a large potbellied man with an appetite for food almost as large as his incompetence. Known for doing as he was told, he had, for years, been an errand boy for senior party leaders. He had danced at party conventions, stuffed ballot boxes, ferried party hooligans to intimidate opposition members, and all without question. His ultimate reward had been his appointment to the district governorship.

'So you're telling me that we have no choice but to engage in a negotiation with these troublemakers? Do we know their full demands?' the minister asked resignedly.

There was a pause before Mr mauve tie spoke up. 'Well sir, their demands are clear. They want prosecution of the five Chinese for murder, a fifty percent increase in wages across the board, and an expulsion of Chinese owners, not to mention, sir, *uhm*, your removal, sir.' There was silence in the room as everyone waited for the minister's reaction.

Minister Zulu leant forward in his seat and said sternly, 'That will never happen; not over my dead body, you hear me?' He sat back slowly and then asked, 'Who are the ringleaders? Governor, I want you to set up a meeting with the ringleaders, I want you all to talk some sense into them. Isolate them and make them understand what consequences might befall their families if they don't let up and agree to go back to work. I want this set up right away, and give me a report on the outcome. Let's at least talk to these imbeciles and give them an opportunity to see the error in their ways!'

Chapter 16

The Negotiation

Hamoonga sat silently in his chair, flanked by Mr Amon Chulu and Mr Zacchaeus Phiri, the only two mine workers who had agreed to accompany him to the negotiating table. They were not willing participants but rather as reluctant as a groom forced to marry his one-night stand. Like all the other mine workers, they were afraid to be singled out as leaders of the rebellion. They feared recriminations by the Chinese employers and the government. In the end, they had hesitantly agreed to back Hamoonga after he had repeatedly said that it would not bode well for their cause if only one man were to show up as the single representative of an entire movement. Hamoonga himself had wavered. Was the whole protest no more than hot air? Were the mine workers, despite their anger, going to let just one man take the rap. He felt the hypocrisy of the situation, and it hurt him.

Sitting across the preposterously large oval boardroom table in a plush, air-conditioned hotel conference room was an intimidating official delegation. Hamoonga's team seemed very thin by comparison, just a shoe-string, not a delegation.

'Your names, please?' asked the officious-looking man facing them, peering over his glasses that were permanently lodged halfway down his nose.

'My name is Hamoonga Moya and this is Mr Amon Chulu and Mr Zacchaeus Phiri,' Hamoonga said pointing to his left and to his right respectively as the two of them fidgeted uncomfortably in their seats. The spectacled man scribbled down some notes into his pad for a few seconds before looking up again. 'So, am I to assume this is the full extent of your party, or are we to expect more?' His tone of voice revealed a certain air of arrogance, a certain '*I'm too good to be wasting my precious time on the likes of you*' quality about it.

'That is correct, we will be speaking on behalf of our fellow workers,' Hamoonga replied.

'Good, so we'll begin with introductions and then get right to it, shall we?' the man announced as he looked around the room.

It took a full twenty minutes for the introductions to be completed and by that time, Mr Chulu and Mr Phiri were ready to wave the proverbial white flag. Present in the room were the District Governor himself, his deputy, and five of his top-ranking staff. There were three senior executives from CMMC China with their interpreter; even though they could speak English reasonably well, they didn't want anything to be lost in translation. The president of the official Mine Workers Union, his treasurer, and his secretary were also in attendance. There was a lady transcribing the meeting, and three or four other people standing in the back with ominous expressions on their faces. The spectacled man himself was a special assistant in the office of the District Governor. Hamoonga and his team were outmatched, outgunned, and outclassed!

'So gentlemen, let us just get the facts straight out into the open. Indeed, let's call a spade a spade!' the spectacled man began. 'You, gentlemen, and your fellow mine workers have engaged in an illegal strike for almost a week now. You have threatened the lives of five Chinese CMMC supervisory staff and you have assaulted three security guards at the mine. Furthermore, your illegal strike has caused disruption to the critically important instruments of government in this city. Make no mistake, gentlemen, you are breaking the law and we are gathered here to make you see reason so that you may abort your current course of action.' With that he sat back in his seat and stared directly at Hamoonga; in fact the entire room had their eyes firmly fixed on the man of the hour.

Hamoonga sat silently for a moment searching carefully for the right words. He then straightened up and began to speak, calmly but firmly, accentuating every word. 'When I was a little boy I would accompany my mother to the market to buy all that was needed in our home. It was quite a distance away, and each time we went, she would make sure we bought enough to tide us over for several days. On one particular occasion, after buying our vegetables, dried fish, tomatoes, and onions, we began the long trek home. Halfway into the journey, a young man pounced on us and grabbed my mother's purse from underneath her arm and ran off with it. We hollered for help but the man disappeared into the nearby compound. Ruing our misfortune, we returned home and I for one quickly forgot about it, for purse snatching was sadly an all-too-common occurrence in our town and surrounding areas. No use crying over spilt milk, as they say.'

'Mr Moya,' the spectacled man interrupted rudely, 'we have no time for your childhood anecdotes here. This is serious business. Can you get to the point and stop wasting our time? If you would just...'

The District Governor interrupted. 'Peter, let the man finish his story. Let's hear what he has to say.'

A little embarrassed, the interrogator adjusted his spectacles, and sat back in his chair.

Hamoonga continued, 'As I was saying, why cry over spilt milk? That was my attitude. My mother, however, would not let sleeping dogs lie. Every day for three weeks she walked that same route and waited at the same clearing. Sure enough, her patience paid off. One day the young man who had stolen her purse walked down the road. He did not recognise her, but she most certainly recognised him. As he reached the clearing, she struck him to the ground with a stick and then grabbed him by the seat of his pants. Brandishing the stick in one hand, she demanded he take her to his home immediately. There were many passersby, all enthralled by the spectacle of this very small woman holding a man in total subjugation. Once at his house, she retrieved her purse before letting him go, humiliated before the entire compound. When mother told us the story, I was full of admiration, but I asked her, "Mama, how much money did you have in that purse? It must have been a fair amount for you to go to all that trouble." She looked at me for a minute and then replied saying there was not an *ngwee* left in the purse when it was stolen, it had all been spent at the market. So I asked, "It must have been an expensive purse, how much did it cost you?" But she said the purse was just a cheap one. Confused, I asked again, "So why did you go to all of that trouble, risking your life to get your purse back?"' Sensing a captive audience, Hamoonga paused for dramatic effect. 'That's when she told me with words that I will never forget: "Son, right is right, and wrong is wrong, there is no in-between in matters of morality." She went on to say: "You must never allow a bad person to take advantage of the innocent, NEVER! If you know in your heart that you are right and that an injustice has been done, never fear, never rest until that injustice is brought to light and corrected!"'

There was a silence in the room as everyone visualised their place in the allegory. It was broken with a sharp rebuke from the president of the official Mine Workers Union. 'You and your friends are nothing but rabble-rousers, troublemakers... instead of following proper protocol for airing grievances, you choose to stage an illegal strike. Who are you? On whose authority are you acting?' He looked flustered. 'I am the president of the Mine Workers Union, duly elected and mandated with great authority to deal with all issues concerning mine workers in this country!'

'With all due respect, Mr President, sir,' Hamoonga said, 'you and your committee have lost the faith and trust of the people, the ordinary mine worker. You are compromised; indeed you should be sitting here with us on this side of the table and not over there fighting for the interests of government and executives!'

The President, stung to the core, jumped out of his seat and banged the table in anger.

'What... how *dare* you? I should castrate your little...' Before he could finish, the District Governor, his deputy, and the three Chinese executives all spoke at the same time trying to calm the man down. It took several minutes for the meeting to resume a civilised tone.

The Chinese Executives spoke among themselves in Chinese before one of them turned to speak in English. 'We understand you have demands. You have very serious demands, *prease* tell us your demands.'

With that prompt, Hamoonga pulled out a single sheet of paper and straightened it on the table in front of him. All eyes were on him as he gathered himself to read out the demands. He cleared his throat and commenced to slowly enunciate the demands for all to hear:

- A swift prosecution of the five Chinese mine supervisors for the murder of Paul 'Kalala' Berg to the fullest extent of the law.
- An immediate change in leadership at Chishimba Mine. The government should revoke the mining license of the Chinese and take interim ownership of the mine until a suitable buyer can be found.
- The resignation of the Minister of Mines for incompetence and failing to protect the interests of the indigenous mine workers.
- An immediate change in working conditions to include a forty-hour week and no less than a 50 percent increase in wages across the board.

The other Chinese Executive then chimed in, 'Chinese government have agreement with government of Zambia. CMMC invest in Chishimba Mine so we cannot leave – you understand? CMMC and Chinese government invest one hundred fifty million dollar in mine and want to invest another two hundred million in five year. This good for Zambia, no?'

Hamoonga turned to address the Chinese Executives directly. 'Gentlemen, I personally have no problem with China nor the people of China. The mine workers do not hate China, but our experience with the current Chinese leadership in our mines has been disastrous. They have overworked the Zambian mine worker. They have had no cultural sensitivity at all, as they show no interest in learning our culture. Wages have been low even though commodity prices and profits are at a record high. We are not fools – we know what is happening in the world.' Hamoonga paused and turned to his right. On cue, Mr Phiri handed him a manila folder. Hamoonga thumbed through the loose leaves of paper in the folder as the room watched. 'This brings me to the aspect of safety.' Hamoonga noticed the Chinese executives look at each other nervously. 'Yes, safety has been totally neglected.' He then proceeded to read from the paper in his hand. 'In a ten-year period since CMMC took over Chishimba mine, there has been an eighty percent increase in incidents as safety procedures have been ignored. Ten percent of them were fatal.' He stopped and looked up at the room. 'This is a Health and Safety Report from the Ministry of Mines itself.'

The officious, spectacled man ripped the glasses from his face. 'How dare you...'

But before the man could finish his sentence, Hamoonga continued undeterred.

'Despite numerous investigations by the government and hundreds of complaints by the workers, nothing has been done. We are tired of it. It has to change!' Hamoonga clenched his right fist on the surface in front of him. Then, looking directly at the District Governor, he said. 'And last but not least, we have the issue of one of our brothers being gunned down at the hands of Chinese supervisors!'

'Let us be reasonable here!' the District Governor interjected. 'Your demands are outrageous. They cannot be met as they are. We are talking about hundreds of millions of dollars at stake for the country. This is money that can and will make a difference in the lives of the very same people you are purporting to represent!'

Just then, in the middle of the District Governor's statements, the door from behind the conference room opened. In walked a familiar figure. Hamoonga almost fell out of his seat. *'Could it be him? Could it be him? Surely not!'* Hamoonga thought to himself. A tall, bald, hefty figure of a man walked in and hovered in the back of the room like a lappet-faced vulture circling its prey. Yes, there was no mistaking it, it was him; there was no way Hamoonga could forget the cruelty, the beatings, the interrogations – he was the one, the devil had reappeared!

Hamoonga's memories from the interrogations at Cha-Cha-Cha prison flashed to the forefront of his mind. He remembered the sick, piercing pain in his sides, the vomiting, the blood, the stench of urine and fecal matter, the dampness, the coldness of the floors, the constant dripping sounds; it all rushed back in an instant wave of unbridled emotions. Yes, it was the man who had savagely beaten him that very first night in the brightly lit cell, the same man that he had seen with Lulu that ill-fated night years ago.

The bald man hovered around for a minute or two and then engaged one of the superfluous people in a whispering conversation before exiting the room. It was but the briefest of moments, but it was a very poignant moment for Hamoonga. He realised then that he and his fellow mine workers were in over their heads. Their rebellion had ruffled the feathers of politicians at the very top, people who always got their way no matter what; things were going to take a turn for the worse, he could sense it. These so-called negotiations were a sham, mere window dressing to try to convince outsiders that civil protocol would be followed. No, he knew now that these talks were just that – talk, nothing more!

Chapter 17

Old Friends

M r Miti shifted uncomfortably in the armchair next to Beatrice. There was an awkward silence as she looked him over suspiciously. 'So, how exactly do you and my brother know each other?' she asked. Mr Miti pulled at his grey beard and cleared his throat before answering.

'We shared a cell as inmates in Cha-Cha-Cha Prison some time ago.' His reply was almost apologetic. Beatrice averted her eyes, embarrassed at her direct question but impressed by his forthright response, even though there was something about him that she couldn't quite trust.

'I'm sorry,' she said. 'I didn't mean to be so blunt; it was rude of me.'

'Not at all, no need to be embarrassed; it was not of your making. We were both victims of a vicious system of patronage.' He spoke with a philosophical air.

Beatrice shuffled her hands in between the sofa partitions, pretending to look for something under the cushions. She then got up and busied her way into her tiny kitchen. A few minutes later, she emerged holding a tray of water and a bottle of Mazoe orange juice concentrate. She pulled the wooden coffee table closer to her guest and then knelt down on both knees to carefully serve him. Beatrice was a well-taught Zambian woman; firstly she knew not to ask her guest if he needed food or drink – that would have been a sure sign of disrespect. No, one had just to offer what one had without asking. Secondly, she knew to kneel in front of her guest – again a mark of respect and welcome. Lastly, she knew to serve him and not let him pour his own beverage; her late mother would have been proud.

'Are you coming from far?' Beatrice asked as she sat back down on the sofa. Mr Miti, clearly thirsty, took three manly swigs of his orange juice before responding. 'Yes, I live in the country now, in my home village near Petauke.'

'Oh my, what brings you here to the city so far away from home?'

'I came two nights ago to visit relatives – they live in Buchi Township not too far from here – so I thought I might stop by and visit my brother, Hamoonga.'

'Oh that is very kind of you; you are welcome in our home, Mr Miti. Hamoonga is not back yet. Ever since that shooting incident at the mine, things have been very tense in this town and I never know when he comes back these days. *Eish, kaya,* I don't know what will happen, I get so worried about him, but he is so stubborn and won't listen to me. All he talks about these days is equal rights and justice. I keep telling him that these politics can get you killed, and we don't want to lose him again.' Beatrice shook her head in resignation. She realised she had gone off on a tangent, but such was the strength of her objections to Hamoonga's recent reincarnation as a local civil rights leader. 'I'm sorry, *mwe ba fyashi,* I didn't mean to go on like that.'

'No, no, not at all. Yes, I have been following the recent events with the mine workers, and I know about Hamoonga's involvement. He's a good man with a big heart, which is something I always remember about him. Hamoonga knows injustice first hand and I'm sure it is killing him to see the injustices being suffered by the mine workers.' Beatrice heard his reassuring words as so much patter.

'Leave it to God, is what I keep telling him. You cannot fight the rich and powerful, not in this country, it's way too dangerous. But of course he will not listen to me.' There was a moment of silence before Beatrice said, 'You are welcome to wait here, I'm sure he will be back soon. He always returns home.'

꙰

It was almost 9:00 p.m. when Hamoonga walked through the front door. The children were already in the bedroom preparing to sleep and Beatrice had long since resigned her attempts to make small talk with her guest.

'Ba Miti! Is it really you?' Hamoonga exclaimed with great delight. Mr Miti rose up from his seat and the two men locked in a warm, brotherly embrace. '*Ah-ah*, what brings you here? I thought I'd never see you again!'

'I was in the neighborhood and I thought I should stop by and see a dear old friend,' Mr Miti replied with a broad smile. The two men looked at each other and embraced again.

'It is wonderful to see you, my elder brother, it is so good to see you.' Hamoonga signalled with his hand for Mr Miti to take a seat as he assumed the position now vacated by his sister. Beatrice, ever conscious of social etiquette, quietly made her way to the bedroom sensing that the two men had much to discuss.

'How long has it been since we last saw each other?' Hamoonga asked.

'I'd say about two years now,' Mr Miti responded.

'You look well.'

Mr Miti nodded. 'Well it's not hard, anything is better than that hellhole we were in for so long.'

'That is true.'

'You look well yourself, I see that you have reconnected with family. Your sister is a great host and you have such adorable nieces.'

'They have really helped me pull my life together. After prison my spirit was broken. I don't know what I would have done without the support of my family.' Hamoonga reflected on his own words for a second before continuing. 'How about you? When I was discharged from the prison, I never heard what happened to you or any of the others.'

'No, they deliberately don't give you information about the others, but my sources tell me most of the others in our cell are living quiet lives in villages across the country. Most just want to melt away and not cause trouble for fear of being incarcerated again, or worse.' Hamoonga averted his eyes, Mr Miti's words had struck a chord. Mr Miti leaned forward and in almost a whisper said, 'You, my friend have been very active, you are certainly making waves. I have my ear to the ground and I can tell you that there are many powerful people unhappy with this mine worker situation. I travelled here specifically to speak with you on the matter. Hamoonga, you are angering many people in high places. Be careful, be very careful, these people can do terrible things to you and to those you love. Think about the price you may be forced to pay!'

Indignant, Hamoonga leaned back into the sofa without saying a word. Emotions welled up inside him like a pot boiling over. He appreciated Miti's show of concern for his well-being, but this was a cause now dear to his heart. How could he dishonour the death of a fellow mine worker? How could he ignore the blatant injustices being suffered by workers at the hands of the Chinese and those in power? How could he waver at this defining moment in his life? How could he let down the hundreds of workers that were now looking up to him to lead them in a fight for basic human dignity?

'Ba Miti, it is with warmth and respect that I tell you this, but this cause is so near and dear to me, it is something that I cannot let go. For too long our people have been shortchanged by corrupt politicians and foreign powers. Working conditions continue to deteriorate as profits increase. There are very low wages, health and safety standards are not followed, we have no decent health facilities, and our people are now being killed simply for demanding change! No, enough is enough, Ba Miti, we have to take a stand. If not us, then who? If not me, then who?'

Mr Miti sat back slowly stroking his beard into a pointed cone. 'So, you are a man with a clear conviction, I see.' He stroked his beard once more before leaning forward again. 'I had to be sure. I had to see it for myself. I had to look you in the eye and make sure for myself that you were willing to do what it takes and to suffer the consequences for this cause.'

'That I am,' Hamoonga replied without hesitation.

'My brother, you have made excellent progress in organising the mine worker rebellion here in Kitwe. It is a remarkable effort but I believe we need to take this further and make it a national revolt. We need to make this revolt bigger than just the mine workers. We need to engage the entire country to finally make real and lasting change.'

Hamoonga perked up with surprise at his old friend's words. Although Mr Miti had provided him with comfort and solace in prison, and told him of his once fateful revolutionary activities, Hamoonga had had the impression that the repercussions had taught him to eschew politics.

Mr Miti continued. 'We need to make this country whole again and free ourselves from the tyranny of this corrupt government and any imperialist powers. I am talking public servants, doctors, nurses, teachers, bus drivers, lecturers, traders in the streets and at market stalls, and more standing up and saying *ENOUGH!* If we can organise the entire workforce in this country to say enough is enough, we can bring this government to its knees and force the regime to secede power. Only then will we see lasting change.' Mr Miti spoke with the vigour of a younger man, and his energy propelled him to keep going. 'As you know many years ago my colleagues and I mistakenly thought we could overthrow the government using military force. We were fed up with the lies and all the corruption. We were willing to do anything to free this nation, but we were misguided. A military coup is not the way; it leads to a cycle of violence and mistrust. During my years in Cha-Cha-Cha I had time to think about these things and I came to realise that true, lasting change needs to be driven by the people themselves – from the ground up. The government can stop a few dozen men with guns but it cannot stop a nation of ordinary citizens who refuse to be cheated anymore.'

'What do you mean? I… we are just mine workers looking for decent wages and justice to be done for the murder of one of our brothers. We are not seeking to overthrow a government!'

'Every fire begins with a spark,' Mr Miti said. 'I firmly believe that this shooting and the ensuing mine worker rebellion is that spark that can ignite into the flame that drives the whole nation out of its slumber. This is the moment, this is the time when we can band together and truly make a change!'

Hamoonga sat back for a minute mulling over Mr Miti's words. It was true that the mine workers had made extraordinary headway; they had attracted the attention of the national news media and they had shut down the District Governor's office. It was also true that no one was happy with the decades of gross mismanagement of the country's economy by the Chibompo government. Even with the recent proliferation of opposition parties, nobody in the country truly believed that change – real and lasting change for the better – was afoot. Maybe Mr Miti was right; maybe this was the time, this was the hour for change.

'So how can I help, what do you suggest we do?' Hamoonga said.

Mr Miti smiled and leaned in closer still. 'We have to set a meeting with leaders of all the powerful civil groups – that is the only way. However, we have to be careful because many of them are infiltrated by government agents looking to sniff out any trouble. Here in Kitwe, I suggest we start by meeting with key leaders in the Marketeers Union. As you well know, marketeers in every Zambian city wield a lot of power; they essentially hold the keys to day-to-day commerce in this country. Chisokone Market here in Kitwe is particularly influential, if we can persuade marketeers at Chisokone to join the plight of the mine workers, the entire city will grind to a halt. This could then spark other cities in the Copperbelt and beyond to follow suit.' Hamoonga followed intently. 'I know some people at Chisokone Market that can meet with us and hopefully help us. I am confident they will be sympathetic to the cause; their members are choking, too, under this nation's corrupt regime. I can make arrangements for them to meet with us and I'm sure we can establish common ground. The meeting will need to be very discrete. I will get it arranged and communicate with you on the details.'

Hamoonga nodded in agreement. The two men shook hands.

'In numbers we can do something to make this country right again, my brother,' Mr Miti said. 'Together we can make a lasting change!'

Chapter 18

On the Road to Damascus

Hamoonga unfolded the creased green paper in his hand. It was ruffled along the top edge where it had been torn out from a ring bound writing pad. He read the two lines again, *'In the name of the Father, the Son, and the Holy Spirit. When the time came, Jesus ate the last supper with his nine disciples. Paul was not one of them but he became transformed on the road to persecute the Christian Church.'* A tiny hint of a smile formed on his face. It was just like Mr Miti to write a cryptic note with Biblical connotations.

The note had been quietly slipped into his hand earlier that morning by one of the dozens of dusty little boys who always seemed to hover around the protesting mine workers. He was sure of what the note meant: Mr Miti had succeeded in making arrangements for the mine workers to meet with the leaders of the Marketeers Union. *'In the name of the Father, the Son, and the Holy Spirit.'* That meant Hamoonga had to bring his fellow leaders of the rebellion to the rendezvous. *'When the time came, Jesus ate the last supper with his nine disciples.'* Jesus didn't have nine disciples, that had to mean the meeting was to happen at 9:00 p.m. *'Paul was not one of them but he became transformed on the road to persecute the Christian Church.'* In the Bible, Saul had an epiphany and was transformed to become the Apostle Paul on his journey to Damascus. Looking at the note, Hamoonga concluded that this could only mean 'Damascus Bar'. The meeting was to be held 9:00 p.m. at Damascus Bar and Hamoonga was to be bring with him the key leaders in the mine worker rebellion.

This play of words was typical of his dear friend Mr Miti. During their stint together in prison, they had frequently passed the time with word play, puzzles, and riddles to stave off the tedium of their days. Back then, the riddles and puzzles had relieved the endless monotony, and now his friend was using them to guard against the malevolent intentions of potential eavesdroppers.

Without question, Damascus Bar was an establishment of ill repute. Steeped in infamy, it was known for entertaining thugs, call boys, laggards, and women of the night. The ignoble establishment was located just behind the sprawling Chisokone Market. To get to Damascus, people had to ply their way through a seemingly infinite array of tightly packed market stalls all cobbled together by a mishmash of wooden planks and tarpaulins. During the day the market was a heaving centre of thousands of day traders with their wares, and customers eager to make a deal. At nightfall, the market was mostly deserted but for the street kids who would sleep in dark hovels, conveniently out of sight and forgotten by society.

Hamoonga was a little nervous as he stood waiting for Mr Chulu, Mr Phiri, and Kibongo to join him. He knew better than to enter the market alone at this hour of the night. It took about fifteen minutes for all four men to converge in the deserted stalls. After the initial obligatory salutations, the four men were silent as they made their way through the narrow passages, each man not knowing what to expect next.

Kibongo led the way. He had spent some time selling *salaula* at Chisokone Market years before he landed a job at Chishimba Mine. Kibongo observed that the market had changed tremendously, even over the last few years since he had been a trader there. He recalled how at times it had felt to him as though the market grew right before his very eyes. Every day new traders would arrive and set up their rickety stands. The number of traders seemed to multiply like acne ravaging a teenager's face.

As the group manoeuvred through the maze of stalls, they could hear the shuffling of feet and the creaking of wood in the darkness around them. The men could feel that their every move was being watched – it was as though the market was alive and balanced in a sort of uneasy slumber. As the group moved deeper into the alleyways they could hear the faint electric strumming guitar sound of Congolese rhumba music playing in the distance. With every turn the electric sounds grew louder. Hamoonga recognised the rhythmic tune of the electric guitar as the climax to a popular Kanda Bongoman song colloquially referred to as *Kwasa, Kwasa*. Reaching the far edge of the market, they could hear loud voices competing in vain against the static, riddled acoustics of cheap speakers mounted in the open air. Turned up to a deafening volume, they bellowed unabashedly into the night sky. At the final turn, Damascus Bar was in full view. There were roughly two dozen people in various stages of inebriation loitering near the entrance. Two scantily clad women were in a heated argument with a slender young man. One of the women grabbed the youth by his loosely fitting shirt, tearing the buttons off as he he tried to wriggle free of her clutches. But his struggle was in vain, the two women descended upon the poor man, and stripped him of the contents of his pockets. None of this seemed to rouse the attention of the other revellers for they were in a world of their own, feverishly gyrating their hips and moving their limbs to the heated rhumba rhythms. The four men exchanged glances, unsure of what to make of it all. After a momentary pause, they proceeded to enter the hive of debauchery, trying their best not to stand out.

The inside of Damascus Bar was surprisingly well lit and not as menacing as the men had expected. There was a small L-shaped bar with a worn grey Formica surface. In front of it were half a dozen wooden stools, one of which was occupied by a hunched solitary soul either drowning his sorrows or celebrating beyond his limits. Behind the bar stood the patron of the establishment – a dark, hefty unshaven man whose expression clearly suffered no fools. There was a half-filled dance floor to the far right, where a man and woman were locked in a primal embrace surely reserved for cats and dogs. To the left there was a dark corner where five men were sitting around a low table covered with empty beer bottles. Hamoonga recognised Mr Miti waving them over.

'I'm happy you were able to make it,' Mr Miti said as he hugged

Hamoonga. 'I'm sorry about the venue, but it's the best I could do under the circumstances – you understand.' Clearly he was joking. Hamoonga smiled and turned to introduce his partners in arms.

'Gentlemen, it is an honour and a pleasure to meet all of you!' Mr Miti said with his customary charm. 'Please sit down, make yourselves comfortable, and we'll make proper introductions.' He pointed to the circle as the seated men made room for the others. Mr Miti promptly signalled to the bar for more drinks to be served. The four men who had been sitting with Mr Miti were all senior leaders in the Marketeers Union. In turn each one of them introduced themselves and declared their admiration and support for the plight of the mine workers. They too described how their members had suffered under the prevailing economic conditions in the country. They spoke of how marketeers across the country had experienced neglect from their local government leaders; lack of decent sanitation, exorbitant taxation on their goods, lack of protection against foreign competition, and so on. Lubricated by the continuous flow of alcohol, the men candidly shared their grievances and spoke about immediate action to address the concerns of their members. They spoke about solidarity and strength in numbers. They talked for hours and as the night naturally ebbed to a close, the men resolved to join forces. Mr Miti summarised the immediate course of action: the Marketeers Union would call for an ad hoc meeting of its members and table a motion to protest in solidarity with the mine workers. The marketeers would stage a co-ordinated protest march in the major cities of Kitwe, Lusaka, Ndola, and Livingstone. They believed that with the mine workers banding together, the nurses and teachers' unions would follow suit. The hope was that within days the government would be compelled to yield to whatever demands they made. They got up, shook hands, and resolved to co-ordinate their efforts through Mr Miti, who was to be the liaison behind the scenes making sure that the mine workers and the marketeers moved in lock step. For his part, Hamoonga and the mine workers would stand firm in their current efforts and wait to hear from Mr Miti. There was an air of hope, as the energy and passion that all had shown for their country was a sure breath of fresh air from the cynicism that had become ingrained in the national psyche. To Hamoonga, it felt like a new beginning, a turning of the proverbial page; he felt proud again of his people and his country!

The men parted ways. Mr Miti insisted that he and the Marketeers Union men leave first, just in case there were any prying eyes. Hamoonga and his group waited for fifteen minutes before leaving the bar. As they walked back through the winding alleys, the four men chatted excitedly like schoolgirls, buoyed by the night's deliberations. The mine worker rebellion had begun under tragic circumstances; one of their own had been killed but maybe – just maybe – something good could come out of it all. Hamoonga thought about the American history books that he had read years ago. He recalled the Boston Tea Party of 1773 when ordinary citizens in the American colonies conducted an act of defiance against the mighty, imperialist British Empire over excessive taxation, thus sparking the American Revolutionary War. Yes, ordinary people could do extraordinary things when compelled to see injustices corrected. This was their time, he sensed; just as their forefathers had defeated the colonial masters, they too would defeat the fiefdom of corrupt politicians that were selling the nation to foreign powers.

'What's that?' Kibongo suddenly asked. Mr Chulu continued talking but was hushed into silence at Kibongo's second attempt, '*Shhhh*, be quiet!' The four men stood in silence. 'That sound?'

Then, as if of one brain, they all realised what it was – *flames!* They could hear the unmistakable crackling sound a fire makes as it consumes everything in its path. Suddenly, their world erupted as frantic screams and rushing footsteps filled the air. The tightly packed wooden stalls and tarpaulins in the market were perfect fodder for a blaze – the entire market would soon be engulfed in flames. Hamoonga and the men had but seconds to find an escape!

As, in panic, he tried to flee, Mr Phiri stumbled and fell to the ground. Kibongo quickly stooped down and heaved him up by the arm. 'Stay calm!' Kibongo demanded. 'If you simply try to run you'll get caught running in circles and the smoke and fire will overpower you!' He now had their attention. 'I know a way, follow me!' he shouted. The men followed Kibongo's lead with no argument; there was no time to waste. Kibongo expertly dodged and wove through the dense thicket of wooden structures. They could now see behind them the giant incandescent flames rising viciously like an angry spirit awakened from its slumber. They could feel the heat from the burning embers getting closer even as they ran as fast as they could. Visibility was waning; the men began to cough as a gust of caustic smoke forced its way into their lungs. Mustering every last ounce of energy they burst out into an open area beyond the grasp of the encroaching flames and lay sprawled on the ground unable to move or speak as each attempted to recover from what felt like a near-death experience.

No sooner had they emerged from the encroaching flames than they heard a hard voice from beyond the darkness. 'There they are! Come on, arrest them, they started the fire, we have witnesses! Catch them!'

Like magic, out of nowhere, a dozen uniformed policemen crystalised out of the darkness. Hamoonga looked up; he could see the men rushing towards them wielding batons. Two or maybe three of them had rifles at the ready. Hamoonga reacted first. Instinctively, he made a run for it. Fortuitously, he was the farthest away from the oncoming policemen and so managed to leap across a shallow ditch before they could catch him. He proceeded to hurl himself across Obote Road ahead of the lights of oncoming vehicles. Then, as if by divine intervention, a large eighteen-wheeler freight truck powered along the road behind Hamoonga, grazing the back of his left foot as he made it to the other side of the street. The driver of the truck, concerned that he had run over a pedestrian, slammed his emergency breaks. In so doing, the truck formed a mountainous physical barrier between the fugitive and his pursuers.

'Move this damn thing now! You idiot! Now, now, now!' one of the policemen screamed as he banged angrily against the side of the freight truck. Bemused, the truck driver exited his vehicle to investigate the commotion. To his misfortune, he was met with a frustrated slap across his face and a barrage of obscenities. The kerfuffle was enough to allow Hamoonga to melt away into the darkness of the night.

His compatriots were not so fortunate.

⌘

Mrs Zulu was visibly pleased with herself; she was beaming in an armchair next to her husband. She never really smiled; whenever she was happy she just seemed to have an effervescent glow about her. Ever calm and confident, her attractiveness was in her bearing; her assured air was what had first drawn the minister to her. Even now, she still exuded that aura; and especially at times of stress, the minister was drawn to her anew, like the first day he laid eyes on her at an independence rally against the British Empire.

'So what do the papers say today?' she asked.

'You were right, my dear. You said we should give them a different bone to chew on and that is exactly what is happening!' The minister felt triumphant. 'Our plan worked swimmingly!' He turned to Babu on his right. 'It's wonderful. I think we're out of the woods now!'

'Yes sir, public opinion has turned on the mine workers, and their rebellion has been broken,' Babu said nodding his head slowly.

'Indeed, listen to this.' The minister pushed his reading glasses further up his nose and read from the newspaper. 'The fire at Chisokone Market caused the death of three people and destroyed property worth millions of kwacha. The police are investigating the matter but three suspects were apprehended on the scene and charged with murder and arson. The suspects have confessed to starting the fire and the police have identified them as leaders in the mine worker rebellion. The hunt is on for a fourth suspect who fled from the scene, a Mr Hamoonga Moya, also a ringleader in the mine worker rebellion of the past few days. Police are gathering evidence but there are eyewitnesses that place all four men at the scene.' The minister shook his head in glee. 'Perfect, perfect!' He brought the paper closer and went on. 'Here you go, it says here that their motives are yet to be confirmed, "but suspicions are that they were trying to cause unrest for their selfish plight for more money. They should be put to death for their murderous ways, we denounce their criminal actions, we denounce their selfish plight and we demand the full weight of the law to fall upon them!" He was ecstatic; for the first time in days the mine workers were unable to gather outside the District Governor's office. For sure the tide of public opinion had turned against them, the rebellion was in tatters.

'Bashi Z,' Mrs Zulu said, 'you were absolutely right, we can always rely on *Agent X* to execute a plan to perfection!'

❖

'Agent X,' as it turns out, was indeed Mr Miti. The government had an army of undercover agents, just like him, who had infiltrated every nook and cranny of Zambian society. Many seemingly ordinary citizens were trained government spies intractably woven into the fabric of communities everywhere. It was an ingenious way for the government to subjugate the masses, keeping them fearful of one another, never knowing who would turn you into the authorities if you said anything untoward. It was an immoral system: you could know someone, a friend, a family member, for years and then one day they would turn against you. Hamoonga had known Mr Miti for over six years; they had suffered through the Cha-Cha-Cha Prison experience together. Mr Miti had been a confidant, a friend, a mentor, a source of strength during those dark times; but alas, it had all been a facade. After the failed coup, Mr Miti had been given an option, spy for us, or die. Regretfully, he had chosen the first option, and had been purposefully planted in the prison by the government to gain the confidence of fellow inmates. He had been tasked to listen and mop up secrets that the state could one day use to its benefit against its citizenry. Slowly, Mr Miti's allegiance had turned to the ruling elite, the likes of the president and Minister Zulu and his vixen of a wife, and they had paid him well for it. A prison experience does not come cheap. All Mr Miti's children had gone to university in the USA, his house had been paid for, and he was given a good life pension.

When the Zulus had been faced with the intractable issue of the mine worker rebellion, it was Mrs Zulu who had had the presence of mind to see about arranging a negotiation with the key leaders of the rebellion. The Zulus had set up the meeting not to negotiate in good faith but as a way to infiltrate the leadership ranks of the mine worker rebellion. Their mission had been to identify the leaders, isolate them, and then decapitate the movement, for with the head goes the rest of the snake. Once they had identified Hamoonga as indispensable to the rebellion, they dug into his past and discovered that he had had a stint in Cha-Cha-Cha Prison. Once they found that bead of information, there was only one man for the job: Agent X.

The leaders of the Marketeers Union were unwitting pawns in the whole affair. While the men conversed in Damascus Bar, the Zulus had put their thugs in place to set the market ablaze at precisely the right moment. Now with the market in ashes, and the Marketeers Union leaders as reliable witnesses placing Hamoonga and his men at the scene of the crime, it was an open and shut case of arson and murder. The three deaths in the fire were an added indictment of the mine workers; the whole city turned against them. Now the narrative was that the mine workers were greedy men who had burned down Chisokone Market to drum up attention for their selfish plight.

Chapter 19

Sic Semper Tyrannis

'Thus always to tyrants'.

Grazed in the left leg by the freight truck, Hamoonga limped off into the darkness like a wounded beast temporarily numbing himself to the shock and pain. His shirt damp with sweat, he scurried away hearing angry voices behind him. He moved with the determination of a runaway slave desperate not to be caught. As he wove his way through the nearby bushes, his only thought was to get as far away as possible from the frantic voices of the men in the distance. Although he was accustomed to heavy manual labour, the thick smoke from the fire, and the speed at which he'd had to run for so long meant that he was struggling to catch his breath and had a sharp stitch in his side. Unable to see clearly in the dark night, he tripped over and fell head first into a shallow ditch. Fear for his life repressed the scream as pain careened through his body. Stilling himself like a possum and taking long slow deep breaths, he looked back in the direction of the now distant voices. He could see several flashlights illuminating the darkness, menacingly darting from side to side like hungry predators seeking their prey. He did his best to control his breathing, slowing it down as much as humanly possible. His mind relived the sudden fire, and the men in uniform descending upon them as if waiting to pounce. How did they know to be there at that precise moment? It seemed orchestrated, like a movie scene pressed into motion at the push of a button. The men had been armed, stationed, ready to catch them as soon as they emerged from the fiercely burning stalls, the screaming petrified vagrants, many of them street urchins. How could it be that a whole squadron of policemen would be lying in wait at that exact moment, at that time of the night, in that part of the city? It was improbable, he thought, someone must have alerted them, but who? Thoughts tumbled through his mind, tossing and turning like a restless child after a nightmare. Who could have set them up like that? The rendezvous with the Marketeers Union leaders had been arranged with the strictest discretion. Only he and Mr Miti had known the details and Hamoonga had kept his colleagues in the dark until just hours before the meeting. Even then, he had not talked about the details of what or who they were to meet, only that it was important that they tell no one, including their wives. They had just escaped being burnt to death; there was no way a sane person would knowingly subject himself to such a risk; no, it could not be one of them – he was certain of it. Lying low in the dank, putrid ditch, he examined different scenarios like the pieces of a jigsaw puzzle, all the while dancing around the dark truth lurking in the crevices of his mind; it had to have been the person he remembered as his most steadfast friend; it could only have been Mr Miti!

The thought repulsed him. Such a betrayal was impossible, inexplicable – maybe Mr Miti had been coerced by the government. Yes, perhaps his life or that of his family had been threatened. Surely Mr Miti was not a Judas Iscariot selling out his friends for a few pieces of silver? It was an idea that sickened him. His memories flooded back – Mr Miti had befriended him in prison, nursed him back to health time and again. He thought back to the questions Mr Miti asked, the advice he rendered, the stories he volunteered. Was it all an act, some indecent ploy to extract information? Was Mr Miti a government agent planted among the inmates like a snake in the grass? Anger welled up inside him, as he thought about his many years incarcerated for something he had not done, and the beatings. He remembered his mother and the anguish she had suffered and how he had been prevented from seeing her, even in death. The long slow hours passed, Hamoonga's leg throbbed as his thoughts grew increasingly bitter until, at last, the light of dawn began to swallow the night, revealing a new day.

♋

Jinan felt no joy in being released from jail. His sense of despair was absolute; misery cloaked him. When the five Chinese supervisors were finally released following the fire and the ensuing media attacks against the mine workers, Jinan returned to his lonely one-bedroom abode. He had no respite from his own thoughts: he replayed the image of the bloodied body of the mine worker over and over again, as he had done in his jail cell. The finality of having ended a life suffocated him; he felt utterly alone, trapped, a prisoner of his own thoughts. He had lost his wife, his son, and now, having killed someone himself, he had lost even the will to live. He loathed what he had become. There was only one way out.

Jinan rolled up the window making sure it was tightly shut. He adjusted his seat, pulling it back to an inclined posture. Taking two deep breaths like a prizefighter preparing for the final round, he reached for his car keys and turned them. The engine spluttered into life. He glanced one last time at the pipe he had expertly routed from the exhaust into the car's interior. He could feel the lulling warmth of the fumes filling the cabin. He remembered being told years ago how carbon monoxide had no scent; maybe it was the impurities in the fuel that he could faintly smell. He inhaled deeply. He filled his mind with the pleasant memories of his wife and son singing nursery rhymes after dinner in their tiny *hutong*, how good those times had been. He smiled and breathing deeply slowly began to drift away, the images growing distant like a fading horizon. The invisible threads that had tightened and tormented his mind, began to loosen their hold and in the process freeing him to drift to a better place, one free of the demons that had possessed him.

❑

Hamoonga awoke to the smell of smoke and charred debris. The huge fire had consumed the market, reducing it to ashes. Smoke and debris had been carried for miles across the city, lingering in the air as a reminder of the events of the night before. Lifting his head, Hamoonga could see clearly where he had spent the night: a shallow compost pit, perhaps dug by the nomadic vendors who appeared at the crack of dawn and disappeared with the setting sun. He could hear women's voices a few feet away, in an animated conversation about the tragic fire that had devoured everything in its path. As he listened to their lamentations, he pieced together what had now become the public narrative concerning the events of the previous night.

'Yes, it was on Radio Icengelo this morning. They say it was an act of local terrorism by leaders of the mine worker's rebellion,' said one lady, clapping her hands in a show of contempt. 'The news said they caught most of them but the ringleader escaped. They are now searching for him!'

'*Yangu!* What has this world come to?' exclaimed another woman. 'There are so many hardships that people are resorting to anything, even violence, to get the government to change.'

'No, *bana* Chibesa!' retorted yet another woman. 'This is not a case of hardships or desperation. We are all suffering, all encountering hardships, but we are not killing people and burning property, are we? No, not at all, these people – these mine workers – are criminals. Do you know that three people died in the fire they started last night? It's tragic and it's unacceptable!'

'*Ehe, Ehe*' echoed a bevy of women.

'I hope they hang every last one of them for this nonsense!' a woman shouted. 'These miners don't realise how lucky they are to even have a job. I say fire them all and give jobs to those who can appreciate what they have!' There was another murmur of collective agreement.

The words bit Hamoonga like a venomous snake. They reaffirmed what he had suspected – he and his compatriots had been setup, and it must have been orchestrated from on high. It had all been an elaborate scheme to eviscerate the mine workers' rebellion. What better way to do so than to taint the character and intentions of its leaders? Remove and discredit the leaders of the movement and the sheep will scatter. Once again, he had fallen victim to the evil machinations of a corrupt system!

◆◆◆

'You are a true patriot, Agent X. You have never failed your country and for that we are truly grateful!' Minister Zulu exclaimed, raising his index finger in the air to accentuate his point. 'This country owes you and others like you a great deal!'

Sitting in the front passenger seat of an air-conditioned black Mercedes, Mr Miti, aka Agent X, turned around to face Minister Zulu and his wife who were seated on the back seat. 'I am grateful, *shikulu,* it has always been my honour and pleasure to serve.' Mr Miti lowered his head and gave two soft claps of his hands, a sign of respect usually given to elders and people in high office.

'As always you have distinguished yourself and shown yourself to be a true servant of the people!' added Mrs Zulu. Mr Miti turned to face her and repeated his respectful gesture.

'My husband and I wanted to show our appreciation in person so we requested that you travel with us back to Lusaka; we have much to discuss and this will give us a chance to talk,' she said.

'You are very kind, madam, sir, I am honoured,' Mr Miti said. 'You know that I am forever at your service. I am but a humble servant.'

In the driver's seat Babu looked into his rearview mirror. He could see Minister Zulu sitting behind his left shoulder. He was in fine form like a fully fed child full of latent energy. He had feasted on the day's newspapers reading each and every article and opinion column with the fastidiousness of a jeweller examining a precious stone. He had reveled in how the editors had impaled the mine workers, labelling them 'criminals,' 'thugs,' 'maggots,' 'less than human'– one paper even called them 'a blight on the national consciousness.' Now with the mine worker rebellion a thing of the past, Minister Zulu was travelling back to Lusaka a victorious man, like an army general returning home with the scalp of his enemy.

'Babu, make a stop at the next filling station. I need you to get us some bottled water,' the minister commanded.

Babu glanced up again at his rearview mirror and nodded. It was a baking hot savannah day, temperatures were above 32 degrees

Celsius; the air was dry and still, almost as though even the wind had resigned, having been defeated by the heat. 'Yes, sir,' Babu replied. 'I actually need to fill up the tank before we leave Kitwe. There's a Total filling station with a decent kiosk coming up. I'll stop there.'

They cruised down Independence Avenue for a few more minutes, then Babu turned left and pulled into a filling station, the letters TOTAL painted in bright red across its main facade. There were four other cars parked in separate bays all being attended to by busy uniformed men. The place was alive with activity – petrol being filled, oil changes being performed, windshields being wiped, fluid levels being checked, and tires being pumped. Set a few feet behind the three parallel rows of fuel bays was a small white kiosk. There was an automated sliding glass door at the entrance of the kiosk; it seemed to open and close every few seconds spitting and swallowing customers of various shapes and sizes. As Babu pulled into fuel bay Number 3, a young female attendant approached and stood ready. She was holding a thick oil-stained receipt book in one hand and a striped *Bic* pen with dirty black smudges in her other. She waited patiently for Babu to turn off the engine and roll down his window.

'Good morning, sir!' she announced with little fanfare. Without waiting for Babu to respond, she asked, 'Regular or Super?'

'Put sixty *pin* of Super,' Babu replied, reaching into his glove compartment to produce a black leather money bag of crisp new bank notes. He pulled out a brick and counted out some notes before returning the bag to its rightful place. Handing the attendant the payment, he opened his door and got out as he barked additional instructions for her to clean his windscreen and check fluid levels. He then shut the door and walked to the kiosk.

◆

It took Hamoonga the lion's share of the morning to make his way out of the city centre. Avoiding the main thoroughfares, he hobbled uneasily through bushes and side streets until he was a fair distance away from the main centre. As he walked, he pondered whether or not to go back to Kwacha East; on the one hand he figured that would be the first place the police would be searching, but on the other, he feared what might happen to his sister and her children. There was no telling what the authorities might do to them – the very thought sent a chill down his spine. He resolved to take the risk; he would go back to Kwacha East, scope out the house from a safe distance, and wait until nightfall to make his move.

The heat was punishing. The sun's rays blazed mercilessly from a cloudless sky. He continued to move slowly, still afflicted by the pain in his leg, only stopping occasionally to smoke a cigarette. He reflected again on the previous night and the cascading events that had led him to this point, events that had irreversibly transformed him from a humble boy into a fugitive wanted by the state. He played and replayed all the pivotal moments, the perverse serendipity of life that seemed to always place him in the wrong place at the wrong time; and always at the mercy of the ruthless greed and malfeasance of a few.

Hamoonga hobbled along on a dusty footpath lined by tall grass that ran parallel to Independence Avenue. He made his way past the roundabout at Kuomboka Drive then past the Second Class Industrial Area, a circuitous route, all the while acutely conscious of police checkpoints. He knew too well that any attempt to use a bus, a cab, or to hitch a ride was fraught with danger. There were several police-manned checkpoints where vehicles would be searched and passengers interrogated and required to show their identification cards. He knew he had to stick to the footpaths to avoid being caught. His plan was to first make sure that his sister Beatrice and the children were safe and then he would figure out a way to head north to the border; he knew he was no longer safe. It would only be a matter of time before the police caught up with him. He knew how much worse things would be for him if he were to be sent back to prison; he would sooner die than allow that to happen.

He came to a clearing with an old deserted train track that had once been used to ferry copper ore during the colonial days. Past the tracks he could see the white facade of a new building; it was one of the latest strip malls built by Chinese contractors. The building stood in a U-shape behind a blue-painted fence with two open gates, one marked 'IN' and the other marked 'OUT.' As he drew closer he could see that most of the stores were empty with only a few cars parked outside. A little beyond the mall and past a set of robots was another new construction. As he edged closer, coming into view to his left he could see in big red letters the sign 'TOTAL.' It was then that he noticed it. Right there in the distance was a sleek black Mercedes Benz with the letters 'GRZ' on the license plate.

His heart jolted as if given an electric shock as he recognised the tall bald figure emerging from the vehicle. It was the man he had first seen years ago with Lulu, the same man who had pummelled him relentlessly in Cha-Cha-Cha. It was the same man that had suddenly appeared only a few days previously at the failed labour negotiations with the District Governor. Yes, he was sure of it! Helplessly drawn in like matter to a black hole, Hamoonga moved closer. He could see the man standing, his car door open talking to one of the uniformed attendants, yes, there was no mistaking him!

Hamoonga moved closer still. Then just as Babu closed the door of his car, he saw the unmistakable face of Mr Miti sitting in the front seat, conversing with someone at the back. In the instant before the door closed Hamoonga clearly recognised Mr Miti's face with its small grey beard before the dark tinted glass hid the inhabitants of the vehicle. Judas himself, he thought.

❏

Babu walked through the narrow aisles of the little kiosk. There were four each shoulder high with merchandise. The first stocked an assortment of potato crisps, corn puffs, salted peanuts, Chalimbana Brittle, chocolates, and sweets – most of them imported from South Africa. The second held bread, coffees, and teas, the third carried perishable foods, and the last vehicle accessories. At the back of the store was the refrigerated section containing milk, fruit juice and bottled water. Babu made his way to the back and opened the glass door of the refrigerator to take out four bottles of water when he heard the girl at the checkout counter scream. One of the women in the kiosk dropped her shopping basket, her wares scattering across the floor. Everyone's attention was drawn to the girl whose eyes were glued to something outside.

Babu rushed to the front and peered through the glass doors. Dropping the water bottles, he hastened outside.

❖

Hamoonga felt a tightness in his chest. Blood rushed to his head.

He was in control, he knew, but he was also mad, and he knew that as well. He reached into his pocket, pulled out his last cigarette, and lit it, his eyes fixed on the gleaming black car now only several feet in front of him. He pulled on the cigarette for a few seconds contemplating his next action. When he saw the attendant move to open the hood of the car, he threw away his fag and walked directly towards the car.

It had been Miti all along – the thought bounced through his mind, unable to escape. Then, he banged on the passenger window raging, 'Miti, how could you? How could you betray us? You set us up. YOU! …'

Then the passenger door was flung open, knocking Hamoonga onto the concrete. Mr Miti had a guile gained from years of military training and he grabbed Hamoonga in an arm lock while giving him a punishing blow in the side. But being the younger of the two, Hamoonga had the advantage of speed; he whisked his legs from underneath his opponent gaining leverage so as to push himself on top. Miti again expertly struck his adversary with a blow to his midriff that left him gasping for breath. He then grabbed Hamoonga by the neck and held him in a choke hold. Hamoonga's legs kicked about wildly. He knocked over nearby containers spilling soapy water all over the floor. Miti did not relent, he squeezed harder. Hamoonga wriggled desperately, this time his foot knocked the nozzle of the petrol pump out of the mouth of the fuel tank. Petrol spewed all over the forecourt.

The Zulus sat rooted within their car, like sheep too frightened to leave their pen. The melée drew the attention of the filling station attendants and the other drivers waiting to be served. As Mr Miti squeezed his arm around Hamoonga's throat, some of the male onlookers descended upon him. Fearing that the older man would choke the life out of the younger one, the onlookers pulled them apart.

☞

When Babu arrived at the scene, Hamoonga was lying on the concrete, gasping for breath. Mr Miti, surrounded by a group of men, was pinned firmly to the ground, one to his right and the other to his left as he wrestled to break free.

'What's happening here?' Babu shouted, 'Sir, madam, are you okay, is everything okay?' he shouted leaning towards the open window of the car. Mr and Mrs Zulu were hysterical, and as the couple talked over each other offering explanations, Babu suddenly emitted a primal, guttural noise as he was engulfed in tongues of fire. The onlookers, screaming in horror, began to flee in every direction. Babu rolled across the concrete floor batting his hands in a futile attempt to extinguish the flames. The flame fuelled by the petrol that had now pooled below the car rose to an incredible height, engulfing it. Mr Miti scampered to safety and watched in disbelief as the flames consumed the car and its passengers.

♦♦♦

Seeing the hefty bald man within touching distance had broken Hamoonga's calm and resilience. Loss, futility, pain and anger repressed for years consumed him.

Possessed by an uncontrollable rage, his neck throbbing from Mr Miti's strangulating grip, he had reached into his pocket, lit a match and thrown the flickering orange tongue onto the translucent pool of fuel. He had watched as the flames foraged over the floor in an instant, circling and engulfing all in its wake. The action was for all the little people, for all those like him, all those who had suffered so egregiously at the hands of people like this man and those he worked for – these people and all they represented: power, greed, hegemony, and corruption. This was a statement he needed to make for all Africans. This was a statement for all ordinary African people tired of tyranny in all its forms, tired of lies, the empty promises and empty bellies, tired of propoganda and deception.

Sic semper tyrannis! And thus always to tyrants!

Chapter 20

All that Matters Now

East Rand Mall, Johannesburg, South Africa

November 2011

Lulu Daka sipped on her soy coffee latte. The bitter aftertaste lingered in her mouth. She nestled her feet beneath her body as she sank into the sofa in a Mug and Bean coffee shop in East Rand Mall. Six years living in Johannesburg, or 'Jozy' as the locals called it, had its perks, and sitting anonymously in a warm coffee shop was one of them.

The shop was empty save for the Asian couple sitting in the corner to her right. The quaint furniture and dim lighting added to the charm of the place. Lulu had adopted the ritual of sitting in the Mug and Bean, sipping coffee, and scanning the international news websites on her laptop. It had become a habit since she arrived in Jo'burg. In those early days she would feverishly browse the Zambian sites for any news of the Zulus. In those first few months, she was paranoid, expecting to see the large, lethal figure of Babu just behind her. But time had passed and now she felt safe, though she was under no illusions that she could ever go back to Zambia!

'We'll be closing up in thirty minutes,' announced a pimply faced teenage barista from across the room. Lulu glanced at her wrist. It was 6:30 p.m. She looked down at her laptop, and typed in the URL for the *Zambian Daily Mail*, and watched as the front page loaded. There it was: the headline in bold letters, 'MINISTER AND WIFE BURN TO DEATH' and two photographs beneath it that made

Lulu start out of her seat.

She read through the story that described how Minister Zulu and his wife had been savagely burnt to death in their car at a filling station in Kitwe. The report went on to say there was another unnamed victim who had sustained first-degree burns and was in critical condition fighting for his life in hospital. The unnamed victim was believed to be an aide to the minister. Lulu gasped, she did not know what to feel; relief that her problems were now over? Or sorrow for the deaths of people she knew well and hated as they were, they had once helped her? Lulu read on, her throat tightened at the sight of the name 'Hamoonga Moya'.

The article said that the Minister and his wife were attacked by a dangerous ex-convict named Hamoonga Moya. He had set fire to their vehicle as they sat helplessly unable to exit the burning Mercedes. Hamoonga had been apprehended by the police and charged with murder in the first degree. He was now remanded at Mukobeko Maximum prison awaiting trial. He was sure to hang.

The memories of her brief encounter with Hamoonga came rushing back to her. Was it the same man she had flirted with all those years ago? She had often wondered what became of him. She'd hoped he was well and that life had been kind to him, but deep down she had feared that the Zulus might reach him in a bid to get to her. She had hoped and prayed that was not the case, but she had done nothing else.

But now this – this was terrible. Hamoonga Moya had now been arrested for murder! Was he innocent? What could she do to help?

Just then, a text message flashed across Lulu's Blackberry lying on the sofa next to her. It was a message from her daughter, Misozi. *'Mum, done with ballet. Pls cum pick me up at Suzi's* ☺'

Lulu stared at the message for a moment. Misozi meant everything to her. They had made a comfortable life for themselves in Jo'burg. It was not Zambia, but they could live in peace and not have to look over their shoulders. Going back to Zambia was not an option. She typed a reply. *'Ok hun, c u in 5!'*

She closed her browser and shut down her computer. Unfurling her legs from underneath her body, she stood up and packed her things. As she made her way out of the coffee shop she thought to herself, 'That is my past. My future, all that matters to me now, is right here!'

♋

Still, despite the nonchalant shrug, the determination to move forward, the news article disinterred old memories of the Zulus and their hold over her which she had tried hard to bury. She had to do something, but what? At least, she knew that they could no longer threaten her.

She stepped out onto the balcony of her third floor apartment and watched as a garbage truck slowly reversed with a sharp beeping sound. Two men in overalls clinging to the side leapt off the truck and started to gather the heaped bins lined up in the street. Her fingers circled the warm tea-cup. She remembered the fresh-faced young man who she'd flirted with years ago in Lusaka; she had always known that her flight might have got him into trouble since he'd been with her when she collected the package. At the time, she could not deal with this thought, pre-occupied, as she was, with her own fears for herself and Misozi. But, by the time she'd established herself in Jo'burg, it was easy to convince herself that it was too late to find out, too late to do anything. Now older, more thoughtful, less selfish, less frightened, news of the Zulu's death by fire, engulfed in flames like witches or heretics, served to remind her that she could or should have done more to find out if Hamoonga had not been caught up in their web of suspicion. She could not believe that the reserved, rather naive young man she had once known would wittingly have lit the pyre. There had to be more to the story and she wondered if Hamoonga was getting proper legal representation. She continued to stare at the men below as they dumped the last bins into the back of the truck, then broke out of her reverie and walked back through the flat into her bedroom to find her old address book.

♦♦♦

Patience Banda scanned the room. She shook her head in disgust. 'No, no, no, you people – what is this?' She raised her hand and beat the air repeatedly. 'No, no, it won't do. It just won't do. I won't have my name associated with such shoddy work!' She pointed to one of the frazzled girls standing next to a gigantic flower arrangement in the centre aisle of the church. 'This is a wedding, people ... and not just any wedding. It's the Mayor's daughter who's getting married! *Awe, awe,* take it down, I'll have to do it myself!' Patience walked hurriedly to the front of the church and placed her handbag in the front pew to her right.

'*Iwe!*' She yelled at another girl. Bring all the arrangements here. I'll need to do them all again. Have you not learned anything?' She tied her long braids in a bun behind her head and began to re-do the arrangements. Ten years in the business of setting up elaborate decorations for prestigious banquets had made her the most sought after florist in the capital. Politicians and wealthy business people all knew her. If you wanted your event to be the talk of the town, there was none other than Patience Banda to make it happen. As she plucked away feverishly at ferns and carnations, her cell phone rang.

'*Iwe,* don't just stand there, hand me my bag... 'One of the girls hurried and picked up her bag. '...honestly, I don't even know why I hired some of you,' she lamented under her breath.

She grabbed the purse and rummaged through it before retrieving the device. The caller display showed an unidentified number. Perhaps it was an international call? In the past few years she'd had some good business from Zambians living abroad wanting to stage lavish homecoming parties or weddings.

'Hello?'

'Patience?'

'Who is this?'

'*Oh mwana,* it's me – Lulu...'

'Lulu?'

'Lulu Daka – remember, Your Day?'

Patience almost dropped her phone in disbelief. 'Lulu – Lulu

Daka? Is it really you?'

'Yes, it's me *mwana!* Her unmistakable laugh removed all doubt. Patience took a few steps away from the uncompleted arrangement. *'Iwe,* Lulu – oh my God! – You're alive. *Iwe,* where are you, where've you been? Are you all right?'

'Yes, yes, I'm fine Patience.'

'Ah-ah, and Misozi, how is she?'

'She's well, all grown up now, quite the lady!' Lulu's smile leant warmth to her voice.

'But ... where did you disappear to? ... I mean, one day we're working together on an event and the next – you're gone? People came asking questions about you but – hey, I didn't know anything-nothing at all. Linda got badly beaten up you know. How could you just disappear like that and forget all about us?'

There was a short pause on the line before Lulu responded so-berly, 'Uhm, it's a long, long story Patience and it's been a long time.'

'Over three - four years? ... '

'Six, nearly seven, to be exact... But I'll tell you all about it. I promise, Patience.' Lulu took a deep breath. Patience understood that there was something weighing heavily on her friend's mind and that the years apart had not undermined their once close friend-ship. *'Mwana,* I know it's been a long time since we talked, and truly I regret having not reached out to you before but for reasons I'll explain when we meet, it just wasn't possible.' Another short pause. 'Patience, I need you to do me a huge favour ... it's really important and...'

'Hold on.' Patience looked up and shooed away one of the girls in earshot of her conversation. Satisfied that the girls were far enough away, she asked in a whisper. 'What is it Lulu, are you in trouble?'

'No, no, it's not me or Misozi, we're both just fine.'

'Okay, go on.' Patience said slowly.

'Patience, I hate to ask, but you're the only one I can turn to .. . Is your father still working as an attorney?'

Patience hesitated. 'Uhm . . . yes, he's due to retire this year, but why?'

Lulu cleared her throat. 'Well . . . it's got to do with someone I knew a long time ago, someone who needs help – big time!'

Glossary

Aba leya? – Who's going?

Alo – Hello

Bali – A father or elderly male

Cheddar – Money

Copped – Bought

Doek – Head scarf or cloth

Chipwile mo fye - It's a deal

Goozers – Girls

Icombela nganda - Small common-law wedding

Imbeka chi saka - The women are plenty

Imwe shuwa – Surely

Iwe – You

Kampompo – Bread rolls

Koma ni au pusa iwe – You are very stupid

Kopala – Copper

Ku kashishi - The HIV virus

L-S-K – Lusaka

Manje – Now

Man-U– Manchester United Football Club

Mayo - Mother

Mealie-meal - Cornmeal flour

Muleya? - Are you going?

Mulishani mwe mfumu? – How are you almighty chief?

Mwashibukeni, - Good morning

Mwe bafyashi – Parents or elderly people

Mwebana – You children

Na ka kadoli – A baby

Nchekelako – Cut me a piece

Nga walya ku shako - Have fun but always leave some for tomorrow

Ni – It is

Ni so tambe – It is (they are) a sight to behold

Owns – Guys

Pin – A thousand
Reggie – Green National Registration Card
Robots – Traffic lights
Rocked – Went
Salaula – Second hand clothing sold at a market
Shabins - Small local bars selling cheap homemade brews
Shi – Father of
Shikulu – An elderly man
Skeem – Think
Skezzah – Woman
Smack – Like
Tata lesa aye – My God
Tiye – Let's go
Tute - Roasted cassava
Twakana – We refuse
Ya li balansa - It's all good

Acknowledgments

It is said that 'if you want to walk fast, walk alone, but if you want to walk far, walk together'. My journey in writing *A Casualty of Power* has been a long and fruitful one with the company of a whole host of people. This book is indeed a collage covered with the thumbprints of many people who have advised me, encouraged me and opened doors for me.

To my dearest wife, Sandra, thank you for all the love and encouragement. You facilitated this whole endeavour through your patience and understanding over my early morning and late night solitary writing retreats. Your candid feedback on my early work was invaluable.

I would not have been able to succeed without the tireless efforts of my first editor, Elizabeth Brown (www.swiftedits.com) – thank you. I am also especially grateful to my publisher, Weaver Press; Irene Staunton performed an amazing job in raising the quality of the book – I have learned so much from you.

My family has played a pivotal role in making this novel a reality. Dearest Mum and Dad, I am because you are, thank you for your constant prayers and for raising me the way you did – all my shortcomings are purely down to my sometimes impervious ears. To my sisters, Saka and Kanyanta, thank you for agreeing to be my filters; your feedback on my initial draft was priceless. To my brother, Mwewa, it was your storytelling on those late nights after school that first inspired me to attempt to tell stories.

This book would have been impossible to write without the cast of colourful characters who I have been privileged to encounter throughout my life; I am eternally grateful for your stories. Last but not least, I would like to give praise and thanks to the almighty God for all that he has given me.

Printed in the United States
By Bookmasters